Signal Seven

Lillian Roth

ISBN: 0990929205
ISBN 13: 9780990929208

Chapter 1

SUSAN CHOKED ON the blood in her throat as she continued to struggle against Bob. The blade continued its slow, agonizing path across her neck while he held onto her struggling form. Susan was unable to cry out because of the amount of blood that flowed from the wound down into her windpipe. Dropping the eight-inch blade onto the ground, he covered Susan's mouth, holding her from behind.

Lowering his head, he whispered into her ear, "How does that feel?"

"Mm…" She groaned for the last time, her last bit of breath whooshing out.

"You think you can take her from me. Well, look who's leaving this circle!" Bob hissed through clenched teeth into her deafened ear.

Pulling Susan's limp body into the enveloping darkness of the building's shadow, he noticed there was no moon out tonight to expose him. The weight of her body was heavy in his arms when he slowly lowered her onto the asphalt parking lot. Checking for a pulse on her neck, he found none. Satisfied, he walked over to her patrol car and turned off the engine and parking lights. He left the radio turned down low but loud enough for him to hear it. Bob knew the police codes and listened for dispatch to call for Susan's status.

He lifted her from behind with his hands under her arms, and dragged her body like a sack of potatoes back to the patrol car. He sat Susan in the driver's seat, slumped over. Hatred began overwhelming his senses, branding him as it sieved through his pores like a pent up body of water finally spilling over a dam. A smile spread across his face from the relief of knowing that this woman was finally out of his way.

Walking over to the knife on the ground, Bob picked it up and walked back to the patrol car to finish his plan. He knew Jade would be all his to seduce now, without any interference. He was proud of his deviltry and relieved by the woman's death. But, he knew if he didn't hurry, someone would see him.

"You won't be in my way now!" he said mockingly.

His adrenaline continued to flow through his trembling body while he carved on Susan's abdomen. Finally he was done. Reaching over, he turned off the radio.

Hell, they'd find her by morning, he thought.

Slipping back to where his car was, hidden behind the building, Bob got in and turned his dome light on. He checked his latex gloves for any nicks or tears, found none, and carefully pulled them off. He looked in his rearview mirror, and scanned his face for any scratches or blotches of blood. He wiped a few crimson drops off his cheek with a couple of alcohol wipes. When he was done cleaning up, he placed the soiled wipes on top of the used latex gloves. After turning off the dome light, and quickly changed, throwing his bloodstained clothes, tennis shoes he wore, latex gloves, knife, and soiled alcohol wipes into a black trash bag. Running his hands through his hair, he straightened it out from the struggle. Bob then stuffed the crumpled black trash bag under the passenger seat, away from any curious eyes.

Still skeptical, he continued listening for anything nearby that might prove to be a problem; he heard only the chirping of crickets. Finally, Bob started his car and made his way onto the road headed west. Turning on the radio listening to the music play, he looked around for witnesses. A car turned onto the street in front of him and then made a quick right into a fast food parking lot.

Almost convinced that there were no witnesses, he continued to nervously monitor his speed and all traffic signs as he drove his way back to his house in Deland. The tension in his shoulders eased, and the profuse sweating stopped the minute he pulled safely into his garage.

Bob let out a long breath as he sat in his car, reflecting on what he had just accomplished. When he recalled why he'd committed the murder, his emotions quickly went haywire.

All she wanted to do was spend too much time with my Jade, he thought.

Instantly he recalled that what agitated him a lot with Susan was that she took Jade to bars, if they didn't know they were considered fresh meat to all the scavenging drunk males.

Shifting in his seat, he envisioned how Jade looked when she was dressed to go out in a short black mini-skirt, a revealing blouse, high heels and her long dark hair flowing down her shoulders. She was downright beautiful. The frustration began to build within him as he remembered watching the men at the bar making passes at Jade. Why didn't she accept that she was his? The memory refueled his anger, and his body began to tremble even more. Still sitting in the driver's seat, he squeezed the steering wheel until his fingers were numb.

"She's mine damn it!" he sighed with exasperation.

His justification for killing Susan was simple. The woman's interference with his courtship with Jade became a thorn in his side. Besides Susan's dismissing him from Jade once she arrived, his biggest issue with her was that Susan's continual insistence that Jade date various men.

Who the hell did she think she was? And what the hell did she think I was? Those thoughts nagged at him.

Smiling, pleased with Susan's death, he knew he could court Jade now.

He reached under the passenger seat, yanked out the black trash bag, and exited his vehicle. He walked to the utility room door and pressed the remote control screwed to the wall. It triggered the garage door to close, groaning and creaking until it was down.

Once inside, he took off his jacket. He piled newspaper and a log onto the metal grate of the fireplace and doused the material with lighter fluid. Standing back with the box of matches, he struck one match and tossed it, igniting the fireplace quickly. He continued to add newspaper to the fire until it roared higher and hotter as he stared into it. The hairs on his hands started to singe from the heat, causing him to take a step back.

He picked up the black trash bag containing the evidence linking him to Susan's murder and tossed it into the blazing fire. The flames threatened to die. Panicking he picked up the can of lighter fluid and doused the bag until the fire burned bright again. The plastic melted immediately, and the clothes ignited and burned. He doused the shoes a couple more times and watched the fire consumed them. He stared into the fireplace, watching the flames dance with the sacrificed items in a rhythm of possession.

He was pleased with the results and stepped back. He sat on the couch, the energy draining out of him. Thoughts of Jade drifted back to him again. He never stopped thinking about her for too long, and then thoughts of her beautiful, bright, intelligent child started to play in his head.

The child…

The angelic image of Jade's daughter, Gracie, filled his mind and made him smile. The thoughts temporarily distracted him. Gracie's innocence and the unconditional love she gave to him whenever he visited her at her elementary school or home were pure joy to him. Even though Gracie had multiple disabilities, she was closer to being normal than any of his other clients.

Thoughts of Gracie faded, bringing him back to reality. Once the announcement of Susan's death was out, he knew Jade would call him. She was going to need his guidance and comfort to help her through the death of her friend, just like she did when her husband died. Bob knew Gracie would need him to be there for her mother and be the temporary father she'd innocently asked him to be.

Soon he'd be her permanent father, once he courted Jade long enough to convince her to trust him and eventually marry him.

Soon.

Chapter 2

THE RINGING OF the phone woke Jade from a sound sleep. She turned onto her side and reached across the oak nightstand to stop the annoying intrusion.

Fumbling through the darkness, she found the receiver as the phone rang a third time. "Alright already…"

She glanced over at the clock across from her bed and saw the time glowing in red: two twenty-two.

"What the…?" She muttered uneasily.

The only people who would rudely interrupt her sleep were her mother, with bad news, or a dispatcher from work. If it was work, she didn't remember being on-call for the evening.

"Hello?"

"Uh, Corporal Davis?" the dispatcher said.

"Yeah, it's me. I thought I wasn't on-call tonight."

"Well, looking at the schedule, you're not Corporal. Sergeant Jenkins ordered me to call you and have you meet him at a homicide."

She rolled over onto her back. She couldn't remember being requested at a homicide scene on her night off ever.

"For what?" Her mind was clearer now, but her heart continued to race due to the familiar, middle-of-the-night phone call of death.

"Corporal I'm only relaying orders from your sergeant." The dispatcher's voice was calm; however, his additional orders were not to inform her of anything about the homicide if she asked.

Since her husband's death over a year ago from an on-the-job shooting, she couldn't leave anytime her job called her out. There was her daughter, Gracie, she was raising as a single parent. Annoyed with the request, she took a deep breath to stabilize the beginning of her anger and let it out slowly.

"Call Sergeant Jenkins on the radio and inform him to call me, please."

"Fair enough. Hold on." The dispatcher put Jade on hold and spoke into the radio.

"Deland, Two-Seventeen?" He waited a moment and repeated the call.

"Go ahead Deland. This is Two-Seventeen."

"I have Nine-Fifteen on the line requesting you to call her at her residence."

"Ten-four, I'll give her a call…" The radio squawked.

"Done," the dispatcher answered.

"Thank you."

Without saying a word, Jade hung up and waited.

A couple minutes later, the dispatcher patched the sergeant through to Jade's home phone.

On the first ring, Jade answered.

"Sarge, what's up? You know I have Gracie with me."

"Jade, look, I need you down here at this signal seven. If this wasn't important, I wouldn't be calling you out," he said firmly.

Her reply was silence.

"You're my best investigator, and I need you right now at this scene. Don't you have anyone that could watch your daughter?" he pleaded.

Annoyed, she knew that if he was right there in front of her at that moment, she would slap him for stupidity.

"But" She tried to argue but wasn't quick enough.

"Jade, it's someone you know," he said with apprehension.

Sucking in her breath abruptly, she realized what he'd just said. An overwhelming feeling of dread started to tug at her heart. She couldn't take it if it was her mother or anyone she was close to. Her mouth went dry as her heartbeat shifted into second gear.

"It's not my mother is it?" Her voice quivered, giving away her fear.

"No, Jade, it's not your mother, but could you call her and see if you could drop Gracie off? I need you here now."

Relief spread through her body. Oh thank you, God, thank you. She thought who could it be? She ran through countless friends and co-workers in her mind.

"Who is it?" She asked hoping he would tell her.

"I'll let you find out once you get here. We're in Daytona, one block west of Best Buy's parking lot. I need you as soon as possible. See you in an hour."

The sound of the phone going dead on the other end stopped her from responding.

"Damn."

Switching on the light on the nightstand, she hung up and dialed her mother's number.

"Hello?" The voice that answered sounded old and confused.

"Mom, it's me. Work called me in. I'm sorry, but I need you here tonight."

"I thought you were off."

"So did I. Apparently they need me at a scene."

"Oh." She knew it was better not to ask more than she needed to know, due to the gruesomeness of her daughter's job.

"Mom, it's someone I know, but I don't know who yet."

"Oh, honey, I'm so sorry. I'll be right over." Her mother's voice was filled with concern.

"Thanks Mom." She hung up and started to get ready.

Fifteen minutes later, there was a soft knock at the door. She knew it was her mother coming from a block over. She grabbed her gun belt, sucked in her breath, and attached the belt hooks to each other. She shifted the belt to fit her waist comfortably as she opened the front door. There her mother stood in her white terry cloth robe and blue slippers carrying a plastic bag containing her breakfast.

"Come on in, Mom." She stepped back letting her in and then locking the door.

"Gracie is sound asleep, I checked her several minutes ago. Go ahead and sleep in my bed. I won't be home until sometime tomorrow." Smiling quickly, she turned and walked into the kitchen, where she gathered her wallet, keys, and a can of diet root beer.

"Good night Mom. I appreciate you coming on such short notice." She leaned over, gave her mother a peck on the cheek, and walked through the utility room and out the back door to her patrol car. Not knowing who had died was beginning to gnaw at her nerves.

Grabbing her jacket from the front seat of her patrol car, she shoved her arms in it and started the car. The red luminous light of the radio burned bright as she pushed the button to turn it on. Voices of fellow officers filled the empty spaces of the interior of her car as she pulled out of the driveway of her ten-acre property and headed north. The voices from the radio had always given her a false sense of comfort. She heard her sergeant ask for the medical examiner's estimated time of arrival.

"Two-Seventeen," dispatch called.

"Go ahead, Deland."

"The ME's ETA is thirty minutes."

"Ten-four. Go ahead and send Daytona Wrecker out here owner's request for a 1999 Ford Crown Victoria, city tag of 15378. Let them know there's front end and left side damage. Definitely bring a flatbed tow truck."

"Standby, Two-Seventeen."

Her thoughts ran rampant as she wondered who the victim could be, and she continued listening to the radio traffic.

A local city unit was involved. She wondered who it could be.

"Damn, who?" The question gnawed at her nerves.

Turning right onto International Speedway Boulevard, she sped towards the crime scene, only slowing at the intersections to make sure no one would hit her in her slick top unit. Her blue lights lit up the night sky as she traveled east towards Daytona Beach. She passed the empty buildings in a blur as her heart raced from anticipation.

"Oh God please don't let it be Susan," she pleaded aloud.

She bit down on her bottom lip, and it began to tremble; Jade fought back the emotions threatening to overwhelm her. She had to know first-hand instead of acting like a worrywart. One of her worst fears was being dispatched to a vehicular homicide and the signal seven being a family member or friend. She'd always would try to calm herself down, reminding herself that it was wrong to assume the worst.

The only Daytona police officer she knew was Susan and her sergeant had just requested a tow truck for a city unit.

Chapter 3

SHE SEARCHED THE front seat for her cell phone then dialed Susan's number. It rang twice before her voice mail kicked in.

"Damn!"

Passing I-4, she slowed down to ninety miles an hour. The limited amount of traffic she passed seemed to all be going in the same direction she was. A car in front of her signaled and changed lanes to the right as she approached. She blew through the intersections, and as she passed I-95, she saw the volunteer fire police red lights redirecting traffic away from a side street. Slowing down, Jade turned left, and the volunteer fire police quickly moved the orange cones aside so she could enter.

The area around the scene looked like a circus of emergency lights, with units from the city, fire department, EVAC, the medical examiner's office, and other departments. It was almost blinding to her tired eyes. She parked, and out of habit, Jade grabbed her note pad and started walking towards the fire truck that blocked her view of the scene. She walked around the truck, and then she spotted a vehicle that had crashed into the driver's side door of a patrol car.

A drunk, more than likely, she betted herself silently.

As she approached, her sergeant turned around and walked towards her with a frown on his face.

"Jade, good you're here." He stopped in front of her.

She stood on tiptoes and tried to peer over her sergeant's shoulder, but he stopped her and blocked her view. Frustrated, she gave him a stern look.

Sergeant Jenkins placed his hands on Jade's shoulders and looked straight into her eyes. She saw worry etched into his face. Evidently, he was not pleased about telling her the news.

"Jade, I want you to know who it is before you see the body."

Anticipation hung thickly in the air.

Sergeant Jenkins continued, "Jade it's Susan. She was…"

"Oh God!" she cried. Tears welded up quickly and fell, causing her tough demeanor to crumble.

Sergeant Jenkins pulled Jade into his arms protectively, letting her cry. A photographer snuck under the crime-scene tape and aimed his camera at them.

"Get that guy out of here!" Sergeant Jenkins barked as he turned his back to block the view of him with Jade.

Trooper Wagner's large frame quickly blocked the camera as well, and he walked up to the photographer.

Jade could hear Bill Wagner yelling at the photographer, telling him he had no morals. She was glad, because her worst fear had come true, and she didn't want her picture plastered all over the news. Pain wasn't new for her, especially pain from the loss of a loved one. Susan was like a sister she wished she had, always caring, but she knew how to keep her emotions in check in scenes like this. Susan confided in her a lot and taught her things none of her field-training officers wanted to teach her. "Took too much time," they said. Jade let the memories of Susan unfold and recalled one of the many important pieces of advice that she gave: have fun even when you're working. Susan had said don't take the work to heart, otherwise, she'd be getting too involved and her feelings would get hurt.

Jade cried in Sergeant Jenkins's embrace for a good ten minutes before she could begin to re-gain control of her emotions. The last thing she wanted was for her department to see her weak like this again. Hard as it was, she forced her feelings deep down for now. Her sobs subsided. Jade began wiping her face with the tissues her sergeant handed to her.

"Jade, she was hit pretty hard by the other vehicle. She doesn't…well…it doesn't really look like her." His controlled expression became somber.

Swallowing, she listened quietly to what he said while she fought to regain control of her emotions.

"But, Jade, there's something else," he warned.

"What?"

When he brushed away the hair that hung in front of her face, he saw a teary-eyed, red-nosed, vulnerable woman, and it bothered him.

"We think there was foul play before the accident occurred," he said with bitterness.

Puzzled, she looked up at him giving him her full attention.

Foul play? What in the world did he mean, foul play?

Reading her look, Sergeant Jenkins continued. "She'd been sliced up prior to the drunk falling asleep behind the wheel and slamming into her." Taking a step back, he gestured her to continue towards the vehicles. "Take a look for yourself."

Jade took a pair of rubber gloves from Jenkins, and quickly pulled them on. She summoned as much courage as she could. Wiping her eyes on her long sleeve uniform, Jade regained her professionalism. Slowly she walked the distance to the group of men clustered around the driver's door of the patrol car. Two of the men were wearing blue uniforms with large print on the back saying MEDICAL EXAMINER. One man, who worked for the local police, was taking pictures of the scene. Two Daytona Beach Officers she recognized as Susan's co-workers. They were hugging each other and quietly crying. Jade overheard a lieutenant and a sergeant of Susan's bickering with each other regarding her last transmission.

Jade's co-worker, who was also a good friend, approached. Corporal Jason Lance gently gripped her elbow for support with his large warm hand and looked down at her quietly. She stopped in front of the crime scene, and the men who stood blocking the view of inquisitive onlookers stepped back, giving way to her. If it wasn't for Jason supporting her elbow, she knew she would have fallen flat on her ass. The scene was overwhelming, with the smell of blood this close mixed with motor engine fluids. The combination reeked of death. She noticed the foul smell when she approached the patrol car, but being this close and knowing the victim was too much for her.

Jason pulled her close, whispering in her ear, "Jade, I'm here for you, just hold on to me, girl." With his support, she looked again, taking in the fact of her friend's death.

The site was gruesome.

Jade noted that Susan's blood was all over the floorboard of the vehicle, on the caged plexi-glass, all over her radio and passenger seat. Jade didn't realize anybody could bleed that much. Looking again at her friend's body, she noted how she was slumped over from the blow to the driver's side. Jade could tell rigor-mortis had already set in as Susan's body laid stiff in a partial fetal position. Noticing the injuries on her friend's broken face, Jade saw that Susan's eyes remained wide open in a fixed stare. Peering down at the floorboard, she saw Susan's internal organs, which clung to her intestinal tract. She scanned the rest of her friend's body for evidence and observed that Susan's back had several bones protruding fighting to break free of her uniform. Looking further down, Jade saw that Susan's hips were partially crushed into the radio. The metal stand for her laptop laid bent from her head striking it. The computer lay in rubble on the passenger floorboard. Bits of bone fragments and brain matter were drying on the passenger seat and window. The site would be forever etched in her brain, but Jade attempted to forget who it was and try to focus on the investigation.

Looking up at Jason, Jade tried to speak, but nausea threatened to overcome her. She pulled away suddenly, walked several steps towards a palmetto bush and vomited her dinner and everything else that she'd had eaten earlier. When she was done, Sergeant Jenkins walked over with more tissue and a bottled soda for her. Willingly, she accepted both items. She wiped her face with the tissue and washed her mouth out with the drink. After several swigs, she closed the bottle and handed it back to him.

She looked around curiously. "Where is the person who was driving the car?"

"He was transported to Halifax Hospital. He sustained serious injuries due to not wearing a seatbelt."

"Is he going to live?" She hoped.

"Possibly," Sergeant Jenkins said with discontent.

Good. That was all she wanted to hear. She needed to talk to that person and get a full interview.

Sergeant Jenkins handed her the driver license of the other driver. Quickly Jade looked at it and then placed it in her top right pocket so she wouldn't forget it.

"Dispatch already ran the driver license. They're going to stick the information in your box for you," Sergeant Jenkins said.

"Is he valid?" Jade asked.

"Believe it or not, yes he is. He's from Connecticut. Probably here for the races."

"Ok. Were there any witnesses?" Her stomach became queasy again, but she continued to fight back the bile that threatened to erupt.

"For the crash, yes, there is one person."

"This person reported the crash?" she asked, taking another swig of the soda to push the bad taste out of her mouth.

Looking around the crowd that gathered on the northeast end of the parking lot, Sergeant Jenkins spotted a Daytona Beach police officer standing next to a blonde elderly woman and pointed. "Yes, your witness is over there, by the Daytona officer."

"Can you have her come over to my car? I'll be there waiting for her."

"Sure thing." Her sergeant quickly walked towards the only witness they had. The old woman would probably be exhausted by having been interviewed by the local police department and now Jade wanted to interview her. Reaching the woman, he gently grabbed her elbow and escorted the grief stricken woman towards his investigator.

Jade greeted the elderly woman.

"Hello, my name is Corporal Davis. I'm going to be the officer in charge of this investigation, and you are?"

"Janet Riley." Her voice had a slight tremble to it.

She guessed the woman was in her seventies. She wore blue jeans, white tennis shoes, and a black racing T-shirt with Dale Earnhardt's signature on the front and a large number three on the back. In her left hand, the old woman held a lit cigarette that smelled of menthol. Watching her, Jade noticed the woman's fingers trembled when she took a long drag from the end of the filter.

"Mrs. Riley, I need to ask you a few questions regarding this accident you saw. I know you've been through a lot tonight and have been asked a lot of questions, but if you could bear with me, I'll try to make this as painless as possible."

The old woman nodded her head.

"I need you to have a seat in my patrol car while I get my digital recorder ready." Opening the front door, she gestured for the elderly woman to get in.

Janet dropped her cigarette on the floor before she got into the patrol car.

Once the woman was inside, Jade shut the door, walked to her driver's door, and sat inside. Finding the recorder, she proceeded with the interview swearing the woman in and obtaining general information of the woman's identity.

"Mrs. Riley could you please tell me what you witnessed tonight?"

"Well, I was driving my car when I saw that car over their plow into the police car. It scared me to death seeing the crash, and the noise was awful. I pulled over, parked and went over to help them. The driver of the silver Mustang was out cold behind the wheel. And for the officer, she was…, well…definitely gone." The old woman shook her head and looked down.

"What direction were you driving and on what road?" Jade asked.

"Oh, I was on US 92, the Speedway, traveling in that direction" she pointed west.

"Approximately what time did this happen? Do you recall?"

Looking down at her watch the old woman began to estimate the time, "Oh… about twelve forty-five maybe."

"Prior to the accident, did you happen to see the driving pattern of the vehicle that struck the patrol car?"

The old woman hesitated a moment as she gathered her thoughts.

"Well, yes, I did!" Her voice grew with excitement as she remembered.

"He kept swerving and couldn't stay in his own lane. Then, when he made that wide right turn onto this road here he continued to drive in the opposite lane right before he crashed." The old woman smiled, smug with herself. "It all happen so fast officer."

Probing further Jade asked, "Would you say he was driving fast?"

"Let me see..., I was going about forty, and he past me, almost hitting the left side of my car, so I slowed down quite a bit more."

"Did he pass you quickly or slowly?"

"Definitely I would say fast."

"What else do you remember?"

"Well I glanced over because he was so close to my car..., I knew it was a guy, and oh yes, he had brown hair."

"Would you be able to place the guy behind the wheel if you saw him again?"

"Well, I can tell you this. I watched him almost hit me, then turn, and drive on the wrong side of the road and crashed into that patrol car. I drove into the Bob Evans Restaurant over there and went to see if everyone was OK. He never came out of the car." She pointed to the crashed vehicle. "So the guy that was taken out of that car there, whoever he is, well, he was definitely the driver."

Jade continued with standard questions regarding the woman's health, vision and any alcoholic beverages or medication she might have consumed that evening. Five minutes later, she was just about finished. "Is there anything else you feel is pertinent to this investigation that I haven't asked you?"

She thought for a moment..., "No."

"Thank you ma'am. I do appreciate your time. End of interview is three fifty-three a.m." Jade knew this woman only witnessed the crash, but at the moment, a short interview was all she could handle. She exited her patrol car, walked around to the passenger side, opened the door, and let Janet Riley out. She escorted her to the woman's own car.

She exhaled slowly and continued her investigation.

Walking back to her patrol car, she reached into her driver-side door and grabbed a scratch pad and measuring tape. With the measuring tape in her pocket, she slowly walked around the scene, trying to get a full 360 degree view. This helped her see everything completely and a better understanding of what happened. She sketched out both cars in their final rest positions on the scratch pad and the building next to them. Next, she sketched out the parking lot and then the roadway. Looking for any type of breakage on the roadway from the first car-the Mustang- she realized she needed the fire trucks and ambulance moved.

Looking around she spotted her sergeant.

"Hey, Sarge!" She tried not to yell too loudly, and she motioned for him to come to her.

Walking briskly over with a lit cigarette in his mouth, he knew what she was going to ask.

"Sarge, could you get the fire trucks and ambulance to move? I need to see my scene completely without all those cars blocking my view."

Blowing the cigarette smoke slowly out, he answered, "I knew you were going to say that. What would you do without my political techniques with the other agencies, huh?" He smiled and spun on his heels. Not caring who he might upset, he yelled, "I need the fire trucks and the ambulance moved pronto!" As he walked toward the group of men, they stared at him, and no one moved.

"Come on, guys. You heard me. Move 'em or I'll have them towed!" He knew that would get their attention.

The men shook their heads and started toward their vehicles.

"Gee, you think you could have said it a bit nicer?" one fire fighter said. He smiled sarcastically at Sergeant Jenkins as he walked by.

"Ah, poor baby. Now hurry it up so we can all go home!" Sergeant Jenkins barked.

The emergency vehicles moved back toward the roadway. Jade walked slowly backward from the other crashed car, searching the pavement intently for any tire marks. The lighting from the parking lot was not enough where they were. She jotted down some of her thoughts on her note pad: Why was Susan there? Was she on a call? Where was this driver heading? Important questions she had to answer.

Jason approached her in long strides, a frown on his face. His body was strong, but not overly muscular, and he had short sandy-blonde hair, blue eyes and a mustache. He was intimidating, at over six foot three, and when he spoke, his tone was usually gentle, but always filled with authority. She liked Jason's calm and playful demeanor. He never patronized anyone, and he was always eager to learn as much as he could. Jade didn't miss how attractive was, but since he was a coworker, she tried not to react to his appearance.

Stopping short in front of her, he looked down intensely at her. "Jade, let me take the pictures while you measure the scene, OK?"

She slipped the camera strap over her head and handed it to him, relieved at his offer to take the pictures. She knew focusing on the gruesome scene through a camera lens would have been too much for her at that moment.

"Thanks, Jason, I appreciate it. Please do be overly thorough with the pictures." She gave him a half-hearted smile before he turned and walked back to the scene.

Bile suddenly filled her throat again. Running to the bushes, she threw up until dry heaves took over. A paramedic nearby walked over and escorted her to the ambulance for privacy. She cleaned her face up, and took a swig of the water that was offered to her. Then she walked the short distance back to the scene.

Measuring off the fire hydrant as the permanent land marker, Jade laid the tape down parallel to the roadway and proceeded to make a field diagram of the evidence. Next, she used the tape to measure off the evidence, documenting the measurements on her diagram in a legend. This was always time-consuming especially for her, since she was very particular about the details. The more evidence she measured, the more it helped in determining important factors, such as momentum, direction of travel for both vehicles, speed, and whatever else she wanted to know based on the givens. She knew it was over-kill, but once she finished documenting the evidence by the tape- measuring method, she had taken the camera back from Jason and took out her markers for photogrammetry. Placing the markers everywhere she needed in the crime scene, she took her photographs and several measurements. Then she was done.

She gave her OK and the first wrecker on scene pulled the silver car off of the patrol car and secured it on the bed of the tow truck. Once the vehicle was safely off and away from the patrol car, Jade forced herself to look at the damage on the left side where it had been hit. Her gaze drifted upward to Susan, or what was left of her, slumped over. A deep feeling of loss weighed heavily on her. Her best friend was gone from her life.

Sergeant Jenkins approached Jade from behind. He had been pre-occupied, speaking to the chief of police for Daytona Beach Police Department and the dead police officer's sergeant.

"Are you ok?"

Her throat ached from holding back from crying. In a froggy voice, she responded, "No."

"I spoke to Susan's sergeant and the chief of police, they're going to give us a copy of the cad tape for the evening and they're going to notify next of kin for us. Apparently, they want to assist us as much as they can. Also, her Sergeant stated she was here, but didn't call in the reason why, only that she was busy at the moment."

"OK, good. Thanks Sarge. I'm going to have the Federal Department of Law Enforcement come out to the wrecker compound to dust for prints inside the patrol car." She looked around, "Where's the transport for the medical examiner's office? We need to get her out of the car."

"Over there." Sergeant Jenkins pointed towards the mass exodus of patrol cars and emergency vehicles south of them.

"OK, have them take Susan out. I want an autopsy definitely done on her for cause of death. You don't mind telling them that do you?" Jade couldn't trust her emotions and didn't want to witness her friend being extracted from the patrol car.

"No problem." Sergeant Jenkins turned and headed toward the people from the medical examiner's office.

She turned to the wrecker driver, who was standing near her.

"You can have this car once the officer is taken out. I don't want anyone in the patrol car. That includes any police officers, unless your office calls me for an approval. Do you understand?"

The driver smiled. "No problem. Your name is?"

"Corporal Jade Davis. I'll be on the inventory sheet and I mean no one is to go into it. I don't care who it is."

"No problem."

Chapter 4

TWENTY MINUTES LATER, pulling into the emergency room parking lot of Halifax Hospital, she grabbed her digital recorder, camera, blood kit, and scratch pad with her jotted notes. She called her location in to dispatch and she placed her equipment into a leather bag. She had her emotions in check; however, she couldn't guarantee how she would react when she met the suspect. Dispatch had informed her that they couldn't get an update on the suspect. They only knew that he was still alive.

She had to see him for herself.

Hospitals tended to give wrong information to callers even if the callers were law enforcement.

As the two glass doors opened by the infra-red motion detectors on the ambulance entrance way, the smell of blood mixed with urine and cleaning detergents filled her nostrils, making her nose crinkle. The emergency ward contained injured or ill tourist, in town for race week at Daytona Beach International Speedway.

Famous racecar drivers such as Wallace, DuPont, Petty, Gordan, Martin, Skinner, Hamilton, Ernhardt Jr. race in Daytona Beach keeping the local community busy. The disrupted traffic, re-direction of traffic after the races, and many intoxicated people walking along the famous International Speedway Boulevard area, which contained scattered businesses, lasted for about a week, twice a year.

A female nurse looked up when Jade approached the information desk, behind which were a number of nurses and doctors jotting down notes on patient clipboards. This was Jade's chance of getting information before anyone had a chance to deliberately ignore her.

"Excuse me. Does anyone know where I can find the male patient involved in a motor vehicle accident? He was brought in around two o'clock this morning?"

The nurse nodded. "Yeah, he was brought up to the third floor. He's in critical condition." She looked at the computer screen. "His name is…Jason McCrugle, and he's in room three ten".

"Thank you."

Jade walked around the corner toward the elevators. Another set of swivel doors opened, and she walked through them and turned left. The hallway echoed with the sound of her footsteps as she came to the south elevators. When the elevator door opened, she stepped in and pressed the third floor button. Slowly the elevator crawled upward to the third floor. Jade walked out onto the hallway, where it was very quiet. All she heard were beeping sounds, somewhere off to the left. Nurses worked quietly as they checked on the critically injured patients.

Walking slowly, she looked at the room numbers on the doors until she came to 310. A young, thin nurse checking her patient's blood pressure turned and raised her eyebrows at Jade. "Can I help you?" she asked.

Jade noted the nurse's nametag.

"Yes…uh, Tracy is it? I'm a traffic homicide investigator for the patrol, and I'm here for Mr. McCrugle." Jade looked at the man in the bed and saw that he wasn't awake. Obviously, he wouldn't be able to talk due to the obstruction down his throat, a tube in his trachea assisting his breathing.

"Was there a blood withdrawal on him?" Jade asked.

The nurse went to the stand that held her patient's notes. Searching through his medical file, she found what she was looking for.

"Why, of course. You want to know if he had alcohol in his blood. That would be obvious just bend down and take a whiff." She handed Jade the file opened to the serology page.

Jade saw that he was more than three times over the legal limit.

Typical drunk, she thought.

She handed the nurse a blood kit. "I'm going to need blood withdrawn from him for our records, if you would for me."

The young nurse wasn't at all pleased that she had to withdraw the blood. Taking the blood kit from the corporal, she opened the box and started taking blood from the unconscious man.

Five minutes later, the blood was secured and the paperwork signed, initialed, and dated. Jade packaged the two vials of blood for evaluation. Taking the camera from around her neck, she started taking pictures of Jason McCrugle while he lay in a coma, unable to protest. These pictures would help her in the investigation. When she was done with her pictures, she packed up her equipment and walked over to the nurses' desk, where Tracy, the suspect's nurse, was at the computer, typing up notes.

"Tracy, concerning Jason McCrugle, what is the extent of his injuries?"

Tracy flipped through the folder and read the diagnosis from the doctor. "Patient has injuries to the pelvic area, contusions to the head with an open fracture and edema to the brain. The patient also has multiple fractures, including to his nose, sternum, and the last three ribs on the left side. Besides having a strong odor of an alcoholic beverage on his breath upon his arrival, he also defecated in his pants unknown if from the collision or other. You saw the serology lab work. What else do you need to know?" The nurse's eyes were blood-shot, and her shoulders sagged probably from working the late shift and not having sufficient sleep prior to coming to work.

"Actually you have been wonderful and very cooperative. Thank you."

Pulling out a business card, Jade wrote down her name and the case number, along with her business phone number. She handed it to the nurse.

"If you possibly could, call me when Jason comes around and is in a clearer state of mind. I don't want to keep calling here about him and interfering with your work, but this is important."

"He killed an officer, didn't he?" she asked.

"I'm not at liberty to discuss this. Criminal charges are pending. But, yes, someone was killed."

"I understand. I'll put this in his record and leave a note for the other nurses, in case he wakes up on their shifts." Smiling, the young nurse placed the business card into the patient's chart. She taped the card to a blank page and started to write a note on it.

"Thank you, Tracy. I hope your shift goes by quickly for you. Take care."

Jade turned and walked toward the south side elevator doors.

Chapter 5

TIME SEEMED TO fly as Bob continued to be patient with his subjects whom he loved to assist. Therapy, it was called, but it only seemed like special attention these kids' needed. Smiling, he glanced at his watch. It was one o'clock already. Gathering the scattered books and stacking them in an orderly fashion, he patted the child on the head.

"You're a smart boy, John. Let's clean up this work area so the next kid can find stuff he likes at this work station. OK?"

John flashed a childish, toothless grin as he began cleaning the table. "Yes Mr. Bob."

Within less than a minute, the workstation was cleared, and the child stood eagerly by the door.

Looking down Bob measured the boy, knowing it would take a long time to get him caught up in reading and everything else. He put his hand on John's shoulder, confident in the relationship of trust they'd built since school had started two months ago. It was a good sign. Normally the children he gave therapy to didn't trust too many people, especially men. Breaking down the wall a child had built up and gaining an invitation into that child's world took time and cleverness on his part. He escorted John from the small windowed room into the classroom. The child walked away, toward a group of boys building what looked like a castle. He dropped to his knees, ignoring everything else that was going on in the classroom.

Bob scanned the room for his next subject, which was his favorite - a dainty girl with long brown hair and blue-eyes who, unfortunately, wore very thick glasses. He spotted her over by the computers, where she was absorbed in playing a computer game. He walked over and tapped her on the shoulder.

She turned around, and her eyes lit up when she saw him. "Hi Mr. Bob." Tossing off the headphones and letting them fall onto the table, she scurried out of the chair and hugged the tall man's leg affectionately. "Is it my turn now?" she asked.

He winked at her and gently took her small, dainty hand. He escorted her into the next room for therapy. Today he would have her read a new book and teach her some more new words from his cue cards, printed large so she could see them easily.

"Gracie how are you today?"

"Fine, and you?" She was so polite and diligent in her use of proper greetings and comments.

"Good. How would you like to learn a new game today?"

Squealing, she clapped her hands. "Yay!"

He knew the game would keep her attention. The key to teaching his star pupil was by telling her it was a game. As for reading, she loved listening to him read her stories, and she would mimic him every so often. This child was his favorite - so precious and so innocent. Gracie was an angel in his eyes, and he wanted to teach her as much as he could in order to get her caught up and ready for the world. As for Gracie's mother, she was exceptional and beautiful, straight from heaven another angel that he wanted to possess, but in a different way. The child needed a father and he wanted to be that person and be a husband to her mother. All he had to do to make his wish come true was be patient and, have a careful plan. His first obstacle was finally out of his way – forever.

Chapter 6

It was already six o'clock in the morning when Jade punched the code into the secured gate at work. The gate slowly creaked open as she patiently waited to enter. Finally, with enough room to squeeze the patrol car through, she drove in and parked. Gathering her leather bag, she exited her patrol car and walked up to the backdoor. The air was heavy with humidity as the sun started to rise over the horizon. The orange-red glow was a warning of another warm day during the winter months. So typical of Florida, she thought.

After she punched in the door code to the back door and then the alarm code to the building, she entered, and went to her desk. The building was quiet so far. Within the next hour, police officers and administrative personnel would be filling the void of the empty building, giving it life again. She made a mental list of who she had to fax information to regarding the fatality. The fatality report had to be input into the computer and faxed to the Medical Examiner's Office, and the Victim Advocate's Office. Turning on her computer she plopped herself down at her desk, feeling miserable. She opened the folder and pulled out the stack of papers documenting her friend's fatality. She had to finish certain required forms before she could go home.

Why Susan? Why her of all people? she thought.

Damn!

Covering her face with her hands, Jade closed her eyes, wishing it were all a nightmare that would be over as soon as she reopened her eyes. Her computer beeped, signaling that it was ready for a password. She lowered her hands from her face and logged in. Then she typed her narrative on the intranet website, the state agency's homicide reporting system. Quickly she typed up possible charges for the homicide. Once she was finished, she did the crash report and submitted it into the server.

"Jade, are you all right?

The sound of the voice startled her from her thoughts. Looking up, she saw her captain standing in the doorway with a look of concern on his face.

"Uh, yes, Captain. Thank you for asking." Her voice faltered just a little.

"Your sergeant called me and told me what happened. Do you feel you can handle this case?"

"Yes sir." This time her voice didn't give her away. Only the hurt look in her eyes told onlookers of her misery.

"OK, if you're sure, but if at any time you feel like you can't handle it anymore, let your sergeant know, and we'll give it to someone else. We'll definitely understand your reasons, OK?"

"I appreciate it sir. Of course it hurts, but I'll do the best I can." Jade swallowed hard and fought to maintain control of her emotions. She refused to give into her emotions again, especially in front of her captain.

He nodded and left the room. Jade looked up at the clock and saw that it was already thirty minutes past seven. Other personnel were walking about the building. Caught up with her thoughts Jade didn't even hear them enter the building.

She called the Florida Climatic Center and requested that the weather report for yesterday be faxed to her. Then she emailed Lieutenant Marlow, who was the court liaison for her department. She requested a certified copy of Jason McCrugle's driving record sent to her station. Next, she called up Daytona Beach Police Department and asked for Susan's lieutenant.

"This is Lieutenant Jarvis," the man on the other end of the line said. "Can I help you?"

"Yes sir, this is Corporal Jade Davis - the one handling the homicide of one of your officer."

"Yes, I know. How can I help you?"

"I'm calling in regards to the notification of Susan's next of kin. I was informed your agency insisted on doing that." Through the phone, she could hear him fumbling with some paperwork.

"Yes," he said. "I have it right in front of me. She has an aunt living up north."

"I'll need that address if you don't mind."

"No I don't mind."

"If you would fax that information over here, I'd appreciate it."

He sighed. "No problem, corporal, and if there's anything else we could do to assist, please do let us know. Susan was a damn good officer and she didn't deserve...no one deserves to die like that. Please let us know if you need any assistance."

"Sir, just a copy of the cad tape for that evening's shift is about all I'll need for right now, but if anything else comes up, whom would I ask for?"

"Me or Sergeant O'Riley, Susan's immediate supervisor."

"Thank you, sir. I'll call if anything else is needed, and I'll let you know when I'm done with the investigation."

He thanked her and they ended the conversation.

Jade hung up the phone relieved she wasn't the one who had to do the notification. That was the one part of the job she definitely didn't like. Everyone reacted differently to the bad news. She remembered the looks on people's faces when they saw an officer at the door late at night. A family member answering the door knew it wouldn't be good news. Some family members would get physical and want to fight, thinking that was the only way to redeem a deceased loved one's death.

She made another mental list. She had to notify The Florida Department of Law Enforcement and have them dust Susan's patrol car for fingerprints at the wrecker yard. She would also have to go back to the scene and take pictures during the daytime. She recalled how nighttime and daytime pictures varied, some more than others. Daytime photos sometimes showed evidence that nighttime photos didn't. She also wanted to look around the scene once again, just in case anything was missed due to the lack of lighting.

It was now eight thirty, and time was flying by. Calling the Florida Department of Law Enforcement, she informed them of what she needed them to do. Next, she packed up her stuff, and she dropped the print-out of her fatality report on her sergeant's desk for when he came in so he could review it before it was sent out. Walking out of the station, she took off in her patrol car and returned to the homicide scene.

Reporters were still at the scene when she pulled up, as was her sergeant and her agency's public affairs officer. They were both being interviewed by a TV reporter.

Her sergeant spotted her pulling up and walked over to her.

"Jade as you can see, we are being hounded by the press. I don't like dealing with them." He popped another cigarette into his mouth and lit it.

"Well, it looks like Lieutenant Howard is earning his pay." She took out her digital camera and started taking pictures of the scene and the tire marks. Sergeant Jenkins stood by, keeping the media far away, enabling Jade to finish taking her pictures.

Once she'd packed away her camera, Jade set down her field notes on the passenger seat. Tucking away her pen, she turned around facing her sergeant who was still puffing on a cigarette and pacing nervously, deep in thought.

"Hey Sarge are you OK?" She'd never seen him act like this and was concerned.

Beads of sweat rolled down the side of his face, leaving a trail from his temple to his jaw.

The morning had turned into a very humid day, with no cool air or breezes.

"Yeah, just wish those reporters would disappear so we could all leave." He tossed his half-smoked cigarette to the ground and stepped on it as he slowly blew out a stream of smoke.

"Well, I put the paperwork on your desk to review, and I already ordered the driver license history on McCrugle. Oh yeah, I called FDLE, and they're going to fingerprint the car for me sometime today. I don't want anyone inside that patrol car for any reasons except for their FDLE fingerprint technicians, OK?"

"Sure." He appeared distracted by the reporter who continued haggling Lieutenant Howard for more information.

"Sarge, I want a raise and a new patrol car." She figured if his answer was yes, he was definitely not paying any attention to her.

"Yeah, sure, whatever," he muttered.

Jade quickly smacked his arm trying to get his attention.

He turned to her, "Ouch! What was that for?"

She was irritated that her guess was correct.

"That was for ignoring me. Did you hear what I said? I don't want anyone except for their FDLE fingerprint technicians in the patrol car without my approval."

He rubbed his arm and frowned, "OK."

Jade watched him with a critical squint and wasn't pleased with his level of distraction. "Sarge, what is the matter with you this morning?"

He sighed, then placed his hands on his hips. Conflict crossed his face for a few seconds before he answered, "Jade, look you didn't hear it from me, OK?"

She shot him a withering glance before answering. "OK".

"Somehow the press got wind of a rumor that's flying around concerning Susan's death. And now they're here, of course, to see if the rumor is true or not. The problem is that we don't really know. Now the lieutenant has to smooth over one reporter who wants an exclusive interview. If she doesn't get it, she says she's going to report the information on the air today."

Jade had no clue of what the rumor was and was irritated that they'd ultimately have to make a deal with the press. Shaking her head in disgust she asked, "What rumor is going around?"

He ran his fingers through his hair, "Look, Jade, the rumor is that Susan was here meeting a boyfriend prior to the homicide. Also, someone's spreading the idea that the only reason we were called to this scene was to do a cover up. Apparently, Susan was having an affair with someone in her department, possibly a supervisor, and they were having secret rendezvous. Now, with this homicide, rumor is that it's foul play." He stared back at her in silence.

Jade stood there trying to digest what she'd just heard. Her body stiffened in shock, causing the words to wedge in her throat. Was he serious? He had to be. That would explain why he was acting the way he was. Jade knew that Susan was having an affair, but for it to end up as a homicide, now that was crazy! She shook her head no and coughed to clear her throat. Her face flushed with anger. Finally, the words spilled out of her mouth. "This is ridiculous! This is just a stunt a reporter is using so she could get an exclusive interview. She knows we would never jeopardize our reputation to do a cover up on a local agency - or any other agency!" Frustrated, fists clenched, she began walking briskly toward the press.

Quickly her sergeant took her by the upper arm and held her back. "What the hell are you doing?" He barked at her.

"This is bullshit and you know it!" She broke free of him.

He reached out and grabbed her again. "Yeah, but you plowing your way over there and showing your ass isn't going to help either!"

She clenched her fists, wanting to make contact with one of them. Suddenly she felt herself spun around by her shoulders.

"Damn it, Sarge, I refuse to have my name smeared because one of them has the gall to make up bullshit in order to get first rights to an interview!"

Her sergeant directed her away from the earshot of the press. "Look, Jade, all of us know its bullshit, but let the lieutenant do his job. There's no point in letting them get you upset. OK?" There was a critical tone in his voice as he spat out his words impatiently.

"Dammit!" said Jade. Turning, she stormed to her patrol car and slammed the door shut. She peeled out and drove to her house. The first phase of the homicide investigation was done. Now she needed to get the hell away from the area before she decided to do something she would definitely regret later on. Traffic was already packed for another race. Torn by conflicting emotions, she made her way back to Deland.

Chapter 7

"Mommy! Mommy!"

The bedroom door burst open. The noise barely woke Jade. Her daughter with her smile cherubic face, jumped onto her bed. The clock on her nightstand read two fifteen. Jade groaned from the interruption of her sleep and buried her face under her pillow.

Then came a knock at the door.

"What?" Her muffled voice was barely audible to the visitor. The door opened and her friend entered.

"Jade, why are you in bed?" Bob asked.

Uncovering her head, she turned around and faced him. Her hair was mused from sleep. She shot him a glare through her swollen, bloodshot eyes in silence.

"Are you OK?" he repeated.

She let out a long raspy breath and replied, "No, Bob. I had a late homicide last night." Raw hurt glittered in her eyes.

"Oh really?" His expression stilled and grew serious.

"Yeah, unfortunately it's someone I know." She could hardly lift her voice from a whisper.

Gracie lay next to her twirling, long curly hair with her dainty fingers. She stopped and turned to her mother, her brow creased with worry.

Jade caressed Gracie's face and then gently pinched one of her cheeks.

"Hey, squirt, Momma's OK." Her faint smile held a touch of sadness.

Gracie smiled back at her mother and went back to twirling her hair.

Bob walked into the bedroom and seated himself on the edge of her bed. His brown eyes brimmed with tenderness and patience.

"Honey, anyone I know?" he asked in a mildly interested voice.

She stared at the floor and nodded her head, fighting to hold back the tears that threaten to fall.

He gently grabbed her arm and gathered her in his embrace. Jade couldn't hold back her despair and wept aloud. The anguish from her friend's death seared her heart.

Gracie looked back at her mother. Instinctively, the child wrapped her arms around her mother's back and hugged her affectionately.

"Momma, you OK?" Her voice held a slight tremor.

Bob put his arm around the scared little girl and brought her closer into their embrace.

"Its OK, honey," he said. "Your Mommy is feeling sad at the moment. She'll be OK once she can cry it out." His voice was soothing yet deceptively calm.

Gracie started to tear up in their embrace.

Jade's body shook from deep sobs that racked her insides. Bob stood his ground and continued to soothe her with gentle squeezes and quick rubs on her back.

After a few minutes spent in tears, Jade swallowed hard and pulled away from his embrace. She turned and reached behind her headboard to retrieve a tissue. Wiping her tear-streaked face, Jade blew her nose and threw the tissue on the floor with the rest of them that were scattered at the side of her bed.

Gracie let go of her mother, wiped her eyes, and lied back down, curling up into a ball watching her mother.

Even though she had little sleep, and was grief stricken, Jade seemed beautiful to Bob. He stood up to let her out of bed. He watched her every move, like a predator with its prey. When she passed him, he inhaled her essence, imprinting it on his brain. He watched her slip her robe over her pajamas and caught a glimpse of her nipples standing erect against the very thin cool white tank top that she wore. Those private glimpses of her, he loved, but they had become rare.

"Bob, I appreciate you picking up Gracie. You know you don't have to do that." Her voice snapped him back to reality.

As Jade walked out the door with her daughter following, he took in the view of her backside with a lot of appreciation.

"I know, but I enjoy spending time with her, and I don't think the daycare environment is really right for her when what she really needs is one-on-one attention."

Gracie's father had passed away over a year ago. If Bob hadn't been there for the girl, Jade didn't know what she would have done. His helpfulness and un-yielding friendship had been a godsend to her. Reflecting for a moment on how many times Bob had been there for them, she realized she'd lost count. As she made a pot of coffee, she realized he'd been there for her through the worst times and had been very patient with them - especially when Gracie went through the rebellious stage after her father's death. Her daughter didn't want to accept that her father was gone forever, and she went through various stages of fits of anger and withdrawal. She herself had been very withdrawn, and again, there was Bob, holding her and comforting her through her depression. Recalling the many times he slept over on the couch worried about them, she wondered what she'd do without him. He had picked up the slack when her husband had passed away and had been a true friend.

She wondered why she hadn't thought about his devotedness to them before.

Gracie took a juice box out of the refrigerator and hugged her mother's leg, not letting go.

"Gracie, honey, I'm OK now. You don't have to worry." Jade bent down and gave her daughter a reassuring hug and a kiss on the cheek. "OK sweetie?"

Gracie's smile convinced Jade that she was better. The child headed toward her room, sipping her drink on the way.

Bob lean against the counter next to Jade, watching as always. Trying to be helpful, he started to escort Jade into the living room. "Come on, Jade. Why don't you relax some, and I'll fix you your coffee and whatever else you like."

"Bob, no, really I can do it." She hesitated, not wanting to bother him with the menial task of fixing her breakfast.

"No, you sit down and let me fix you something. Bagel?" He asked, picking up the remote control and turning on the television for her.

"OK, Bob you win. A bagel would be great. They're in the refrigerator, and I want honey on it. Oh yeah, and cream and sugar with my coffee."

"I know your flavored cream. That's in the refrigerator too. Don't worry. I'll handle it. Relax and I'll be back in a moment." He smiled sheepishly and disappeared into the kitchen.

Plopping herself down onto her couch, she could hear the cabinet doors open and shut until he found whatever he was looking for.

Within a few minutes, he was done making her breakfast, and he brought it out to her. She was watching an old John Wayne movie that was playing on cable when he placed the food and drink in front of her.

Smug with himself, he thought about how well his plan was working. She's so beautiful, he thought as he watched her cradle the coffee cup in her hands and sip the beverage. He sat down on the couch next to her, and she began eating while watching the television, completely engrossed in the distraction. The friendship they had was strong, he knew. Trusting him with her daughter and even giving him a key to the house was a big step. The invitations to dinner were many, always with Gracie included, but none of the times had it been with just the two of them. Something he was planning to fix. Now with Susan gone, Jade wouldn't be so busy and wouldn't have any excuses to give him.

An erotic thought occurred to him. Scooting himself behind her, he placed his large warm hands on her shoulders and gently started to massage her.

"Mmm...," she said. She closed her eyes and slowly chewed her food, enjoying the sensation of the massage, something her husband use to do almost every night to relax her.

The sound of her purring voice caused a surge to go through him, starting from his chest, moving through his body, through his arms and legs, and, more strongly through his groin. Aroused just from hearing her voice and touching her shoulders, he bravely started massaging down her back. Jade moved forward, letting him kneed out the tension in her back, enjoying every minute of it.

He could feel the tension release while he massaged her through her silk robe. He pulled her slowly back toward him, and continued, working up her back to her shoulders and then her neck. Placing his thumbs on her spine in her neck, he rotated them both clockwise, while the rest of his fingers wrapped around her neck ever so gently, soothing her stress away.

Jade continued to purr unconsciously at his touch, as his magic whirled her into oblivion. Her body reacted to his touch as his fingers left a trail of goose bumps on her skin. She could feel her breasts swell as he slowly moved his hands up to her head and massaged her scalp. She scolded herself silently, knowing his touch was arousing her, and at the same time, she didn't care. She could trust Bob. He was her good friend and confidant, and at the moment, her masseur. Sometimes she wondered why he was so good to them, but she realized it wasn't good to be so skeptical about everything. She told herself to just enjoy it.

Leaning forward as he massaged her scalp, he gazed down at her lovely face and body. His arousal was no longer partial, but a full-fledge hard on when he saw her nipples harden, brushing up against her very thin shirt and silk robe. His blood pressure started to increase as he continued to move downward from her scalp to the front of her shoulders pulling her robe off of her shoulders and letting it drop to the floor where she was sitting. The thin white fabric of her tank top left nothing to imagination, as the nipples on her swollen breasts stood erect.

The feel of Bob's warm hands against her skin was erotic as he continued to massage her, moving down her left arm and then her right arm. She was lost in the sensation of his hands against her skin, feeling completely secure with him.

Oh, God I got to have her, he thought.

He adjusted his arousal momentarily with one hand. The pain was getting to him. Next, he started down her back again, this time kneading her soft skin farther from her spine, working toward her sides. Then he took a chance and bravely started rubbing her sides from her waist slowly upwards towards her shoulder blades. His fingers touched the sides of her small but swollen small breast massaging away any tension, and she raised her arms slightly, letting him continue his work. The pressure in his groin threatened to burst as Jade brushed her back against his arousal.

I need her badly! he thought.

He lowered his mouth to her ear. His lips grazed the soft skin of her ear. In a husky, low voice he asked, "How does that feel Jade?"

"Mm…great," she said. Her voice sounded almost like a purr as she reveled in his touch. His breath against her ear sent an erotic shiver down her body.

Resisting his desire to taste and kiss the delicate skin on her neck, instead he inhaled the fragrance of her perfume she'd put on the evening before and that still lingered. He imagined his lips gently grazing her neck as she accepted every bit of his touch.

Maybe she'll let me kiss her just once, he thought.

His passion was blinding his inhibitions as he continued to go further and began to lose control of himself. He began to kiss her neck. Pushing away her hair, he boldly continued kissing and tasting her neck, her earlobe, and then the side of her face, quickly.

Jade finally turned toward his mouth and returned his kiss for the first time.

He couldn't believe it, but his body demanded to be taken care of. His body ached for her touch. Turning her around by the shoulders, he continued to kiss her. Her arms slid around his neck, and he pulled her into his embrace. His body threatened to burst. He felt her breast lay up against his chest. He trailed a row of kisses down her neck, wanting to take off her shirt. His inhibitions put aside, he started to pull her shirt off her.

Realization of their actions snapped her back to reality. Guilt rushed in and caused her to blush from her neck up. O God, what in the world was I thinking? she thought.

"Bob, this isn't right."

A glazed look concealed his thoughts. All he could hear was his heart roaring loudly in his ears and the word '*no*'.

She attempted to ease his embarrassment and hers by taking his hand in hers. "Bob, are you OK?" Her voice was low, almost a whisper, and filled with concern.

The fog started to lift, bringing Bob back to his senses. On the other hand, his body was still alert with his need.

"What?" he said, his voice hoarse. He sat back, rebuffed.

"I'm sorry," she said. "We shouldn't have…are you OK?"

Recovering, he sat motionless on the couch, staring down, lost in his thoughts.

He hesitated, torn by conflicting emotions. Should he just tear off that flimsy shirt and take her, or shouldn't he? His body ached to be touched, but the look on her face was definitely not of desire.

Her eyes were sharp and assessing. She reached out, placing a hand on his shoulder. It was a simple jester, out of concern, nothing more. This act seemed to bring him out of his closed thoughts.

His cold, intent stare seemed to burn right through her like fire.

Quickly she retracted her hand, as if she'd touched a lit flame. His eyes, which once glowed with deep longing, now glared angrily at her.

"What did you say?" This time his voice grated harshly.

"I said are you OK?"

He stood and walked to the front door, leaving her waiting on the couch. His fists were clenched down by his side. He stood next to the doorway, silently composing himself.

Finally, he answered her.

"No, Jade, I'm not OK. I need to leave before I do something stupid." He openned the front door, hurried passed it, and shut it behind him.

A few seconds later, Jade heard his car door slam, and he drove away.

"God, help me." Looking up to the ceiling, she said a silent prayer for Susan and for herself.

"Mommy, is that you?" said Gracie from the back of the house.

"No, honey, it was Mr. Bob. He had to leave."

Jade went into her bedroom, discarded her clothes, and took a cold shower. She had to be at work in less than an hour.

Chapter 8

JADE ANSWERED THE phone, hoping it wasn't Bob not just yet. She'd only been at work for two hours and was bogged down with her caseload.

"Homicide, Corporal Davis."

"Hello, Jade?"

Relief filled Jade as she realized it was Lieutenant Jarvis.

"Hello, Sir, how can I help you?"

"I wanted to inform you of Susan's funeral arrangements. Our agency is going to take care of everything, once the medical examiner is finished with his investigation."

"I'll let your agency know when the body can be released. Did your people notify her aunt yet?"

"Yes. We spoke to her, after the Michigan State Police informed her of Susan's misfortune. Her name is Margaret Hensley. She's sixty four. I faxed you her information right before I called you. I included the information you needed: the time of notification and her address and phone number. We also got her verbal approval for her burial arrangements."

"Oh, really?"

"Yeah, she told us she was retired and couldn't afford to pay for her funeral. Apparently, they weren't close at all, and the last time she saw or heard from Susan was over three years ago. So we offered to pay for an airline ticket and hotel if she could make it out here, but she refused."

"That's sad. Susan told me she had no living relatives she was close to."

"Unfortunately. I mailed her a release form for Susan's body, and she's mailing it back to us, notarized. I enclosed an overnight envelope so that it would get here quickly."

"OK. Once you get that back, I'll need a copy of it, and so will the Medical Examiner's Office so they'll release the body to your agency."

"No problem, Jade. The funeral is set for next week on Monday morning at nine, at St. Paul's Catholic Church. She should be released before then."

"Yes, Sir. Thank you. I do appreciate your help."

"No problem. If you could just keep me informed of the case, that would be wonderful."

Yeah right! And mess up my homicide case? Don't think so, buddy! she thought.

"Sure."

"Good. Have a good day, Jade."

"You too, sir."

At the sound of the receiver hanging up on the other end, she placed hers down. Of all nerve, him asking that of her. He knew better. Or did he?

Next, she called the tow-truck agency to find out if Florida Department of Law Enforcement had been out there to fingerprint the vehicle.

"This is Corporal Davis," she said into the phone. "Has anyone come to finger print the Daytona Beach patrol car yet?"

"Yes, ma'am they're about done."

"Good. If you could have them leave a business card with their case number for me, I would appreciate it. I'm on my way up there to do measurements on the patrol car. I should be there in about thirty minutes, in case they ask."

"No problem corporal. Just ask for Kenny, that's me, and I'll have the information for you."

"Thanks, Kenny." She hung up the phone and gathered her equipment and her partner.

The sun was turning the high clouds up in the sky bluish-purple with a splash of pink and orange, signifying the end of the day. There was rush hour traffic, it was almost a quarter after five, and Jade knew she only had a good hour until sunset. She knew she'd have to come back out tomorrow to finish measuring the vehicle, but at least she could get a quick rundown on the damage.

Her partner, Corporal Jason Lance, was extremely helpful and steadfast in his work, and she regarded him highly. She was relieved that Jason was at the scene this morning assisting her. It was very difficult for her. She was also grateful that it was him there helping her instead of her other partners. Turning her radio to the detail channel, she called Corporal Lance.

"Yeah, go ahead, Jade." His voice was deep and calm.

"Jason, let's process the patrol car before the sun goes down. I need some day pictures taken of both vehicles, and if we have time left, we can try processing Mr. McCrugle's car. If not, I'll have to come back another time."

"Whatever you say."

Both police vehicles pulled into the fenced wrecker yard and parked next to the office. Gathering the equipment they would need, they walked to the front door of the business, where a skinny, unshaven, mop-headed young man was waiting, grinning at them.

"Hi, I'm Kenny. You must be that female cop in charge of those vehicles we towed early this morning?"

Jade noticed the young man smelled of grease and sweat. His white uniform and blue pants were smudged with dirt. His occupation had him to scoot under various sized vehicles in order to hook them up for tow. She knew he also did menial labor, assisting stranded motorists with tire changes, or simple mechanical issues. Kenny definitely had his work cut out for him. He was dirty and tired, yet dedicated, waiting to let them in to gather their information.

"Kenny, we appreciate you waiting for us. You probably had a long day, but if you could just let us have about an hour with both vehicles, we promise to leave."

"Yes, ma'am."

He thrust his hand into his back pants pocket, retrieved a card, and handed it to her.

"Here you go, before I forget. This here is the business card from those agents who were here earlier taking finger-prints from that patrol car over there." He pointed to where both vehicles were parked.

"Thank you, Kenny." She took the card from him and smiled as he escorted them inside the garage.

It was getting darker by the minute, and both of them snapped pictures of the inside and outside of both vehicles. Jade measured the two points she needed for photogrammetry and placed markers on top of the patrol car. She did the same thing with McCruggle's vehicle, as Jason processed the vehicles' interior and exterior conditions. Afterward, Jade would be able to download the pictures into the computer at work, along with her two measured points of interest for reference into the photogrammetry program; this would calculate accurate measurements for her. Once they were both finished with their inspections, they gathered up their equipment, and with Kenny's help, they were escorted out of the compound yard.

"Kenny, we'll be back tomorrow, early, to finish up with our inspections," said Jade. "I don't want anyone else near the vehicles without my approval, OK?"

Grinning a chipped-tooth smile, he answered, "Yes ma'am, no one is to touch those vehicles until further notice from you."

This time Jason spoke up. "Thank you, Kenny, have a good evening."

They both walked back to their patrol cars and put away their equipment. "Jason lets go eat."

Chapter 9

"MEXICAN?"

"You read my mind." Jade smiled.

"The Mexican restaurant located in the Sears shopping plaza?"

"Yep. I'll follow you, Jason."

They both started up their patrol cars and headed back west to Deland. The sun had just sunk over the horizon, and they sped down International Speedway Boulevard, the lights of the businesses twinkling as they drove by. Fifteen minutes later, they drove past Deland's city limit sign, and continued west. Four miles later, they pulled into the shopping plaza, parked, and walked into the restaurant.

Jade ordered her favorite, the shredded beef chimichunga with refried beans, sour cream, and guacamole and cheese sauce. The food arrived quickly, and she devoured hers, enjoying each bite. It had been days since her last full meal. Her partner chose cheese enchiladas and a taco for his meal. They both ate quietly, thinking about the case.

When they were done, they sat there letting the food digest before they had to return to the station.

Jade was curious about what Jason had to say.

"Jason, what do you think about this case?"

He looked directly into her eyes, admiring the way they changed depending on her emotions.

Reluctantly he told her how he honestly felt.

"You really want to know?"

She nodded her head, raising her eyebrows inquisitively.

"All right, I am only going on the limited knowledge of the case so far. I didn't know her like you did, so bear with me."

"Fire away."

He took a deep breath.

"From the look of the scene, I would say she was with someone last night who she knew and felt comfortable with. Whoever that person was killed her. The way she was butchered and then put back into her patrol car, I definitely have to say it was a man. He would have to be strong and convincing enough to have her meet him there and not call in her intentions to the station. The drunk driver who struck her car, unfortunately, had to be unlucky enough to crash his car into hers after the murder. Dumb luck for McCrugle, I would say. Again, like I said earlier, I don't know her well enough, and I am only going by what I saw at the scene."

"Bingo." She thought the same thing. Susan normally wouldn't call in if she was visiting a friend and chatting awhile. So for her not to call in what she was doing, only that she was busy, would mean she had to be comfortable enough with the person, so that included whoever she was dating.

The next question would be who she would be meeting with, particularly in that area, which was secluded from public's view, being a block off of the main drag. Again, that would limit the number of people she'd see. Susan never mentioned having a boyfriend or someone she was having an affair with. It didn't add up now. Susan dated, but wasn't serious about anyone. She hadn't dated anyone more than twice, and to the best of Jade's knowledge, she wasn't seeing anyone recently.

Jade frowned, deep in thought as she sipped on the straw.

Jason, intrigued as he watched Jade's quickly changing expressions, decided to ask her what she was thinking. He never told her that he learned something new in just about every case when they were paired up together. He was a logical thinker and careful about what he put into his reports. He knew that in order to meet the increasing demands of the job regarding deadlines, there were some corporals who had become professional report writers. Every so often, when the case was more than a mere traffic infraction or simple misdemeanor, he put more effort into his work. It seemed like for the past year, he had been over-loaded with single-vehicle homicide crashes nothing as exciting as this case he was now assisting Jade on.

What was even more exciting was working with his beautiful partner. His increasing attraction to her awkwardly intertwined with his need to protect her even when they weren't working together. This occurred when coworkers would make chauvinistic remarks about her, and he would end up defending her. They knew he would protect her, maybe that was why they said the negative remarks. More than likely they complained just to see his reactions. If he only had enough nerve to take the next step and ask her out. That thought tore at him because if she declined, then their friendship would more than likely be jeopardized or maybe not; he wasn't sure.

"Jade, what's on your mind?" he said.

Surprised, she quickly looked up at him.

Jason smiled at her and shrugged.

"Steam is coming off of your head. You're obviously debating about some-thing - more than likely this case - so spill it out."

She laid her arms on the table as if balancing herself.

"Well, you and I are thinking the same thing it had to be someone she knew. You said you think it was a man, due to the physical evidence at the scene. Well, I think your right, since Susan met in a secluded area. This would make the list of suspects shorter, since it had to be someone she trusted."

Frowning, she glanced down, her voice soften as she continued.

"She obviously was sliced, with what I'm not sure, but the ME will let us know. Now, where she was attacked is a good question obviously not in her car, but outside of it. After this person attacked her he…killed…her and…"

Her eyes filled with tears as she imagined the gruesome scene as she spoke.

"He…dragged her or carried her back to her car, placing her in it. Now, at the scene, there wasn't any blood on the ground that we could see. That will be something for us to look for - possibly in the pictures or when we return to the scene. That will definitely be our first task when we get back to the station - re-trieving those pictures."

"OK."

"As far as the idea that it was a man I think your right. To overtake her, someone would have to be a lot stronger than her. She definitely wasn't a weak person. So who could it be? That's the golden question. How long she was dead before Mr. McCrugle struck the patrol car is another thing we have to get from the ME. Oh, God."

"What, Jade?"

"What if she was still alive when her car was struck?"

It was a thought that tore her insides apart. The tear that traveled down her cheek escaped untouched. She took a deep, calming breath, telling herself that, hopefully, Susan had a quick death, not the slow agonizing death she was starting to form in her mind's eye.

"I doubt that, Jade. With the extent of her injuries, I'm sure it wasn't possible. Don't torture yourself with those thoughts."

She sighed.

"Yeah, you're right, it just…so…"

She turned away trying to regain her composure.

"Look, the best way to help Susan is to find the killer. Let's get back to the station and download those pictures to see if we can find anything. If not, we'll return to the scene and look there."

She nodded.

"Ready to go?" He dropped a twenty dollar bill on the table definitely enough to cover the bill and then some.

"Yeah."

They both left the restaurant, walking back to their patrol cars as passers-by watched the uniformed officers. Jason walked Jade to her patrol car and pulled her into his arms, gently hugging her. He hated to see her so distraught and only wanted to comfort her.

Surprised struck Jade by the sudden kind gesture from her partner. He never held her; he was always somewhat distant with her when it came to physical touch. She always thought he was just too shy to act on his feelings. Even so, she laid her head on his shoulder, resting it there as he held her. She liked his comfort, this time without anything promised in return. Clearing her mind of the insecure thoughts that were invading it, she pulled away.

"Thanks, Jason, I needed that."

He looked down and smiled at her. He wanted to kiss her badly.

"I'll see you at the station." She turned and unlocked her door as Jason returned to his patrol car two cars away. Once inside, they both drove away toward the northeast side of town.

Chapter 10

TOWARD THE WEST end of the parking lot, located directly in front of Sears, Bob parked his dark, four-door, medium-sized sedan facing east. Exiting his vehicle, he walked to the plaza sidewalk. His first destination was the grocery store for some soda. He whistled a happy tune. Nothing could ruin his day, or so he thought. As he walked by the store windows, he casually looked in, glancing around as he normally did to see if anything interesting would catch his eye. He noticed the uniformed officers in a local Mexican restaurant. Curious, he slowed his pace to see if he could identify any of them. One of the officers was facing away from him, but the other one looked like someone he knew. The one not facing him was a woman possibly Jade.

He wanted to linger, but he past the window, unable to walk any slower without getting people's attention in the restaurant.

Damn! He thought.

Was it her?

He stopped abruptly.

Pedestrians walked by, glancing at him as he stood there with a perplexed look on his face. He wanted to walk back and see who it was, but he knew it would draw attention, so he decided to walk on to the supermarket.

Twenty minutes passed. He was irritated at the lack of speed of the cashier and the bag boy as he inserted his key into the keyhole of his vehicle. Tossing the grocery bags into the back-seat, he sat in his car with the windows down.

He decided to wait.

Five minutes passed.

Two uniformed officers exited the Mexican restaurant, casually talking to each other. He recognized one of them as Jade.

Jade with another man. That was the panicked thought that invaded his mind.

His blood started to boil.

He couldn't control the trembling.

He watched them walk to Jade's patrol car. The tall male he recognized as Jason turned and took Jade in his arms. He watched her expression change from surprise to enjoyment.

His fingers turned white from gripping the steering wheel. Why was Jason hugging his Jade so freely? Sweat started to pour into his eyes, burning and blurring his vision. Quickly wiping it away, he started up the ignition. He wanted to drive over there and run the son of the bitch down, but he decided not to follow through on his urge.

However, what he couldn't understand was why Jade was with this guy, especially after she knew how he felt about her. Didn't he mean anything to her? She was everything to him. He would give his soul to the devil if he could convince her to be with him. She had everything: beauty, intelligence, financial stability, a beautiful child. And wasn't he now a big part of her life?

Damn it!

He *was* part of her life, and Gracie's too. She just wasn't thinking right at the moment, with Susan murdered. Normally, any normal human being who'd lost a close friend would be distraught. But having to be the investigator in one's best friend's murder would cause turmoil in any sane individual.

Isn't that right? he thought. He tried explaining the insane behavior, but it was difficult for him to digest.

Patiently, he stood where he was at.

Jade smiled at Jason, and they both got into their patrol cars and drove away. More than likely, he decided, they were traveling toward their station, which was east of the plaza.

He had to think. The scene disturbed him. He wasn't sure if she was avoiding him and seeing someone else or accepting support from other coworkers.

He needed time.

He had to focus his anger.

Should he discipline her?

Or the guy?

He drove away, containing his anger and contemplating his next move.

→⊨◉ ◉⊨←

Jade and her partner downloaded the pictures into the computer at the station and found nothing further to assist in the investigation. Ten minutes later, they drove back to the Daytona Beach crime scene and scanned for possible clues they could have overlooked.

Nothing.

Absolutely nothing.

"Damn it, Jason! There should have been something left here." Jade was frustrated at finding nothing.

"I know."

"There should have been something."

"This guy is good."

"No kidding!"

Jason stopped and looked at her, waiting for her to give up the search. They had checked and rechecked for any further evidence left at the scene. Unfortunately, when there was a homicide involving another agency, the whole world seemed to show up. Then if you were looking for further clues after everyone left, it would be a miracle if anything was found.

Jade shrugged her shoulders and looked back at Jason. He was obviously finished, but he didn't walk away until she gave the say so.

"I guess we're done here for now," she said.

"Yeah, I think so."

She quickly scanned the area one last time before she finally gave up on the site for any further leads.

"Thanks, Jason."

He winked at her and smiled.

"Let's say we head back to the station and finish up our reports?"

"Sure," she said.

They both walked back to their vehicles and got back to the station thirty-five minutes later. Checking her voicemail, Jade found that Susan's lieutenant had left a message indicating the time of Susan's funeral and the location of the cemetery.

"I'll see you there, Jade," the lieutenant said on the message. "- Oh, by the way, I'll have the documents for you at the funeral."

Two days away, she thought.

The finality of her best friend's death hit her again pretty hard. She left to take the rest of the evening off. Jason was sweet as he wished her the best before hugging her one last time.

Chapter 11

EVEN IN LATE January, Florida always had a weird spell of unpredictable weather. Instead of the temperature being in the forties and fifties this morning, a warm front had found its way to the Sunshine State, bringing a dramatic change again.

Walking out through her back utility door, Jade handed Jason a cold glass of lemonade. The two of them sat in the warm, eighty-degree sunshine, watching their children play together. Once a week, they made a point of getting together with their kids and trying to enjoy an afternoon together. Lately they'd both had to cancel due to an abundance of single-vehicle traffic homicides.

"Whose wagon is this?" the young slender girl asked as she struggled to pull the wagon out of the screen in porch.

Jade smirked at her daughter's continual rambling questions. She watched her coworker's two-year-old toddler follow faithfully behind Gracie.

"It's yours, honey. Why do you keep asking me those silly questions?"

Like always, Gracie ignored her questioning, but continued pulling the wagon around the yard. Pushing her glasses back up to the bridge of her nose, the little girl wiped sweat from her forehead. Pulling the wagon was difficult for her; she had to take each step carefully due to her lack of poor vision.

Jade watched her daughter and sighed. She only wished things were different for her daughter. Gracie's vision problem had held her back, since her birth. Due to being severely premature, Gracie weighed only one pound twelve ounces at birth. She had, and would continually have a difficult struggle with life. Jade knew Gracie's brain damage also affected the child's learning abilities. How much, she wasn't sure. No doctor was sure.

"Jade, is everything all right?" said Jason.

The deep voice penetrated Jade's thoughts, lifting her furrowed brows and changing her frown into a pleasant smile.

"Yes, why do you ask?"

"You had a sad look in your eyes, and like always…" He looked away for a moment, trying to gather the right words. "You don't or won't share them with me." His deep blue eyes stared deeply into hers.

Staring back, not sure of what to say, she suddenly reached over and squeezed his hand for comfort and reassurance. "It's not that I don't want to share, Jason. It's just "

A shrilling scream came from around the car that the two children were standing behind. Both Jade and Jason jumped from their patio chairs and ran over to their screaming children.

"Momma, Momma, it's a snake! It's a snake!" Gracie stood frozen, tears streaming down her face, as the coiled up black snake hissed at her and Junior.

"Junior, don't move, son!" Jason commanded.

"Gracie, honey, stay still and it won't hurt you! I'm going to get a stick. Stay there!" Jason turned and rushed away toward a nearby group of bushes.

Gracie stood frozen, crying hysterically, unable to move as Junior stood next to her, watching the wavering black snake.

With her heart beating erratically, Jade ran fifty feet away to where her flat-headed shovel was leaning against the wall of her house and returned in less than five seconds. Jason ran back and grabbed the shovel from her, positioning himself slowly behind the snake. The snake wavered, hissing at him now as he stood there waiting for the right moment.

"Gracie and Junior," he said. "Slowly, very slowly, step backward." He carefully raised the shovel, distracting the snake as the two children backed away. Once they reached the back of the vehicle, Jade snatched both of them, pulling them away as Jason struck the snake repeatedly with the shovel. Looking down at the mutilated snake, he inspected it, realizing it was a moccasin.

"It's dead," he said. "Don't worry." He saw the relief in Jade's eyes as she started inspecting both children for any bites.

"Are you both sure you weren't bitten?" Jade scanned the children's legs and arms as they shook their heads.

"Momma, it didn't bite us. It just scared us." Gracie's lower lip started to quiver as she nervously picked at her hands.

"Oh, honey, it's OK." Jade hugged her daughter reassuringly and then wiped away the child's tears.

Jason leaned the shovel up against the house then walked over to his son, who looked frightened and worried.

"Come here, son." He squatted down, gathering his son in his arms.

"Gacy sad, Daddy!" Tears were falling from his face as the toddler started wailing. "Gacy, don't cry!"

"Junior, she'll be OK, but you need to stop crying or she won't stop either." He tried to convince his son with logic, but in the end, letting both kids cry out their fears seemed to make them feel better.

Once both children were calmed down, Jason handed Junior off to his partner and friend, wishing their relationship was more.

"I'll bury the snake farther back." He had to finish his role as the two kid's hero and get rid of the remains of the snake.

Jason grabbed the shovel, scooped up the snake, and walked away.

"Come on, you two," said Jade. "Let's go in and have some ice cream. What do you say?"

Both children's eyes lit up as they beamed a smile at her, cheering, "Yay!" Jade held hands with the children and went into the house.

Ten minutes later, Jason walked in, sweating.

"Here you go, hero." Jade stepped up, planting a quick kiss on his cheek then handing him an ice cream cone.

He wished her kiss was not a platonic one, but he just couldn't muster enough courage to make a pass at her, knowing it could ruin their friendship. He just smiled, took the ice cream cone, and started to eat it.

→⊨◎ ◎⊨←

It was near dinnertime as Bob drove by Jade's house. Glancing at the front of the house, he saw the green Ford pick-up truck again. He knew who drove it and knew his Gracie played with the male child who accompanied the guy who seemed to be in Jade's life more and more. His left temple started twitching as he passed Jade's house, contemplating what he should do. The decorated present on the seat next to him jiggled from the bumps in the dirt road.

Chapter 12

"Five o'clock, Momma!" Gracie bellowed from her room, answering her mother's question.

"Thank you, honey!" Jade smirked as she turned to Jason. "Why did you want me to ask Gracie what time it was when you know darn well? You just looked at your watch a minute ago." She looked suspiciously at him with her arms crossed across her chest.

"Hmm?" With one eyebrow raised, she waited for his answer.

The sound of cars driving up her driveway distracted her, and she turned and looked out her window. Six cars pulled in and drove toward the backyard. Then two Deputy patrol cars, several city patrol cars, and eight more various civilian cars pulled into her driveway and parked in the back.

"What the hell?" Turning, she looked to Jason for an answer.

He smiled at her, and he turned to Gracie and Junior, who both came running into the living room.

"Ready Gracie?" he said.

Smiling her toothless grin, she cheerfully replied, "Ready, Jay!"

"One, two, surprise!"

"Surprise!" both kids chanted.

"What's going on?"

"Everyone is here for your birthday party, Jade." He smiled, proud of himself, because he'd wanted to tell her from the moment he saw her this afternoon, but he waited.

"There's going to be lots of food. We're going to use your barbeque, and Sarge says he wants to be the chef. Jade, please don't kick us out; say you'll let us do this for you?" He knew how she cherished her privacy and that this was her first birthday without her deceased husband. No one wanted her to be alone. All of them her friends, her coworkers everybody cared a lot about her.

Jade saw how happy Gracie acted. She knew it was difficult for her daughter to hold a secret. "So all of you planned this?"

"Yeah," they all answered in unison.

"How could I pass this up? Thank you, Jason." She reached up and hugged him.

"Let's go outside and get this party started," he said. He grabbed her hand and motioned for the kids to follow them out the back door before he stole that kiss he desperately wanted.

Two hours later, music filled the air as the group gathered inside to light the cake. Laughter and chatter could be heard from the roadway as a single vehicle pulled into the driveway, parking in the front. A male exited the vehicle, walked to the front door, and let himself in.

Gracie watched through the front window and waited for Mr. Bob. As he came into view, she started jumping up and down, yelling, "Momma, Mr. Bob's here!" She ran to the front door and threw herself into his open arms.

Jade turned to see who had entered, unable to completely hear what her daughter had just yelled. Her smile broadened as she saw her friend. Her stomach knotted as she saw the joy and love between her daughter and her daughter's therapist. Just as quickly as her smile formed, a frown made its way back. A quick stab of guilt crept into her heart. She recalled their brief embarrassing moment a couple weeks ago. She knew she shouldn't have let her defenses down when Bob made a pass at her. She had no feeling for Bob except as a friend. The only problem she had now was trying to find the courage to have that talk with him. She hugged Bob quickly and motioned him toward the gathering crowd.

He returned a smile to her, and she was unaware of the captivating picture she made just standing there. It gnawed at his insides. Walking over to Jade with Gracie's hand in his, he stood protectively next to her as she blew her candles out. The crowd cheered. He scanned the room, and realized most of the people in the crowd were males.

Competition, he realized.

He swallowed hard, uncertain, and he watched the crowd take turns hugging and some kissing his beloved Jade.

The first male to do it was definitely drunk. He had a cold bottle of beer in one hand as he roughly kissed Jade. The crowd cheered gaily. A warning voice whispered in his head not to show any feelings, but his anger mounted as each male took turns congratulating her. A few were obviously under the influence, giving her longer kisses than necessary. Others were timid, giving just a peck on the cheek. Jade laughed, obviously not annoyed with the behavior.

The last one was a uniformed deputy, and he whispered something in her ear. Bob's anger mounted, and he was now glowering with rage. The deputy started to kiss Jade on the cheek, but this time Bob's temper exploded. The voices in his head couldn't be heard reasoning with him any longer. Briskly walking over, pushing people aside, he grabbed Jade and pulled her away from the deputy.

Annoyed by the sudden interruption, the deputy reached out to Jade. "Hey, man, what's your problem?" He spat out the words impatiently as the guy stepped between him and Jade.

The barely bridled anger in Bob's voice betrayed him. "Your behavior is unacceptable. If I were you, I would step back." His nostrils flared with anger. He clenched his fists prepared to fight.

The crowd quieted suddenly. The alcohol had clouded the people's senses, but the air sizzled with intensity between the deputy and the man who stood next to Jade.

With both hands on her hips, she stood in between the two men who glared at each other. "All right, enough, the two of you! Otherwise, I'll have to call the cops." She waited, hoping the humor would sink in.

The crowd started laughing as one of the deputy's friends' pulled him toward the kitchen.

Jade turned and grabbed Bob's arm, pulling him along as they walked into the hallway. She looked into his face and saw his disapproving gaze.

"Bob, what were you thinking?"

A war of emotions raged within him as he glowered at her. "Me? What the... No, this isn't going to be turned around on me!" His tone had become cold. "You were letting those guys kiss you and..." his voice trailed off as his rage was quickly consumed, leaving him confused.

Sighing, she reached for her confidence deep down inside and gathered his hands in hers. "Bob, you're a wonderful man, but..." She looked over her shoulder for any unwanted ears that might be near. "I just want us to remain friends nothing more. I'm sorry about that kiss we shared; I have no excuse for that. Please just try to enjoy yourself and "

His dark eyes showed his tortured disbelief at her words. His voice was almost a hoarse whisper, but she heard what he said. "I don't believe this." He turned away, not waiting for an answer, and strode to the door. He walked out, not saying a word.

Looking around, she realized no one saw their spat. She was still embarrassed about the kiss they had shared a while ago and about his behavior this evening. She had tried to make her peace with Bob. He just refused to let it go. Taking a deep breath, with a stab of guilt gnawing at her conscious, she walked back to the crowd and continued with the party.

One pair of eyes did see the quarrel. Gracie had followed Mr. Bob all evening and didn't understand what was going on with her mother and him. In the shadows, she leaned against the front windowpane, with her thick glasses sliding down her nose. The tears ran down her face. Gracie watched as his car pulled out of the driveway. It caused her little heart to break. She wished Mr. Bob hadn't left so quickly, but the reason was something her innocent mind couldn't comprehend. The crowd settled down and started to eat cake, while Gracie isolated herself from them and everyone there. Leaning against the windowpane, hoping she would catch a glimpse of Mr. Bob returning, she waited.

Another pair of eyes also witnessed the argument. He felt tipsy from the alcohol he had consumed, but he wasn't drunk. He walked over to Jade and leaned over, whispering into her ear as she sipped on her drink.

"Are you OK?"

Surprised, she glanced up to see Jason watching her. He was handsome, with wild sapphire eyes and a secret expression on his face she hadn't quite figured out.

"I'm not sure yet." She flashed him a quick grin, attempting to reassure him but failing miserably.

"This time, you are you going to share your thoughts or..."

He had asked her earlier that day about sharing her thoughts, and she had been interrupted prior to telling him. She decided for once she'd open up to him.

"Jason, we did have this conversation earlier, didn't we?" She glanced around, sipping her drink again and watching everyone chat with each other, ignoring them.

"Yes we did, but we were interrupted."

She sighed and decided to tell him.

"You really want to know?"

His gaze was soft as a caress as he nodded his head.

She felt vulnerable, but she continued.

"Jason, sometimes I think about Gracie's problems, and it's overwhelming. Being a single mom now, there are some days I feel at a total loss, and I wish my daughter's life could have been different." She bowed her head. "And as for now, no, I am not OK. I take it you saw me arguing with Bob?"

His steady gaze bore into her in silence as she looked back up at his face. He nodded his answer, hoping she would continue.

Reluctantly she did.

"To make a long story short, he wants more than I can give as a friend." She flushed miserably. "And to make matters worse, Gracie loves him like a father figure, and I'm not sure how tonight is going to change his relationship with her." She fought back the tears and looked away from him.

Jason looked around to make sure no one noticed them; he had to get her out of the house so she could clear her head. His fingers were warm and strong as he grasped hers. He whispered in her ear, "Follow me." They walked unnoticed out the back door and around to the side of the house. A few people gathered outside, drinking and smiling at one another, caught up in their conversations of work.

She wiped away a tear that fell and fought desperately not to cry. Too much had occurred this past year, let alone this past couple of weeks; it was getting to her.

Jason stopped and turned to her. The sad look on her face tore at his insides. He watched her push back a wayward strand of blonde hair as another tear slid down her cheek. Capturing it with his thumb, he cupped the side of her face and gently lifted her head up to look at him.

She saw the heart-rending tenderness of his gaze, and her emotions started to melt away her resolve. No longer did she feel like the stable, strong, independent woman; now all she wanted was to feel his comforting touch. Her tears fell, and her body trembled as he pulled her into his embrace.

Rocking her back and forth, he whispered reassuring words. She buried her face in his chest and relaxed, sinking into his cushioning embrace. Her quiet sobs subsided, and he tenderly pulled her hair away from her face. Her skin tingled where he touched her, slowly arousing her. No longer did she feel sad and at a total loss. His closeness awakened parts of her she thought were dormant. Secretly she had been attracted to Jason, but she had kept those thoughts to herself. Reluctantly she stepped back.

He cupped her face with both his hands, and gently wiped away her tears. Without thinking, he leaned down and gingerly placed a kiss on her forehead. She didn't flinch or pull back. His heart thundered in his ears, and he decided to continue. Kissing each eyelid slowly, he looked down at her face and read her reactions.

A delightful shiver of wanting ran through her as each kiss was planted. His nearness was overwhelming. Her cheeks colored under the heat of his gaze.

He kissed the tip of her nose, wanting to taste the sweetness of her lips. His mouth only inches from hers, he hesitated.

She parted her lips and raised herself to meet his kiss, wanting to know this intimate part of him. It had been a year since her husband's death; she knew it was time she tried to move on.

Their lips met at first grazing each other's, testing, and then the kiss deepened. The intimate touch sang through her veins as her blood coursed through her like an awakened river. As he roused her passion, his own grew stronger. Her arms slid around his neck as he placed his hands on her waist, drawing her form into him. His kisses were slow and drugging. His tongue explored the recesses of her mouth. She responded, coaxing him on as a soft whimpering moan escaped from her. This felt right to her. Jason was who she wanted to be with, but that secret would remain unspoken.

His body was filled with need. Fully aroused, he felt intoxicated from her kisses. He was amazed Jade returned his kisses; he had only dreamt of kissing her and never thought this would really happen.

Moving even closer against his hard body, she ignited his passion even more. He pulled away. He had to catch his breath. She was the first woman to ever do that to him. Fully aware Jade's touch had significant power over him; his heightened sexual state was demanding more of her.

His intense gaze caused her heart to flutter in her chest. She had a burning desire an aching need for another kiss as she looked up at him. His mouth met hers again, this time more demanding. She felt her knees weaken, as he grazed her earlobe and then kissed down her neck, leaving a burning path of desire.

Fully aroused, his manhood pushed against his jeans, begging to be released. He wanted her more than anything in his life, but reality was sinking in; they were a few feet around the corner from other people. Reluctantly, he pulled back.

Dazed, she relished the tingling sensation his kisses awakened in her; they were kisses her tired soul could melt into.

He gently held the side of her head with his open palms, gazing into her face, trying to read her reactions. He knew full well their actions just now had changed their relationship completely and he hoped she wouldn't ignore it. He watched her, waiting for her reaction.

She slowly opened her eyes. They were still glazed from desire.

"Jade I didn't mean to…" His voice was low almost apologetic. Not sure what to say, except that he didn't mean to act like a teenager, he fumbled on. "I only wanted to…"

Damn what do I say? he thought.

Fully recovered, she could sense his failing attempt to explain his actions. She took a step back. She needed to think clearly. Being near him only clouded her judgment.

His blue eyes were filled with pain, warmth, and desire. With no conscious thought, she took a step closer and kissed him, lingering, savoring every moment, hoping he understood her unspoken message.

He was surprised, but recovered quickly. His mouth met hers with savage intensity.

A door slammed. A child's voice cried out, "Momma where are you?"

Jade and Jason stepped back, recovering from Gracie's sudden interference.

Not sure how to react, Jade left Jason breathless and walked around the corner to meet her daughter.

"Honey, I'm here. I didn't go anywhere."

"I thought you left me."

"No, baby, I would never do that. Let's go back inside before you get bit by mosquitoes. Just give me one minute out here. Go back inside."

Her daughter nodded and walked back inside waiting at the window, watching her.

Jason walked around the corner with his hands in his pockets. "I need to get…"

"Jade!" said a man, his voice booming from inside. "Where are you?"

Jason grinned with amusement as he watched her squirm. "Your friends are calling you."

She turned and walked into the house.

⊷▬◉ ◉▬⊶

Chapter 13

BOB'S VOICE HARDENED ruthlessly, and his face contorted in an angry sneer. "That bitch!" His knuckles turned white as his grip on the steering wheel tightened. Anger caused his body to shake, black fury moving throughout his body. It started to fuel his anxieties and fears.

"What the hell was I thinking?" Filled with self-doubt, he drove aimlessly, not paying attention to traffic signs or oncoming traffic.

"What more can I do for her to love me?" He felt his temper rise and then drop just as quickly. Mixed emotions swirled through him as his eyes blurred with tears that threatened to fall. He turned the steering wheel left. He didn't see the red sedan traveling south on the truck route that he traveled along. A loud noise caused him to look up right as the red sedan collided with his passenger door. His vehicle rolled twice from the T-bone crash as he traveled south on the truck route. Traffic came to an abrupt stop. Finally, his vehicle settled in an upright position as he lost consciousness.

⇥═◉ ◉═⇤

"Hey, Jade, I'm sorry about what had just happened with that guy. Was he someone special to you?" said the deputy who'd almost gotten in a fight with Bob.

"Well, yes, he is. He's my daughter's teacher and a friend to the family. But he is not a boyfriend or anything like that; he's just become more protective of us since my husband's..." She still wasn't comfortable saying "my husband's death."

"Jade, it's OK." The deputy suddenly stopped and turned his radio louder listening to his call to a crash nearby on the truck route. "Hey, I have a call to go to some crash on the truck route. It's an overturned vehicle blocking traffic. Got to go. Duty calls." The deputy placed a quick kiss on her cheek and left.

Gracie watched as the patrol car turned left from her driveway with his lights and siren on. Odd. She thought it was the same route Mr. Bob had taken. But she quickly dismissed the idea.

Her mother came up behind her and wrapped her arms around her small figure.

"Sweetie, what are you doing?"

"Momma, I'm waiting for Mr. Bob to come back. Is he coming back?" Her eyes were gentle and filled with eagerness as she looked up at her mother.

A look of tired sadness crossed over Jade's face. "No honey I don't think so."

"Oh." She turned and looked back out the window and casually blurted out, "That policeman just went the same way as Mr. Bob. Maybe he will get him to come back."

A sudden foreboding started sinking in when her daughter spoke those words. Jade calculated the time in her head between when Bob left and the time of the deputy's call. It had been approximately fifteen minutes. There was a possibility. She tried shrugging it off. She didn't want to be negative and made a quick prayer for her friend.

"Come on, Gracie. Come away from the window and have some food with me." Jade gently pulled her daughter toward the kitchen.

⤚⬤ ⬤⤙

Chapter 14

A COUPLE HOURS later, Jade watched her friends drive out of her driveway. That dreaded feeling came back, sinking down to the core of her soul. Dismissing it, she tried to convince herself it was because of her friend's funeral tomorrow afternoon.

Her phone rang.

"Hello?" Jade couldn't think of who would be calling her at this time of the evening. She glanced up at the kitchen clock. It was 8:32 p.m.

"Jade, it's me, Scott. I need you to stay there. I am on my way to see you." His voice carried a definite commanding tone.

"OK, can you tell me why? It's a bit late, and I need to get Gracie into the shower."

"No, I can't." The phone went dead.

She hung up, puzzled and irritated.

Five minutes later, Scott pulled into her driveway in his patrol car. Quickly getting out, he walked toward the front door dreading the news he had to tell her.

She stared, stunned not able to say anything. The sound of Gracie crying and running down the hall to her room brought her back to reality.

"Gracie, honey, come here." She went down the hall to comfort her daughter, with Scott directly behind her.

"Momma, Mr. Bob...Mr. Bob..." She threw herself hopelessly into her mother's outstretched arms.

Jade gathered her into her arms, kissing her head and hugging her. She stood up with the crying child in her arms. Tears welled up in her eyes as she fought to keep her voice from cracking so as not to upset her daughter even more. She turned to Scott.

He wiped away the tears that were running down his friend's face with the open palm of his hands. He frowned. He felt terrible being the bearer of bad news, especially after he almost had a fight with the guy Jade cared about like family.

"I'm so sorry, Jade, to be the one to tell you the bad news," he muttered hastily.

"I know, Scott. I know. He's at Halifax, right?" Her blue eyes were full of life but glittered with raw pain as she looked into his.

Nodding his head silently, he turned and left her comforting the small child. He felt like a total idiot.

Once Gracie was calmed down enough for her to put her down, they gathered their items they needed, locked up the house, and left to see Bob. Jade watched her daughter draw her therapist a get-well card. Once she was done drawing, Gracie did something totally unexpected. She kissed the card and then held it to her chest. Jade tried to clear the lump in her throat. If only I cared about Bob as much as Gracie did.

Arriving at the emergency room Jade parked her Honda Accord. She gathered Gracie, and they walked into the hospital. A salty, stagnant smell invaded Jade's sinuses, causing her to crinkle her nose up. She walked up to the Daytona Beach officer stationed at the entrance to the hallway she needed to go down.

She stopped and presented her badge to the officer.

"Hi, my friend was airlifted here earlier from a bad car crash, and we were hoping to be able to go back and see him."

The officer eyed her badge, but continued to look at the child, who was clenching a card in her little fist as if it was very precious to her. "Young lady, do you want to give that to your friend you're here to see?"

The tears started to roll down her cherubic face as she nodded her head. A recent grandfather, the officer had a soft spot for children. He looked up at the child's mother and smiled, pressing the button to the glass doors to open them. "Go on, you two."

A few minutes later, they found an emergency room nurse who was able to direct them to the correct room. She walked into the room and saw him.

She swallowed hard and gulped back her tears, failing miserably at her attempt to look strong for Gracie.

The child's trembling voice filled the air as she walked up to the battered man asleep under the covers with nasal cannulas taped to his face. "Mr. Bob," she said.

No response.

"Mr. Bob?" Reaching up, the child shook his arm.

His eyes slowly opened to the voice calling him.

Jade wiped away the tears from her face, happy to see her friend awake.

Looking up at both of the people standing at his bedside, recognition gleamed in his eyes.

A trembling crying voice caught his attention. He looked at Gracie, and his heart was torn in two. He saw the raw hurt in the girl's eyes. He reached up with the arm closest to her, and wiped her tears with his thumb.

"Mr. Bob, we were so worried!"

Pain throbbed throughout his entire body from the crash and from being jostled around for X-rays. He'd swore silently to himself that he would never come back to this hospital again. As he tried to talk, his tongue felt thick, and he concentrated on every word, trying to enunciate them correctly. "Gracie... honey...I'll be...OK." Sucking in a breath after each word took a lot of effort.

A nurse walked in with his chart. "Oh, good. Are you two family?"

Jade couldn't count on her voice now, so she just nodded.

"I'm sure you want to know his condition. Don't worry. He'll be OK. We have him on some heavy pain medication right now, so he might sound like he's under the influence, but it's only the meds making him sound like that." The nurse flipped through the chart some more and frowned.

Finding her voice finally, Jade said, "What's wrong?"

"Well, he did suffer some cracked ribs, and a concussion, and we had to stitch up that cut above his eyebrow. It looks like the doctor wants him to stay a couple nights for observation. So if you don't have any further questions, I need to get him a room upstairs."

Jade shook her head and turned back to the injured man on the bed with his eyes closed. Gracie had her head lying on his arm stroking it.

Jade's eyes roamed upward as she studied his face. Again, his eyes opened and found hers. He analyzed her reactions. In a voice she hardly recognized she greeted him. "Hi there."

He didn't say anything. He couldn't. The medication fogged his brain, and he fought to keep his eyes opened. The last thing he saw was Jade leaning over him, and he felt her lips gently brush his cheek before he passed out.

⋅⊱⊰⋅

Hours later, he opened his eyes and blinked several times, attempting to focus. The lights were bright, a dull pain erupted in his head. He tried to move, but his entire body ached. A moan escaped his lips as he tried again to move. His ribs detained him, causing more pain to spread throughout his body.

Bob's moaning woke Jade from her light sleep on the chair. Getting up, she walked over to his bedside.

"Bob, you OK?" she asked.

Perspiration beaded on his forehead. He turned his head to the direction where the familiar voice was coming from. He sucked in his breath and held it. He saw her hovering over him like an angel.

She's so beautiful.

She surveyed him to see if there was any way she could help him without bothering his nurse. His eyes found hers.

A slow smile spread across her face, giving her an angelic look. "Hi there." she said.

Even her voice seared his soul, causing him to forget his pain momentarily. His voice cracked, but he was able to whisper, "Hi."

Her eyes filled with tears. "You had us worried there. Do you remember what happened?"

He looked around the room and spied what he needed at the moment. "Water…please."

"Oh." Jade found the styrofoam cup with the straw hanging out and retrieved it for him. She put the straw to his lips, and he sucked in the cool, pleasant water that hydrated his burning throat.

Placing his head back onto the pillow, he felt better. "Thank you."

"Bob, I am so sorry." Her voice trembled from the stress of her emotions.

He cut her off. "Jade it's not your fault."

Guilt settled in her like a heavy weight, she recalled the evening before, and what had made him leave. Her shoulders sank as she looked down and bit her lower lip.

He said in a grudging voice, "If I was paying attention, I would have noticed what was going on around me."

"Yeah, but if I didn't have…"

Before she said something he knew she would regret, he said, "Didn't what? Tell me you only wanted to be friends? Well, shit happens."

"Bob."

"Jade, you and Gracie" He sucked in a short breath. "Mean the world to me." He took in another breath. "But you need to figure out what you want out of life." Pain gnawed at his chest.

"I know," she answered.

"I've been there trying to show you" He took another breath. "That you can lean on me in your time of need." Sucking in his breath in short gasps quickly limited him to what he really wanted to say.

Worry crossed Jade's face as she nervously put her hands in her pants pockets.

A short, stocky nurse walked into the room, rolling a blood pressure machine behind her. "I see you're finally up. Try not to talk too much; your ribs will hurt you even more." She noticed his breathing and the woman who stood over her patient looking guilty.

"I strongly suggest you don't over excite Bob too much until he takes his pain medicine. And, honey, he's going to be busy with us coming into his room for one thing or another. Why don't you go home for a while. When he's ready to come home, we'll contact you. OK?"

Glancing down at Bob, Jade blurted out, "Sure, but no matter what you say, Bob, you're going to let me take you home." She gathered her stuff and walked out the door, feeling a little bit relieved.

Chapter 15

A FLUTTERING NERVOUS feeling quivered in Bob's stomach as Jade's Honda drove up. He had been expecting her and was relieved to see Gracie in the backseat, waiving her small hand in his direction, and smiling from ear to ear. He couldn't help but smile back at her.

The vehicle stopped in front of him, and he stood up slowly with the help from the male attendant.

Jade quickly got out of her vehicle, and jogged to the passenger side to open the door for Bob. She didn't miss the grimace of pain on his face as he moved from the wheel-chair to her. After quickly planting a kiss on Bob's cheek, she thanked the male attendant. She helped guide Bob into the front passenger seat. Gripping the roof with one hand and holding onto Jade with the other, he lowered himself slowly into the seat. Beads of sweat formed on his forehead, and he could still feel the pain even with the pain medication running through his system.

Inhaling Jade's sweet scent, he let her put a seat belt on him.

Always caring about everyone, he thought.

A squeal from the backseat startled him.

Gracie wrapped her small, slender arms around his neck, and planted a wet kiss on his cheek.

"Mr. Bob, are you better?"

After the sudden attack, he had to gasp for breath. Gracie's little arms tightened around his neck, blocking the airflow. "Yes" he said in a suffocated whisper as he loosened her grip.

"Sorry." Biting down on the inside of her cheek, she tried to keep from squeezing him again.

Jade's hair brushed against his face as she sat back down in the driver's seat. He closed his eyes, and relished the fresh smell of strawberries mixed with perfume on her hair. Her hair was one of many traits he loved, and he fantasized about how it would feel on his chest.

She put on her seat belt and mumbled, "Here we go." She drove the vehicle out of the parking lot and toward Deland, where they lived. For the first time, she realized how many bumps there were on their route. Bob groaned with everyone. She had been debating about whether she'd have Bob stay with her or let him heal at his home. She wasn't sure. The last thing she wanted was for him to take her generosity as a come-on, but at the same time, she didn't want him to be suffering.

Loneliness was eating at her. She missed her husband more than anything at this moment. He isn't coming back, and I need to move on, she thought. Raw hurt ate at her constantly, some days more than others. She wanted male company, but wasn't ready for any commitments. Bob had been there, filling a small void, making her family seem whole, but she wasn't in love with him.

Watching emotions run across her face, Bob realized she was debating something. It had to be something she felt very serious about, otherwise she wouldn't have been debating this long. Gracie was sitting in the backseat, rocking back and forth to the music, laughing occasionally. "Hey…what's bothering…you?" he said. He took quick breaths between words, trying not to aggravate his wounds any further.

Startled out of her thoughts, guilt stabbed at her. Should I or shouldn't I? she thought. What to do! Impulsively she blurted out, "You're staying with us. No excuses. I'll feel better knowing you're not alone and in need of anything." She glanced in his direction momentarily for his reaction.

Yes! he silently screamed.

"OK. I'm in your debt." He got out each word slowly.

Gracie giggled, more excited with his answer. "Mr. Bob will be with us!" She hopped in her seat with excitement, clapping her hands.

Relief swept over Jade with his answer. "Thank you for letting me do this." She continued driving west on International Speedway Boulevard toward Spring Garden Avenue, closer to home.

Chapter 16

THE NEXT DAY arrived. Jade was holding Gracie's hand in hers as she walked up the steps to the Saint Paul's Catholic Church. Today was Susan's funeral. Jade's mother was helping with Bob while she visited her friend one last time. Law enforcement folks from all over the United States were visiting, filling up the church pews. Some were standing. Others waited patiently throughout the building. When a law enforcement officer dies in the line of duty, his or her department has a well-decorated funeral for the officer a funeral filled with dignity and honor. A representative from every agency in the state attended, and as many attended from other states, if they could. The sermon was beautiful. People dressed in class A uniforms, looking even more official than ever, were all affected by the kind words of the priest. The procession that followed had pedestrians watching, waving flags as the black limo with Susan's body drove by. Traffic was held up until all the patrol cars following in the procession cleared the intersections. It was incredible the honor that was shown for her best friend. Tears blurred her vision as she sat in the rear passenger seat of the marked patrol car with her daughter. Jason drove her, still the caring zone partner. He continued his support for her by being there. She guessed there had to be almost a hundred patrol cars following in the procession. Twenty minutes later, everyone arrived at Daytona Memorial Park, where Susan was to be buried. With everyone standing around the casket, the twenty-one gun salute was done, the folding of the flag completed, and Susan was lowered into the ground.

Jade stood with Gracie, silently crying, standing in the family reserved area. She watched everyone walk by the casket and drop flowers into the grave. It seemed like forever, but the line of people finally dwindled to a few and then none. Jason wrapped his arm around her shoulders as she laid her head against him. She looked at the flowers, and she took a step forward and handed her daughter a few.

"OK honey, if you want to say goodbye to Susan, this is the time." Her voice quivered as she tried like hell not to get too emotional.

Confused and unsure of what was happening, Gracie looked up to her mother. Tears were ready to fall as the child cleared her throat to speak. "Mama, it's OK. Susan be back soon. Don't be sad." Even with broken grammar, Gracie could sound so much older than she appeared to be.

Jade dropped the flowers into the shallow grave, and her voice faltered. "Susan…I'll find the bastard who did this to you."

She wiped the tears away. "I promise." A cold feeling crept into the pit of her stomach, causing her to sit down momentarily.

Gracie mimicked her mother, dropping the flowers she had into the grave. "Love you. Bye-bye. See you soon." Turning, the child ran into her mother's arms and hugged her.

Jason rubbed Jade's back, trying to soothe her.

"Ready to leave?" His voice was calm, his gaze steady as he watched her.

When she nodded, he gathered both of them into an embrace, and they walked to the marked patrol car.

⇢▷◉ ◉◁⇠

Jade took a week off from work. Her sergeant had agreed with the idea, knowing she needed the time off. During the week, she took care of Bob, taking great care not to give him any wrong signals. Gracie was extremely helpful whenever she could be. She spent the most time with him. Escaping his presence, Jade took care of Susan's affairs and mailed her belongings to the relatives. It was the least she could do for her friend. By the end of the week, Bob appeared to be healed to the point at which he could fully take care of himself. The day before Jade had to return to work, he took the hint and asked to be driven home.

Gently hugging Gracie, he said his goodbyes and promised to be back at school working with her soon. The child was sad to see him go, but she had been so helpful and entertaining while he stayed there. He knew he'd miss her. His heart pounded hard in his chest as Jade drove with him away from her house. Looking at the outside mirror, he saw Gracie waving continuously, with her grandmother by her side.

At this point, he actually felt like he had a family of his own, but Jade was distant with him the whole week. Not that he was ungrateful; she was patient and made meals for him, washed his clothes, and talked to him. He knew she was distancing herself from him and didn't like it. That wasn't his plan. Convinced more than ever, he knew he needed to woe Jade the proper way. She knew how he felt for her and Gracie; she just needed time and more of his attention.

Smiling, he reached over and gently placed his hand on Jade's free hand, which was lying on her gear shifter. She turned toward him, smiled quickly, and then drew her attention back to the traffic ahead of them.

"Jade, I want to thank you for everything you've done for me this week. I don't know how I would have managed without you," he said in a low and composed voice.

In a voice that seemed far away, she said, "Our pleasure. We just hope you'll be fully recovered soon." Concentrating on the young pedestrians playing in the street, she did not look at him and pulled her hand away placing it back onto the steering wheel. The feel of his hand on hers did not feel right. No matter how much she tried to feel anything for him, the only feeling that kept emerging is friendship.

Pulling into his driveway, she did not turn the engine off, but jumped out of her vehicle and walked quickly to his side. Opening the door, she helped him out. As he recuperated, Jade fumbled through his keys again opening the front door. She turned on the kitchen light, and went back to the door to help him in. His figure blocked the doorway startling her.

He shut the door and slowly strode to his startled beauty with thoughts of only kissing those opened lips. He didn't want to let her go just yet.

Her eyes widened in alarm as he approached. She saw a devilish look that gleamed in his dark eyes.

Letting his cane fall, he cupped her face in his palms. The pounding of his heart was deafening, and the feel of her warm soft skin exciting him.

A cold knot formed in her stomach. She reached up and grabbed one of his hands with hers. His thumbs rubbed in a slow teasing circular motion around her jaw as he slowly bent down, drawing her into a deep kiss. She felt awkward, but she made her final attempt to see if there were any feelings in her for him and kissed him back.

Nothing, she thought.

I feel nothing except he doesn't kiss very well.

At first, his kiss was gentle, and then they were filled with hunger. His grip tightened as his other hand grabbed her butt cheek squeezing while pulling her into his groin. His breaths were quick, as his hands roamed not being gentle. She could feel his manhood pushing against her stomach as he continued his assault.

She pulled free, and he groaned, pulling her back and placed wet kisses down the side of her throat.

"No, I can't do this." She said while trying to free herself from his grasp.

There was no response, but his continued assault of her body.

"Bob, no!" Her voice penetrated his fogged senses. Finally, he let her go, but he felt completely aroused.

Stepping back, she regained her composure quickly. The raw need in his eyes and showing on his body was overwhelming.

"Bob, I can't, please. It's just not going to work out this way." She ran out of the house and sped away, leaving his door open.

He walked up to the door, and watched her leave. Shutting the door, his blood boiled with need as flames from their passion rocked him. He ached with need. The pounding of his heart was still deafening. He laid down in his bedroom with the picture of Jade on his nightstand haunting him. Placing her picture on his chest, he fantasized of her.

Chapter 17

"Hello?" said Father John with some degree of warmth.

"Father John, how are you?" Jade's voice was shakier than she would have liked. Her misery felt like a steel weight. She needed to talk. She needed the incredible weight on her shoulders to lighten and quickly.

"Jade, is that you?"

"Yeah, are you busy?" She started to feel like she was sinking from the weight.

"Are you OK? Is Gracie all right? What's wrong?" Worry echoed in his warm voice. It called to her.

"Oh, Father, I need to talk to you. Can we meet?"

"First tell me you and Gracie are OK, and then we'll talk more."

She closed her eyes, sighing heavily, "Yes."

"Stay there; I'm coming over." His voice carried a unique force, filled with authority yet with the same amount of concern.

"Thank you."

Hanging up the phone, she waited for the only person she felt she could speak to. The last couple of weeks were too much. It had been too long since she called Father John. He was like a brother to her. After Chuck died, he counseled her up until November of last year. She felt her life was moving forward, Bob had been there to help with Gracie, and her friends had been supportive.

An hour later, she watched Father John pull into her driveway and park. She greeted him at the door. Strong arms enveloped her.

"Where's Gracie?" he worriedly asked.

Hearing her name, the child came from the hallway shyly. She pushed her glasses back up on the bridge of her nose and slowly walked to the familiar, open-armed man who smiled at her.

"Come here, Gracie. I promise I don't bite." His voice was tender and coaxing.

Embracing her, he planted a kiss on her forehead then gazed into her inquiring blue eyes. "Silly girl, you remember me? I'm your mama's friend and a priest. I work at the church. You remember?"

She nodded and grinned back at him in recognition.

"Good girl." He stood up and followed Jade into the living room.

⇢⇥◉ ◉⇤⇠

Hours later, tired and troubled, the priest left the house unaware of a pair of eyes watching him from the empty wooded lot across the street.

Who the hell is that? thought Bob.

His nostrils flared with anger. He waited for the rest of the day for her to contact him, and she didn't. Yet here she is running home to call some guy over, he thought. What the hell is up with that? Well, I can't blame the poor bastard. Once she smiles at you that's it.

Watching the Buick pull away and head north, he couldn't recall who the guy was. His mouth took an unpleasant twist as a sick feeling spread from his stomach out to his limbs. Not sure if it was the pain medicine, he returned to his car, using his cane. He really didn't need it, but the terrain was uneven, and he didn't want to risk injuring himself worse. Fumbling for the drink he brought, he drank the cool liquid hoping it would ease the bad feeling he had.

No luck, nausea started to set in, he fought it as he sat back down in the driver's seat and drove the rental car away.

Chapter 18

THE FOLLOWING WEEK, Jade avoided Bob and gave him time to cool off and realize they weren't going to be a couple. She realized how hard headed he was. First he told her to make up her mind, and then he'd made a pass at her. She couldn't find in her heart anything more than just friendship for him. Chastising herself for her foolishness, she realized she'd jeopardized their friendship because of their intimate moment.

She'd dialed the familiar number to her faithful ride along, and waited for him to answer.

The masculine voice was old, but that was deceptive. Jack was in his late sixties, but definitely in great shape. Smart too. Whenever he could cut in with a cunning remark, he would do it with no hesitation.

"It's about time you called!" he said.

"How'd you know it was me?"

"Caller ID honey. I can finally afford it."

She could imagine him smiling right now.

"Welcome to the new age of technology, Jack," she said with a chuckle.

"All right, darling, are you coming over to pick me up today?"

"You know I am. Just making sure you want to come along?"

"Hurry it up," he barked.

The phone went dead. That was Jack's way. Good ol Jack, trusty and arrogant, his communication skills won over many people's trust. In this job, it's important to know how to talk to people, especially when you catch them doing something they aren't supposed to be doing. Grinning from ear to ear, she pressed harder on the accelerator.

Ten minutes later, she pulled into Jack's driveway. He was waiting outside smoking a cigarette.

Seeing her, he dropped the cigarette and stepped on it, and then he picked up his bag.

"Hello darling." He placed his bag in the backseat and took off his campaign hat before sitting in the front passenger seat.

"Hi, Jack, glad you can make it."

"Smart ass. Keep it up." His southern drawl fit his lean, tall form.

Driving away, she began to tell Jack about her misjudgment with Bob.

He sat there taking it all in.

"What do you think?" She realized the more she talked about it, less terrible it seemed.

Jack hesitated, thinking. She liked that about him, he didn't just say anything to please her. He weighed it out and then told her his thoughts.

"Well, honey, you screwed up. Clean and simple rule of thumb with friendship is, once you cross that line and mess around…well, there is no turning back."

"Are you sure? If I give him time to himself and don't call him, he should realize…"

He cut in, starting to get impatient with her. "Look, honey, men see the world black and white. There is no gray, like you women love to think. I'm telling you, Bob had to have been attracted to you. That's why he was hanging around so long. You're a beautiful girl, and he sees it. Why do you think he made that move on you when you dropped him off?"

She shook her head. She couldn't think that. Bob loved Gracie too. No man would hang around as long as he did just to get laid. Her daughter's relationship with Bob was a strong one. He wouldn't just use a child to get into the pants of the child's mother. "Jack, I think you're wrong. I know Bob better than that. He's not like that. I think we can mend our friendship."

"Fine, honey, you do what you think is best, but remember what I told you."

"Yes, Dad, I will."

"Fine then. Let's get to the station and work. Or do you want to drive around and pull some violators over?" His eyes gleamed with his last statement. The adrenaline rush was addicting. Whenever a violator was pulled over, any ride along could feel it.

"Hey, Jack, how about you drive and pull them over, and I'll just sit where you're sitting?"

"Bullshit! I'm just an auxiliary sergeant; I don't get paid to do your job."

"OK then, don't be an old fart and tell me what to do." A smile was threatening to plaster itself on her face. Hiding it was difficult.

"Fine," he answered. They drove north to the station.

The sun was starting to set. It was late February, and the weather was still on the cool side this evening. She realized how quickly time had flown and how little she knew about Susan's death. Pulling into the station parking lot, she gathered her equipment and went in, with Jack in tow.

Keying in the security code on the digital pad, she opened the door walking to her office. Once the door was unlocked, she placed her equipment on her desk and checked her voice mail. Jack sat down, keyed in the password on the keyboard, and started his reports.

Jade listened to her voicemail.

Finally, some clues. An anonymous caller had left important facts on her voicemail. Quickly she scribbled them down. Her fingers drummed while listening to the next message, from the Florida Department of Law Enforcement.

"Corporal Davis, this is Quinten Farrell from the Florida Department of Law Enforcement. I am the crime scene analyst. I first want to give you my condolences for the loss of your friend. I also have some good news. I've search and finally found something in the patrol car. There are black hair follicles belonging to a human, not animal, found in the front driver's seat and on her uniform. Importantly these hair follicles do not belong to the officer. My guess is that they belong to the suspect. The hair came off of this person during close physical contact with your friend. I found it on the driver's seat and on the top part of the blouse uniform. I also found several black threads on her uniform not belonging to the uniform. The thread is very common. Its cotton, and the particular dye color of black was most commonly used on sportswear, like sweat shirts or T-shirts. I need you to call me so I can get a preliminary report on what happened. My telephone number is three-eight-six-two-seven-four-three-eight-two-nine. Thank you."

Jotting down the information, she clenched her jaw to stop the sob that was forming in her throat. She felt a warm glow flow through her body with the new information. Every bit helped.

Looking down, she analyzed her data. A dark, four-door sedan, male, black hair, and black clothing were her clues. Obviously, the suspect concealed himself in the dark shadows, didn't want to leave evidence behind, and obviously had some issues with her friend. Susan would never meet someone alone unless she trusted this person. Who the hell was it? It had to be someone Jade might know; Susan told her everything - well just about everything.

Looking up from the computer screen, Jack saw the frown, and her expression grew still and intense.

"Darling, what's eating you up?" His southern drawl was extremely soothing to her emotions.

She eyed him, aware of his scrutiny.

"I need to check out the photos of the other officers in Susan's precinct. I need to rule out any possibilities of any suspects from her department."

"Oh?" His eyebrows shot up.

"Rumor is going around that Susan had a boyfriend. Normally, Jack, she told me everything, including what guys she dated or was involved with. She'd just started secretly dating someone in her department, but she wasn't clear who, but I need to be sure." She glanced at him for a sign of objection and found none.

"You're the investigator, honey. You tell me what you want me to do, and I'll do it." His eyes glowed with new purpose, and he stared back in waiting silence.

"Let me call her lieutenant and see if he can help us first. If so, we'll head off there and take a look." Picking up her radio she said, "Nine fifteen, Deland."

"Nine fifteen," the voice squawked back quickly.

"I need Daytona PD phone number to dispatch."

"Can you copy?" the dispatcher quickly replied.

"Go ahead, Deland." She had the pen ready.

Dispatch squawked back the phone number.

Picking up the telephone receiver, Jade dialed the number.

A woman answered.

"This is Corporal Davis with the patrol. Is Lieutenant Jarvis on duty?"

There was silence for a several seconds.

"Yes, Corporal, he is. Do you want to speak to him?"

"Yes, please."

The phone was quiet for several more seconds.

"Corporal, can he call you?"

"Yes." She told the woman the phone number to the station and her extension. She hung up and waited, tapping her pen on the desk in anticipation.

A couple minutes went by. The phone finally rang.

"Corporal Davis," she said.

"Corporal, can I help you with anything?" His voice was resigned.

"I need your help with Susan's investigation." She hated to say that, but honesty was the best approach.

"What can I do for you?"

"By any chance does your agency have an updated yearbook of your employees there?"

"Yes, we do. Why?"

Blowing out the air she'd been unconsciously holding, she continued. "To eliminate possible suspects." There I said it, she thought. God, I hope he cooperates.

There was silence on the other end.

"Lieutenant?" She waited for his answer.

"I'll be in the office in thirty minutes. I'll see you there." He answered in a stern, clipped voice that forbade any questions.

The phone went dead on the other end. She hung up.

Chapter 19

"WELL, JACK, I pissed him off. Gee, making friends use to be so much easier." Her attempt at humor failed.

He saw raw emotions flash in her eyes.

"Sure, honey." He gave her a smile that turned into a chuckle.

Gathering her equipment, she smiled back. "Let's get going. He gave me only thirty minutes to be there, and he wasn't happy to say the least."

"I could tell from your expressions that he wasn't please with you." Turning off his computer, he held the door open for her.

They locked the homicide room door, and walked down the hallway to the back door. Rounding the corner, they bumped into Jason.

He was dressed in civilian clothing and holding onto his son's hand.

He appeared not to be surprised at their meeting.

"Hi." His voice was low and smooth.

The child smiled up at her. "Hi!" The cheerfulness of Junior's voice caused another smile to spread across her face. Jason's smile was as intimate as a kiss, and she found herself blushing suddenly.

Jack bent down and held out his hand to the child. "Hi, young man, remember me?"

The child shyly extended his hand and shook the extended one slowly. "Yes, sir." He quickly retracted his hand and hid behind his father's legs, peeking out.

Jack laughed aloud at the child's reaction to him.

Gathering her wits, Jade silently chastised herself for reacting foolish. I can't figure him out, she thought.

"We need to go," said Jade. "We're on a time limit. We're enroute to Daytona PD to meet with Lieutenant Jarvis." She felt she needed to explain herself to him at that moment.

"Oh?"

"Process of elimination." Looking down, she smiled at the child. "Hello, Junior." She caressed the child's cheek gently.

She glanced back at Jack. She couldn't afford to be distracted by Jason. "Let's go, Jack".

As she brushed by Jason, his stare was sharp and assessing. She could feel his eyes following her, but she refused to be distracted. At the same time, she had known lately that his behavior toward her was changing. Or she had finally realized it.

Driving away, she glanced back at the station. She had to. It felt like she'd betrayed Jason by ignoring him. Determined to force her mind back onto the case, she focused on her task and drove quickly east toward Daytona Beach.

Jack shook his head. He couldn't hold his thoughts back. "That boy back there burned a hole into you the way he was looking at you." He pulled a Marlboro from his pocket and placed it in his lips. A bad habit he had - if he couldn't smoke one, he left one pressed between his lips, waiting for the next available opportunity.

She shrugged, stealing a glance at him before returning her attention to the roadway. "I don't think so."

"Darling, that boy is smitten with you. Don't you see it?"

She was glad of the semi-darkness. It hid her blush. "Jack you think everyone is attracted to me. I'm just an average girl - nothing more. He just wants to help; he's a coworker, you know." The words came out of her mouth sounding foreign to her. A part of her had wanted Jason to like her more than a coworker, but she had no confidence in herself regarding the laws of attraction. Sure, he's handsome, she thought. But! but! but! I'm just chicken.

"Yeah right!" He laughed, lounging against the door panel, watching her.

"All right, Jack, let's not get distracted by what we really shouldn't be talking about." She really didn't want to talk about her love life.

"Sure, honey, whatever you say."

The city limits of Daytona Beach came into view as she sped along, hurrying to the city police department.

"Look, what I want you to do is to take a look around. Act as if you're interested in the building or whatever you can think of. We're looking for a black-haired male, and with Susan's taste, it'll have to be an attractive male in his mid to late thirties or even in his forties. This guy will have to be in shape and have no facial hair. She didn't like mustaches or beards. I'll look through their yearbook for any possibilities, but, Jack, if you see a potential, try to get a name. I just hope Lieutenant Jarvis doesn't kick me out of his station too soon. I want to be sure so I can start the elimination process. I want this son of a bitch who did this to her, Jack." Anger filled her quickly, giving her voice a harshness.

"Sure thing."

Within minutes, they pulled into the parking lot of the city police department. Calling into the dispatch, she gave her location and exited the vehicle.

Lieutenant Jarvis was smoking outside, watching Corporal Davis's patrol car park. Waving the two officers over, he dropped his cigarette on the ground and stepped on it.

Extending his hand, he greeted the two. "Hello, Corporal Davis. Hello, Sergeant." He leaned forward, reading Jack's nametag. "Porter." His smile was forced. He knew why the corporal was there, and he didn't like it.

Opening the door for them, he waved them in. All three of them walked down the corridors of the department to the back offices belonging to the lieutenant. Walking in, Jade sat in the seat he indicated for her.

"Hey, Lieutenant, where's the men's room?" Jack asked, playing his role.

After getting directions, he walked past the men's room to look around for clues, leaving Jade to do her investigation with the lieutenant.

The lieutenant sat down behind his desk and leaned over. In his grasp was a thick, leather- bound book, which he handed her. Page by page she examined the photos of the male officers, scanning for attractive, dark-haired males.

Ten minutes later, the lieutenant didn't seem to notice Jack was still gone. Shuffling papers back and forth, he focused on his work, ignoring her.

Half-way through the yearbook, the tenseness in the room seeped into her bones. Looking up, the lieutenant gave her an unfriendly stare. "Have you found what you're looking for?" There was an edge to his voice.

"No, not yet. I'm sorry, but you have to understand, I'm just doing my job, nothing more." Her tone was apologetic; she felt just as uncomfortable as him.

His face began to relax, giving him a friendlier look. When he spoke again, his tone was warmer. "I know, but you have to understand that we don't like it." He used the term —we- meaning his department, and she knew it.

She proceeded through the photos, trying to hurry but not being sloppy.

The lieutenant stood up and looked toward the door. "Is your auxiliary sergeant OK?"

Oh, great, she thought. What to say? Come on, think!

"He's been suffering from the Mexican food we had earlier."

His expressive face changed and became sober. "Oh, poor guy."

He bought it, thank God! she thought. Come on, Jack, hurry.

She silently prayed, hoping Jack would return before she finished looking through the book or before the lieutenant became suspicious again.

Thirty minutes went by. She took her time with the last page. Jack walked in, blowing out air loudly.

The lieutenant acknowledged his return with a slight nod.

"Are you almost done?" Jack said to Jade. Looking down, he noticed she was on the last page and winked at her when she looked up at him.

"Yeah, I think so." She closed the book, and stood up handing it back to the lieutenant. "Do you have any employees not appearing in this yearbook?"

"No," he replied

"Thank you, sir. I appreciate all your help." A small smile touched her lips.

Taking the book from her outstretched hands, he returned her smile. "Did you find anything?" Curiosity was gnawing at him.

She took a deep breath and let it out before answering, "No, thankfully."

"That's a good thing, I think. If there is anything else I can do for you, Corporal, let me know." He came around his desk and escorted them out to the front door. Shaking both of their hands, he locked the door behind them, turned and walked back his office, feeling relieved.

Once they were both inside her patrol car, Jack proceeded with his assessment of his task. "Well, I looked around. Not too many people were there, unfortunately. Not one of them fit the description you gave me, honey. Not one. I even looked at photos on the walls. No luck."

"Yeah, and there were only two employees with black hair in the yearbook. One was too old, and the other was definitely Susan's type - Lieutenant Jarvis."

That information bothered her.

She drove away, heading back west. Jack popped the unlit cigarette back into his mouth and waited.

Chapter 20

THE DRIVE BACK to the station was quiet. The sun had already set. Lights from the area businesses blurred as she pressed harder on the accelerator. She wanted to get back to the station. Something was bothering her, but she couldn't put her finger on it. A sense of foreboding began eating away at her. She knew her premonitions were never wrong, and she learned early to never question them.

Twenty-five minutes later, they were back in her office. The message light blinked on her phone like a beacon. She reached for the receiver, and the pain in her stomach increased as she punched in the security code to hear her message.

"Corporal Davis, my name is Joanna Kincaid. I work for Halifax Hospital intensive care unit. I'm Jason McCrugle's nurse. I'm informing you that he died today at six thirty this evening from his injuries. Doctor Monroe from our unit called his time of death. I'll also let your dispatch know just in case you don't get this message."

"Dammit!" Her lips thinned with irritation.

"What?" Jack asked.

She felt a stomach spasm.

"McCrugle died not long ago. What more can happen?" She covered her eyes with her hands. She concentrated on her breathing, trying to calm herself down. Anger was gnawing at her. Rubbing her eyes, she rested her head on her hands, feeling defeated.

At her disbelief, he shrugged. "Look, honey, you know this guy's death was inevitable. Talking to him more than likely wouldn't have helped you. He was drunk, and like most drunks, he probably didn't remember a whole lot of what he was doing or what he saw.

His southern drawl softened the blow she was feeling.

She couldn't argue his logic; he was right. "Yeah I know, I know," she answered solemnly.

"You have leads don't cha?"

"Yeah, but not enough to have a definite suspect," she answered tartly.

"Honey, you have more now than you did yesterday. Don't be negative. There's always tomorrow, don't give up."

Jack was only trying to help. She had to give him credit. Good ol' Jack, keeping her on track and, of course, acting like a protective father figure.

"You know I'm not a quitter. It's just that I'm frustrated, that's all." Her stomach growled loudly, surprising them both.

"Let's get out of here and get something to eat," said Jack. "I'm done with my stuff. What do you say? I'm buying." Hands on his hips, he waited for an answer.

"I don't know if I can eat, but I'll try. Since you're done, we can go. I just need to get out of here to clear my head." They both left the station and locked up. The night sky was clear, with all the stars twinkling like Christmas lights. Driving away from the station, they continued chatting and teasing one another.

The pair of eyes observing them from the church parking lot across from the station was disapproving.

⋯⟨⟩ ⟨⟩⋯

After dinner, she returned to catch up on the homicide tracking system to include McCrugle's death. Jack stood outside, smoking his Marlboro lights cigarette. The quietness inside the station could almost be spooky, but she had a gun and knew better. With the homicide door left ajar, she could hear if anyone came into the station.

She caught up on the paperwork to include the Post-it notes of McCrugle's time and date of death in the investigative folder. She typed the information in the field packet notes. Organizing her desk before she left, she noticed a small bulging object under some loose papers. She lifted them and discovered a single red rose with a note attached that read, "To a beautiful woman who inspires me." It was unsigned.

"Jason," she whispered.

She brought the rose up to her nose, inhaling the fragrant scent. A smile slowly spread across her face as this simple gester of his caused her to take her mind off of everything. She was momentarily happy, with no regrets.

She was by no means blind to his attraction to her; his thoughtfulness had pushed away the shield she kept around her heart since her husband's death.

It's been over a year, and you seem to be so right for me, she thought.

Using one of the blank sheets of paper, she scribbled a note, thanking him for the rose.

Dropping Jack off at his residence after her shift was a ritual for both of them. She watched him unlock the front door and step inside, and she felt relieved and started to drive away.

A dark sedan drove by slowly, causing her to stop in the driveway.

Unconsciously, she looked at the license plate for expiration and for a tag light. She knew that most criminals would get pulled over for simple faulty equipment violations on their cars because they fail to do a vehicle inspection. So out of habit, she always checked cars that passed her.

The sedan had dark-tinted windows, making it impossible to see inside. The tags appeared current, and the tag light worked.

Making a right turn out of the driveway, she stopped at the stop sign and looked both ways. A light in the rear view mirror caught her eyes.

The same sedan had turned around and started driving slowly toward her.

Turning right, she continued south to the next stop sign then on into a residential neighborhood. She watched her rear view mirror and waited.

The sedan turned right, heading slowly in her direction.

I must be paranoid, she thought.

Turning right again, she followed the twists and turns the road and traveled around a lake, one of many in the city of Deltona. She drove the speed limit, curious to see if the vehicle would follow.

She almost stopped but continued to inch forward at ten miles per hour, waiting.

The sedan suddenly came into view and slowed to a crawl.

Increasing her speed, Jade continued traveling her path out of Deltona. Every once in a while, she glanced in her rear view mirror. The sedan continued to follow her.

This person must be heading in the same direction as me, she thought. Who would want to follow me?

At Kentucky Avenue, she turned right and headed north to State Road 472; the sedan followed, leaving a cushion of several car lengths behind her.

Still not convinced she was being followed, she took an alternate route to make sure. After a left turn onto State Road 472, she increased in her speed to see if the vehicle following her would do the same.

It did.

The hair on the back of her neck started to rise, giving her a creepy feeling. No way, she thought.

She made a quick decision and took the southbound exit to US 17-92 instead of the northbound exit.

It still followed.

Once off the ramp, she went into the left lane immediately and did a U-turn in the median and headed north.

A few seconds later, the sedan did the same U-turn.

She was being followed. Jade was definitely convinced.

She traveled north until she came to the truck route. She turned left and sped up to over twenty-five miles over the posted speed limit. She was convinced the car would follow.

The Handy Way Service Station came into view; she quickly drove in and parked at the gas pumps. She started pumping her gas and waited for the same sedan to approach.

It drove by. The person driving turned his or her head in Jade's direction, but she was unable to make the person out at all.

The vehicle passed her.

As she released her breath slowly, relief replaced the anxiety that had been building up inside her. After topping off her gas tank, Jade drove down Beresford Avenue heading west, away from the sedan's direction.

She looked at her watch and saw that her shift was just about over. Pulling into her mother's driveway, she made sure she wasn't being followed. She retrieved her sleeping child from the couch and she placed her in the backseat. Then she kissed her mom goodbye and Jade headed home.

She frowned when she realized her front gate was open. Her house was dark, and there was no movement near the windows or around her property.

Not sure if her mother left the gate open she parked in the back and called into dispatch to end her shift. Gathering Gracie in her arms, she started to her back door.

The same sedan drove by slowly at that moment.

Jade's heart hammered in her chest violently. It was the same vehicle that had followed her earlier, and she became acutely aware of her vulnerability, having her daughter with her.

Oh, my God, she thought as she approached her back door.

Fumbling with her keys, she found the back door key and quickly unlocked the door. Once inside, she locked the back door and laid Gracie down in her room, leaving the lights off. Out of paranoia, she peeked through the blinds and watched the sedan drive slowly by, never stopping.

Chapter 21

THE AIR HAD changed to a crisp bitter cold early in the morning. The humidity had vanished, and dry air drifted in, making the air seem colder.

Gracie peeked out of her dewed window, trying to catch a glimpse of any squirrels running around in the yard. She loved how they would play or quarrel with each other. Today her mother was going to be driving her to school again she was disappointed.

Jade walked into her daughter's room, quietly peeking to see what she was doing. Tip toeing, she reached the window and looked out to see what she was looking at. The dew on the windows made them hard to see through, but near the bottom, there was a clear spot.

She giggled when she noticed her mother hovering above her.

"Hi, Mommy." The child's mussed hair resembled a rat's nest; Jade reached down to smooth it out.

"Good morning, honey. How did you sleep?" She was exhausted from not getting enough sleep. Paranoid that whoever was in the dark sedan last night might do her and Gracie harm, she barely slept during the night. Instead, she had peeked through the windows constantly, looking for any signs of the vehicle or any person.

"Good, Mommy." Gracie hesitated. "But the noise coming from the window…" Peeking through the window again, she didn't think anything of the sound.

Stiffening, Jade raised her brows unconsciously. "Oh really? What kind of noise did you hear?"

Pushing the covers off of her, the child looked annoyed by the question. Defiantly she crossed her arms in front of her chest and frowned. She squinted. "Why, Mommy? You make it go away?" Even with her broken sentenced, her point was made.

Jade couldn't understand why Gracie was acting the way she was, "Honey, why are you upset that I asked you that question?" She had to know.

"Humph." Gracie continued her antics, not answering her mother.

"Gracie, young lady, answer me." Sitting down on the twin size bed, Jade stared her daughter.

Gracie's little head turned back and forth indicating she wasn't going to tell her.

Irritated now, she pushed her anger down and tried a new approach, hoping it would get her daughter to talk some more. Most of the time, her child wouldn't say much, let alone explain herself, so Jade had to think in different ways to get an answer out of her.

"OK. Let's try this again. The noise you heard last night - what kind of noise was it?" She smiled at her daughter as she leaned on the mattress for support.

"Why? All you're going to do is make it go away!" She pouted.

"Gracie, please cooperate with me. The noise is as important to me as it is to you. I promise I won't scare whatever it is away. I just need to know what could have made that noise. Can you tell me what kind of noise it was?" Fear was slowly slipping in, replacing the anger that had mounted in Jade.

The child was quiet, thinking. Finally looking up, Gracie bore her baby blue eyes into her mom's with a perplexed look.

"Gracie, can you make the noise for me?" Jade knew her daughter was battling her inner demons, trying to make her injured brain work. Her daughter had a hard time explaining her feelings, let alone most of anything else when asked.

Nodding her head, Gracie stood up from her bed and started tapping on her window. "Like that, Mommy. It sounded like that." A slow smile spread across her daughter's lips from the accomplished task.

"When you heard that noise, what did you do?" Jade gently caressed Gracie's arm, encouraging her to continue.

Suddenly, Gracie jumped back into her bed and hid under the blankets.

"Gracie, were you scared of the noise?" Jade asked.

Her daughter's voice squeaked, "Yes."

Pulling the covers from her daughter's head back down, she continued her questioning. "Honey, what happened after that?"

"It kept doing this," she said, tapping on the window again.

"Did you ever look out the window to see what it was?" The fear was spreading quicker now as Jade finally was able to obtain answers from her daughter.

Gracie nodded.

"And…?"

"It was dark, Mommy. It hid from me." Disappointment spread across Gracie's face.

"Did the noise continue after you looked out the window?"

"Yes." Her daughter nodded her head.

"For how long?" The rapid thumping of Jade's heart continued from the anticipation of Gracie's answer.

"A long time." Gracie rocked back and forth, soothing herself from the memory. Realizing her daughter was scared yet intrigued, she gathered Gracie in her lap and hugged her. "Honey, don't worry about the noise. What I want you to do next time is come and get me when you hear the noise. Remember to be real quiet when you leave your room to get me, OK?"

"OK, but the squirrels won't like me telling on them."

Her logic was silly, and Jade laughed at the thought. "Gracie, I won't be mean to the squirrels, but I don't want them bugging you when you should be sleeping, OK?"

"OK, Mommy."

A few minutes later, she had her daughter dressed for school. They both walked out of the bedroom and went into the kitchen for breakfast.

Making a mental note to look outside next to her daughter's bedroom window, Jade smiled at Gracie, attempting to make the child feel at ease. She didn't want to scare her by telling her a boogeyman was at her window or someone resembling one. Thirty minutes later, she drove Gracie off at school.

She made it home in record time, parked, and hurried to the spot outside Gracie's bedroom window. There on the ground were footprints large ones. The ferns under the window were bent down due to the weight of the person who had stood on top of them. Fear was causing her heart to do summersaults.

Jade realized here was another clue of someone's presence. Oh, my God, she thought as she adapted to the realization that she and Gracie were now victims.

She had no idea what to do at this point.

Going over the scenario again in her mind, she realized there was no evidence of who it was. She hadn't seen anyone, but her daughter had heard the noise. "Great!" The deputies would respond to this call but wouldn't be able to help her. Looking around more for footprints, she found some that lead toward the southwest corner of her front yard. Whoever it was didn't want to be seen, but would tap on a window to get attention? What kind of person would do that? And why? She thought.

Shaking her head, Jade decided to call Father John a fresh person to evaluate what had happened to her. She didn't want an officer. He was logical, and he would be able to help. Maybe she could get him to sleep over just in case just to ease her mind. Maybe.

Inside, she dialed the number for Father John. After the second ring, he answered.

"John, it's me, Jade. How are you?"

"OK. The question should be how you are?"

"Not good, Father. Is it possible for you to come over today and so we could talk?" Her voice quivered from the fear that had rooted itself deep inside her.

He looked through his calendar and saw that he was free that afternoon. "Yeah how about one today?"

"Sure. I'll see you then." Without a second thought, she hung up.

Chapter 22

Jade's black hair was tied back giving her a much younger appearance and with a better view of her high cheekbones and delicate features. As her friend and priest, John still couldn't shake off her beauty, which he'd always admired. He envied his deceased friend, Jade's husband, Chuck, but he always had that stronger pull toward helping others. So becoming a priest, devoting his time to the church, fulfilled him much more than being just a counselor. The nervous look in Jade's eyes bothered him as he sat there at the table watching her.

She prepared a simple meal of club sandwiches, chips and soda. Handing him a napkin and a drink, she started explaining what had occurred last night. "Father John, I know I probably sound paranoid, but I'm telling you it's true. Someone was following me last night and was messing with Gracie's window. I think this person was attempting to go through her window but realized she was there." Frowning, she took small bites of her sandwich.

"Jade, why would this person follow you?" He still wasn't sure of the whole story. She tend to leave bits of information out whenever she told him her problems. He had a feeling this time she did the same thing.

She finished chewing a bite of her sandwich and washed it down with some of her diet soda. "Oh, I'm sorry. I'm investigating a homicide involving my friend Susan, remember?"

He nodded and continued to eat.

"Well I have a feeling this person...well murderer, is still out there." She placed her sandwich down and seemed lost in thought. "Father John, I think this murderer is now coming after me."

He was quiet, not sure what to say. Then he fell into the role of Priest and started with the questions. "The big question is why, Jade? Is there a link between you and your friend Susan in some way? Do you think you might know this 'murderer'?"

"Well I've had time to think about this for a bit and I think somehow this person feels I know something. Susan and I told each other just about everything except certain information about work. So if this is about work than I really don't know who this person is, but if it's about her personal life then…"

"You might know this person?" His brows rose as he leaned toward her over the table. His inquisitiveness had just peaked.

"There's a good chance I do, but, Father, who? Who could do such a thing?" She continued to rack her brain recalling the guys Susan had dated. There were many, the names, well, she couldn't remember them all. Only the first names were what she could recall. "Damn!"

Reaching across, he gently placed his hand on her arm, attempting to comfort her.

"Father, it has to be someone she knew personally, otherwise how would they know about me?" The sorrow in her eyes reflected her pain as she covered her face with her hands.

"Think Jade. Only you can answer that question."

Looking back at him, she nodded her head.

Time ticked by slowly. Quietly she recalled the guys she could remember who Susan had mentioned. Getting up, she brought a pad of paper and a pen back to the table jotting down names while she picked at the chips on her plate. Completely abandoning her sandwich, she took one last drink from her glass. Picking up her plate, she headed for the kitchen as she continued thinking of possible suspects. She put the plate in the sink and leaned against the counter, completely absorbed in her thoughts. A few minutes later, a hand came down on her shoulder from behind, causing her to jump.

"I'm sorry. I didn't mean to startle you, but I am going to have to get going. I have a meeting in thirty minutes back at the office. Smiling down at her, he gave her a quick hug.

She walked him out to his car, they chatted back and forth. Before he left, they hugged again and gave each other a peck on the cheek. Watching him leave, she waved. When Father John had driven out of site, Jade decided to walk around her house for any other signs of potential intrusion.

Chapter 23

As he lay on the ground hiding, the sand began traveling up his nose with each breath he took. Glancing at his watch again, he saw that forty-five minutes had passed since he'd been there watching Jade's house. His leg felt a bit stiff and started to tingle warning him of the numbness to come. Irritated because it had been over a week and he hadn't heard from Jade, he'd followed her last night. Deep down inside, it made him feel better, but he knew he made several mistakes. Swearing to himself, he knew if he let his guard down again, he could really slip up, and Jade would catch him. But damn, he had to make contact with his special little girl Gracie; she was the one suffering the most out of all of this.

If he had only restrained himself better and not become so overly jealous of Jade's other friends, he might still have a chance with her.

Damn her for making me act like a fool! he thought.

The bugs started to bite him. Bob knew this was a good location up on the small hill in the wooded lot across from Jade's house. He could watch her and not be seen as long as he stayed close to the ground the brush would conceal him.

Longing for her attention was starting to overwhelm his daily thoughts and now she was teasing him even in his dreams.

God I miss her, he thought.

Watching Jade was the only way to know what was going on with her. She had failed to stay in contact with him lately.

Women! he grumbled.

But who was that guy? Thinking back, he recalled seeing him come over to spend time with her not long ago.

Why was he spending time with her? The thought bothered him a lot. Jealousy started to eat through his gut, slowly gnawing at his insides. Knowing he screwed up, he didn't want to completely lose her. He watched the woman he loved walk the perimeter of her house, and he ached for her.

What was that kiss for, too? Bob knew the answer wouldn't be sufficient. Jade's mine, damn it, and no one else's! he thought. He continued watching Jade, mesmerized by her every move. Then as casually as she could be, he watched Jade slowly pull the band out of her hair letting her long flow of blonde hair fan across her back. With her hair down, the contrast of her tanned skin against her hair gave her an exotic look. I love it when she leaves her hair down, my beautiful Goddess, he thought.

"God, I want her." The words escaped his lips in his mesmerized state. His body became alive. The tingling of his extremities eluded his overwhelming thoughts, causing him to forget about his environment momentarily.

She was so exquisite.

Bugs started to bite his hands and right leg, but he didn't feel it. He was numb. His fantasy of her sludged his brain as he continued watching. Jade bent over to examine something on the ground in front of the house giving him a view of her backside.

Thoughts that are even more erotic slammed into him, causing his breathing to quicken. The fire ant that crawled onto his chest under his clothes bit him hard, bringing him back to reality.

"What the!" Leaning back on his side, he scratched hard at the bite mark. His numb hands tingled coming back to life at his sudden quick movements. A few seconds later, he looked back, and she was gone.

"No." he whispered.

Scanning the area quickly, he couldn't see her. She must have gone back inside, he thought.

Who was that guy to her? He still could not recall who that man was. Convinced he was to have her, he thought out his plan to take out his competition and soon.

Chapter 24

BACK AT HIS house, Bob rubbed ointment on the ant bites to help soothe the burning feeling. Damn insects! He should have been more observant!

Thoughts formed into a plan to take out his recent competition from this afternoon. Whoever that guy was didn't matter anymore. Another swift flow of anger swept through him. Swearing under his breath, he applied more ointment to his injuries, and he failed to hear the knocking at his front door.

When he finally did notice it, he was startled.

"What the...?" He quickly put his shirt back on and then a pair of shorts, before walking into the living room. The knocking was loud this time, causing him to rush over to answer it.

Hopes of his beautiful Jade at his door came to his mind.

Quickly swinging open the door, his disappointment was reflected in his eyes as he stood in the doorway. The uniformed officer standing there seemed familiar, but he couldn't quite place him.

"Can I help you, officer?" He asked in a calm voice.

The deputy was average height with dirty blonde hair and a mustache. In his hands, he held a ticket book, and he stood watching him. "Yes, I'm Deputy Kemp, and I am here in regards to your traffic crash a couple weeks ago."

Understanding flooded over him, washing away his sudden nervousness. "Oh, yes, I remember. Were you the officer in charge of my crash?" he asked.

"Yes, sir," said the officer.

"Come on in." He opened the door wider for the deputy to enter.

The deputy followed Bob into the dining room and took a seat at the table when offered. He laid his citation book on the table in front of him.

"How can I help you, Deputy Kemp?" Bob inquired, trying to restrain his irritation.

The deputy answered in an authoritative voice. "I am not sure if you are fully aware of your crash and what had happened." His brows rose as he looked questioningly at him.

"Actually, I have been preoccupied lately and haven't had a chance to think about it. How about if you tell me more about it?" Bob's eyes narrowed.

"Well, you were traveling east on Beresford Avenue and entered the Spring Garden Avenue intersection. When you entered the intersection, you ran a red light and traveled into the path of a 2003 Ford Expedition. Thankfully the driver of the Expedition saw you in time to be able to slow down before crashing into you."

"Are you sure that I ran a red light. You weren't even there, were you?" Bob asked.

The deputy said, "No, sir. There were three witnesses to your crash. Two of the witnesses were traveling southbound on Spring Garden Avenue, and the other was at the red light facing west on Beresford Avenue facing you. All of them stated you had a red light."

Bob was quiet, letting the information seep in. He couldn't shake the feeling that he knew the deputy for some reason. What really bothered him was the fact the feeling he had toward the deputy even before he was informed of the crash was of definite dislike. Before he could stop himself he blurted out, "Where do I know you from?"

The deputy cleared his throat and shifted in his seat. "Well, sir, from Jade's birthday party. You interrupted me as I was giving Jade a kiss."

Realization dawned on him. He sat there, silently observing the deputy. His voice was cold and exact. "Oh, yes, now I remember." His instincts were dead on.

"Back to business. I am here to issue you a traffic citation for running a red light." The deputy opened the small metal case that held the citation and turned it around facing him.

"Let me explain this to you." Quickly, he explained the citation to Bob and Bob's options.

A boiling rage began building up in Bob's gut.

"If you would just sign here real quickly, I will be on my way." The deputy pointed to the bottom of the citation holding out a pen to him.

Snatching up the pen, Bob scribbled his name and handed back the pen. With a smirk, he took the citation from the deputy and stood up. Walking toward the front door, he clenched his fists trying to hold back a sudden urge to wrap his hands around the deputy's neck.

The radio squawked. The deputy held the radio close to his mouth and responded, "Roger that. I'm on my way out and will be en-route."

Bob's mind snapped back to reality. Reasoning won over. Sliding his free hand into his pocket to keep it busy, Bob opened the front door with the other. The deputy walked out onto the front step and started to turn around to say something. The door slammed into his face muffling out any noise. Clenching his teeth Bob locked the front door not caring what so ever of his actions.

"That son of a bitch!" The words spewed out through his clenched teeth.

Pulling the citation out of his pocket, he turned it over and saw the fine amount, and his sanity snapped.

"You prick! One hundred and fifty one dollars? That fucking prick!"

His nostrils flared as he paced back and forth, crumpled up the citation and flinging it at the wall.

Chapter 25

RUBBING AWAY THE sleep from his eyes, Bob continued watching Deputy Kemp from his vehicle. Across from him were binoculars, lying on the front seat. The air in the car was very cold, keeping him awake. Smiling to himself, Bob knew renting the car from Orlando International Airport was the best idea yet. In case anyone saw him driving away they would be looking for a completely different vehicle then what he drove.

"Hmm," he grumbled.

He couldn't take his eyes off of Deputy Kemp. "Well, Deputy Kemp, tonight's the night you die." Complete satisfaction swelled within him knowing his plan would be successful.

The night came and swallowed the horizon. Just a quarter moon shined through the puffy clouds. Bob had watched the Deputy go to numerous calls and pull several cars over. Waiting patiently and leaving good distance between them, Deputy Kemp wouldn't realize he was being followed.

An opportunity had just risen. Bob scanned for any witnesses.

No one was around in the quiet dark outskirts of the southwest Deland neighborhood. Beads of sweat developed on his forehead instantly his adrenaline started to kick in. Rolling down his window, Bob grabbed the BB gun from the backseat and pointed it out the window. Getting the deputy out of his car was a challenge, and he brought the gun to see if his plan would work.

Aiming, he started pulling the trigger. He pinged the car a number of times.

Smirking, he patiently waited. The sweat slowly rolled down the sides of his face as he watched in the car.

Inside his patrol car, the deputy looked up. The computer glowed in the darkness displaying his silhouette. The patrol car door opened, the deputy exited. Walking around his patrol car inspecting it and finding nothing, he scanned the area.

"Good. Stay there," Bob whispered to himself. Putting the car into drive, he started slowly toward the deputy. The scene played slowly in his head as he watched Deputy Kemp finally look up and see him approaching. His heart raced into overdrive as Deputy Kemp walked out into the roadway flagging him to pull over. Only two houses away, he pressed down as far as the accelerator pedal would go at the same time steering toward his unsuspecting target.

Realizing too late what was happening, Deputy Kemp tried to move out of the way. The car slammed into him. His body flew onto the windshield and off to the left side of the car.

Looking into his rearview mirror, Bob watched Deputy Kemp roll on the roadway and not move. He smiled and made his way back to his house and parked the rental vehicle in his garage. In the next couple of days, he would have the windshield replaced and returned back to Orlando after he made sure there was no evidence of what he did tonight.

Chapter 26

PULLING INTO HER driveway, Jade parked her patrol car in its usual spot. She looked around in the darkness and waited to see if she saw anything moved. A few minutes passed and no cars drove down her street. Having Jason hidden in her backseat made her feel secure, but at the same time, it awakened a new awareness in her. She didn't want to take any more chances and called Jason telling him what had happened. Being overly protective and upset that she didn't ask for his help sooner he insisted on staying with her for a while. She worried for Gracie's safety, and she arranged for her daughter to stay with her mother overnight.

"I don't see anything. It's clear," she whispered.

Jason continued to slowly scan the area.

"Why don't you unlock the back door and go in. I'll follow you." He whispered loud enough for her to hear. For some reason it seemed like a more intimate moment than his attempt to protect her.

She gathered her equipment in her arms, and exited her patrol car, with Jason following right behind her. As she stopped to slide her key into the lock, he gently placed his hands on her hips briefly before taking the computer bag off her shoulder and holding it for her. She found his closeness comforting yet so compelling that it drew her attention away from the potential danger at the moment.

They entered the dark, quiet house. Jason closed the door behind him, locking it.

Reaching out, he gripped her shoulder gently and stopped her in her tracks. Without saying a word, she turned her head toward him and waited. He took the keys from her hand gently and leaned into her whispering, "Is the kitchen door locked too?"

Her voice had drifted into a whisper as hushed as his. "No, it's unlocked."

"Stay here. I'm going to check your house first," he ordered.

Annoyed at falling into the victim role, she couldn't just let Jason walk in by himself. "I appreciate your bravery, but I'm a cop too," she replied defensively.

She could feel his body stiffen behind her.

"Jade, stay here!" His tone was coolly disapproving.

"I'm not letting you go in there by yourself. What if something happens to you, then what?" Her words were cool and clear as ice water.

Shrugging, he stepped in front of her then turned. "Then stay behind me, down here." He pointed.

She knew he was annoyed, but this was her house and by God, she wasn't going to let him go in alone without back up.

"Let's go." As quietly as he could, he opened the door. They walked through the dark house together. Jason led with his service weapon in one hand and her hand in the other.

They both searched her house thoroughly, and with the last room done, he breathed a sigh of relief. He holstered his service weapon and turned back to her. "It's all clear."

Placing her weapon back into the holster, she nodded silently and walked into the hallway, with Jason following. She slid the hall closet doors open, un-buckled her gun belt, and placed it on the top shelf.

Realizing what she was doing, he proceeded to checking the windows making sure they were locked. Next were the doors, he had to make sure she would be safe.

Walking back to her, he observed Jade had most of her uniform off except for her undershirt and pants. As she started unzipping her boots, he approached quickly, mumbling, "I checked the doors and windows. They are secured. I'll be in the other room." He turned, running his hand through his hair with uncertainty.

Damn, I need to get it together, he thought as he fought the urge to turn around and take her in his arms.

She watched Jason push the French doors open and enter the living room. Taking in his tempting, attractive male physique, she turned and walked into her bedroom to finish undressing.

Ten minutes later, showered, changed into her usual tank top and long, thin cotton pajama pants, the feeling of tension slowly started to dissipate. She walked toward the living room.

Tired, she walked into the dark room with the glow from the television illuminating her way. Her hair was undone from the tight bun she had it in earlier and fanning across her breast bringing out a different appearance.

Jason's eyes froze on her compelling image. His expression grew serious.

Noticing Jason's reaction to her presence brought back memories of their kiss a while ago. She walked up to him, and heard him suck in his breath. She was completely unaware how alluring she looked.

He stood near the window, silently watching her.

Awkwardly she cleared her throat, feeling foolish now. Unable to look up at him, she fumbled with her words. "I, uh…I probably am over reacting, but, Jason… I saw the footprints, and Gracie heard the noise and…"

His hand gently cupped her chin guiding her to look up.

Surprised by the physical contact, she stopped in mid-sentence, seeing the flash of desire in his eyes.

"It's OK." His voice was low and smooth as he stared deeply into her eyes.

He radiated a vitality that drew her like a magnet. Slowly he lowered his large warm hand down her arm where it lingered on top of hers causing a tingling in the pit of her stomach to develop.

She bit her lower lip. She glanced away, trying to gather her thoughts.

Without a second thought, he leaned forward and brushed a gentle kiss across her forehead.

The heavy lashes that shadowed her cheeks flew up. She gazed into his eyes intently. Her heart began its tribal beat of attraction, pounding thunderously in her chest. The quiet around them sizzle. Her face flushed, and she recognized the spark in his gaze.

Reaching out, he cupped her face gently and slowly lowered his head to hers. Not once did he blink afraid that it was all a dream. Jade stood there, lips parted, waiting for his kiss. Her warm breath fanned across his lips while he hesitated just for a moment.

She never moved.

He continued.

Their lips grazed each other at first, testing, then gently his lips covered hers. Shivering from the kiss, she drank in the sweetness of him. His tongue gently massaging hers was sending currents of desire through her body. Her arms came up as she subconsciously placed her hands around his neck while leaning into him.

Her soft curves molding to his hard body as his hands explored the hollows of her back.

He continued kissing her slowly and more deeply drugging her senses.

Her heart played a strong, loud beat, deafening her. His tongue danced in and out of her mouth while a slow burning of desire continued spreading in her stomach, threatening to override her senses.

His hands massaged her neck, down her shoulders, and then slowly up her back. One of his free hands brushed away her hair from her neck as his lips seared a path down her neck leaving a delicious sensation. The blood from his brain rushed straight to his groin blocking out any conscious thought.

Erotic was the only thought that made sense in her mind. Logic started slipping away. Her burning desire spread its way down between her legs, up to her breasts, fogging her mind completely. His lips recaptured hers becoming more demanding this time as his fingers slipped under her shirt. A moan escaped as her breath quickened.

His manhood pushed against his jeans as he pressed against her slim form with one hand on her lower back pulling her closer. His other hand cupped her breast, bringing her shirt up, exposing one side of her to his view. A low growl rumbled from him as he lowered his head to suckle her breast.

Through glazed eyes, she looked at him and she ran her fingers through his hair. Her breathing continued to quicken as he pushed her shirt up higher to suckle both of her breasts. Her body heat suddenly heightened as his mouth teased, nipped, and sucked each nipple. Then suddenly he stopped.

A terrible need was reflected in his eyes as he stood drinking in all of her for several seconds.

Jade felt no shame at returning her gaze to his attractive male physique, particularly his jeans. She didn't feel any need to pull her shirt down as she slipped her small hand into his. Looking up she found him devastatingly handsome with his rugged good looks.

He made no gesture to retrieve his hand.

She walked silently toward the double French doors, and Jason followed.

At her bedroom door, he turned her around. His expression was tight with strain as he hesitated. His deep voice simmered with barely checked passion as he spoke in a low tone. "Are you sure? I don't want you to have any regrets."

Stepping closer to him, impelled involuntarily by her own passion, she looked up with a mischievous smile, whispering against his lips "Yes." She kissed him, lingering and savoring every moment.

Her kiss was as tender as a summer breeze sending shivers up and down his body in a quick jolt. That simple act sent a surge of excitement from his head down to his toes. Sweeping her gently up into his arms, he walked toward the large bed.

She could feel his uneven breathing on her cheek when he held her close. Burying her face against the corded muscles of his chest, she inhaled his musky scent before he laid her down. In the dark, Jason pulled his shirt off over his head in one fluid motion. Kicking off his shoes, he laid down on his bed next to her. His lips recaptured hers, this time more demanding. Giving herself freely to the passion of his kiss, he slipped his hand under her shirt exploring every inch of her. His hand seared a path across her taut stomach, and then roamed higher intimately over her breasts. Pushing her shirt upward, his tongue explored the rosy peaks of her breasts.

Moaning softly, she instinctively arched toward him while caressing the back of his neck. Her nipples hardened from the sweet agony of his warm teasing mouth.

His lips continued its searing path as his hand explored further down her torso. An electric shock scorched her when his fingers slid sensuously down under her panties finding its mark between her legs. His fingers expertly teased her tingling sensitive skin while he massaged her delicate folds of her woman hood. As he roused her passion, his own grew stronger aching to be released from his pants.

She couldn't control the outcry of delight, and she abandoned herself to the whirl of passion he was awakening in her.

His finger slid down dipping into her intimately finding her damp, ready for him.

She rocked against his hand drawing herself to a heightened state of arousal. His touch was divine ecstasy. Her body began to vibrate with liquid fire as her insides began to quake clasping his fingers that continued to thrust to a rhythm inside her.

"Oh baby, please come for me," he whispered, and he continued whispering how beautiful she looked.

The world started to spin as Jade felt her body shatter into a million pieces. Quivering, she smiled. She lay there enjoying the moment.

He kissed her. It was a kiss that left her mouth burning with fire. Pressing his manhood against her thigh, he slowly removed his fingers from inside her. Tugging at her panties, he pulled them off her and onto the ground.

She sat up as he pulled her tank top. Jason stood and quickly discarded his clothes.

His manhood pulsed as she drank his naked body in with her eyes. Reaching out she grasped his erection in her delicate hands tracing her thumb around the tip of his swollen shaft. His hardness aroused new desire in her to erupt.

He groaned. He knew that he was too close to losing to her thrilling touch. Wanting to feel himself deep inside her, he crawled back onto the bed lying on his side next to her. The moonlight peeked through the bedroom curtains giving him a dim view of her. His eyes drank in her nakedness.

The glimpses of his aroused naked body sent a delightful shiver of wanting him through her. Gently lowering his head, she met him half way recapturing his mouth with hers as she leaned her body toward him.

He smothered her lips with demanding mastery as his leg slipped between hers gently, yet possessively. His mouth, warm and moist, possessively caressed her nipples as he slid his other leg between hers.

She was very much aware where his body touched hers as he roused her passion even further. Her pulse, erratic as desire spiraled through her, pounded through her chest as his manhood teased the entrance to her warm moistness of her womanhood.

He raised her arms above her head whispering in her ear in between each kiss to keep them there.

Squirming beneath his body, she enjoyed the exhilarating sensation his manhood aroused in her.

His breathing quickened as she continued rocking her hips against him. With one quick thrust, he entered her.

A moan escaped her lips from sheer delight as her folds encased him. He filled her completely.

Flesh against flesh, she matched his urgency with her own lusty needs. Her arms instinctively came down as her hands explored his strong back, his waist down to his hips. Their bodies were in harmony together as they found the tempo that bound their bodies as one.

His hardness electrified her as she felt him with each thrust. Then suddenly he slowed his pace then with drew himself from her. Small beads of sweat had formed on his forehead as strain showed on his face.

Puzzled at first, she looked up at him in confusion.

He smiled back at her, "Honey we almost forgot the protection."

Reaching above her, he grabbed the condom, ripped the package open, and placed the condom on.

Her wildly beating heart was the only sound audible to her, but she understood as she watched him. Shivering laying there waiting, she admired his thoughtfulness. She been taking birth control for years and wasn't worried about a possible pregnancy, she'd been prepared. Thank you for double protection, she thought.

Gathering her gently back into his arms, her body tingled from the familiar contact as he kissed the hollow at the base of her throat. His lips came down on hers as he entered her body with a slow agonizing thrust.

She rocked her hips, wanting more of him, and he slowly increased his pace within her. She felt her passion rising in her like molten lava, clouding her thoughts.

Moaning softly from the sweet tight sensation of his continual thrusts inside her, he watched, as she lay there with her rosy peaks of her swollen breast taut from their passion.

Fire started to build up inside him as she cried out quivering from her release. It was a raw act of passion as he held her hips and buried himself deeper inside her with each thrust. She wrapped her legs possessively around his buttocks not wanting him to stop.

She met each thrust with her own increasing his mounting passion.

Out of control as waves of pleasure shuttered through him, he surrendered to his fiery need of release. With one last thrust, he lay down on top of her as his seed was released. Wave after wave of sensations crashed through him causing him to see stars shattering behind his eyelids. Breathless, he couldn't think of any other woman that made him feel this way.

A few minutes passed as they lay with their bodies entwined. Their bodies glistened in the moonlight that peeked into the bedroom. He gently kissed her. Not knowing what to say now and not wanting to withdraw himself from inside her, yet he knew he had to. Sighing, slowly he withdrew himself as she unlocked her legs, sliding them down from his hips. Regretfully he left the bed and went into her bathroom to remove the condom and clean himself. When he returned to the bed, a slow smile spread across his face. Gathering her in his arms, he realized he didn't want to leave her side.

She snuggled closer to his warm naked body, and the contact reassured her of a feeling she felt in a long time. Sleep came quickly, taking both of them in its spell within minutes.

Chapter 27

REACHING UP, SHE turned off the alarm clock. She lifted her nose and sniffed the air.

Coffee, she thought. Hmmm.

She turned and realized Jason had already woken up and was making coffee. She reached across and grabbed the pillow Jason had slept on, inhaling his scent. Memories of last night flooded her thoughts; she smiled hugging the pillow to her chest. A few minutes passed, and she rolled out of bed and went to shower.

Gathering two cups and placing them next to the coffee maker, Jason looked out each of the windows into the dark. The house was dark. He finished his rounds, going through the house, looking into the darkness for any movement. There was none.

Hearing Jade in the shower, he took the opportunity to slip his jeans and shoes on. For the next ten minutes, he walked around outside in the night, listening, looking for any movement around her house. There was nothing just the crickets singing and an armadillo digging for food.

Walking back in, he waited for Jade to finish up in the bathroom. Another ten minutes went by, and she exited with a towel wrapped around her.

Kissing her neck slowly and nibbling down, he pulled her into him, cupping her buttocks. He couldn't help himself and definitely couldn't keep his hands off of her. Tugging at her towel, it dropped to her feet exposing her naked body.

His hands roamed intimately over the swells of her breast, causing her nipples to grow taut. A wave of desire swept through her as a soft moan escaped her lips.

The sound of the telephone brought her to her senses. She answered it. "Hello?"

"Jade, it's Jenkins. I need you in the office this morning as soon as possible."

The urgency in his voice started to bother her and brought a terrible foreboding. Automatically she responded, "Sure, Sarge, I'll be there right away".

He hung up with no further explanation.

She placed the receiver back down.

"What was that all about?" Jason asked after lifting his head from suckling one of her breast.

"I have to go." She panted from the delightful feeling of his mouth on her nipple. " Sarge wants me in right away," she moaned. "He didn't say why."

Turning her around, he gripped her hips and started rubbing his arousal against her firm rear-end. He massaged her breast and planted kisses down her neck.

Purring like a cat, she rubbed against him.

His breath quickened as she naughtily continued her rubbing against his raging hard on. He couldn't think.

Suddenly Jade turned around and dropped to her knees in front of him, smiling ruefully. Tugging his jeans open, she pulled them down.

He looked down at her naked body turned on at the view.

Jade grabbed his shaft and licked the tip, tasting his saltiness. Holding his breath, he focused on not coming immediately as her soft lips circled around his shaft taking him into her mouth. First, her actions were slow teasing him by circling her tongue around the top part of his dick. Then without warning, she used one hand to stroke his shaft as the other hand gently massaged his sac in a continual motion. She did this as she continued torturing him sucking harder and slowly, ever so slowly increasing in her strokes on his shaft.

Feverishly he grabbed the edge of her bureau for support. Jade was a master at this skill of driving him absolutely out of his mind. He had to stop her or he would come in her mouth at any moment. He stood her up kissing her swollen lips gently. His hand went down between her legs to gently rub her already swollen clit. Two of his fingers slipped in to her finding her already aroused and wet for him.

Moaning and rocking her hips against him, she whispered how much she needed him inside her, deep inside.

That was it. He lost all control. Gently slipping his fingers out of her, he growled and turned her around again. This time, he bent her over the side of the bed and entered her with one quick thrust. Her tightness enveloped him incinerating his cock. Primal thoughts of possession over-took him as he continued thrusting himself into her.

Jade lost all reasonable thoughts; her lust took over. She met each of his thrust with her own. Bucking wildly her moans of desire escaped her lips uncontrollably. His thickness filled her completely as she felt him engorge even more. At this point, she couldn't control the trembling in her legs.

Jason stopped pulling out of her, he turned her around lying her on her back. Panting hard he asked, "Are you OK?"

She nodded her head. "Uh huh."

The last bit of his control slipped from his mind. His mouth found hers as his cock slid back inside her once again. This time he knew he didn't want to stop.

Too full, too big, she thought.

Involuntarily her inner muscles pulsated against his hard length inside.

He thrust with vigor releasing his passions on her. She raised her back, trying to get more bucking beneath his hands. The pleasure was unbearable, and when she thought she couldn't take it any longer, he slid his hand between her legs, and pressed her clit. She screamed.

Brilliant sparks of light burst behind her closed eyelids.

Wildly, he plunged into her, spilling his sperm deep inside her and neither of them cared about the repercussions.

Gradually he withdrew. With a devilish grin, he bent down picking up the towel he took off her and handed it back. "If you don't mind, I would like to have my turn in the shower." He turned and walked into the bathroom shutting the door.

⤗⤐ ⤔⤖

Chapter 28

PULLING INTO THE station parking lot, Jade saw that most of the secured parking spaces were full with patrol vehicles. "What the hell?" A white Crown Victoria parked toward the west side came into view. "Why is a deputy here?" Confused, she parked on the grass. A foreboding started to develop in the pit of her stomach as she approached the rear door. She pressed the code to get in, the back door dinged her presence as she entered the building. She heard a group of men arguing.

The intense argument increased, and she stopped at the entrance to the homicide room. Everyone stopped abruptly and looked at her. Feeling suddenly awkward, she walked in and placed her stuff on her desk.

Sergeant Jenkins walked up to her with a look of irritation written across his face. Turning toward him, she could feel the tenseness in the air, her stomach tightened into a knot. "What is going on?"

"Jade, last night a deputy from this county was run over and is critically injured." A look of surprise crossed her face. She opened her mouth to say something, but he cut her off. "Hold off let me first tell you everything."

She nodded and sat down at her desk and leaned back in her chair.

"The deputy"

The blonde haired deputy that was sitting across from her with a disgusted look on his face interrupted him, "His name is Scott Kemp."

Frowning Jenkins continued. "OK, Deputy Kemp was apparently finishing up his paperwork from a call at the Botts Landing Apartments near the river when he was run down. A neighbor apparently witnessed the incident but didn't get to see the driver of the vehicle." He watched the realization form in her eyes and knew she would be upset, but he wasn't sure how much. If he didn't let the deputy get on his nerves so much, he would have pulled Jade aside to tell her the news.

A sudden pounding in her head became deafening to her. Leaning her head down, she covered her face with her hands and prayed the pain would go away. Oh God, she thought. Oh God, oh God.

The tears came suddenly as she rubbed her temples in her feeble attempt to ease the pressure in her head.

Feeling suddenly like an idiot, Jenkins placed a hand on her shoulder. "Jade, I'm sorry. I knew you knew him, but…I'm an asshole. I'm sorry."

She patted his hand, but she couldn't say anything at the moment. The pain in her head was slowly subsiding.

"Jade, Deputy Thomas is here because his supervisor wanted one of his men assisting in this investigation." He walked over to the bookcase grabbing the box of tissue and placed it in front of her. "The midnight shift trooper, Hernandez, handled the crash. Basically, since this is the second police officer victimized, Sheriff Franklin feels we need assistance. Personally I think since he knows you're handling these cases and know the officers, he thinks you're letting your personal feelings cloud your judgment."

She opened her eyes and glared at him. "What the hell did you just say?" Disgust filled her voice.

"Look, Jade, I'm sifting through the bull-shit I was told." Glancing back at the deputy sitting across from her, he shook his head.

"Go to hell, Jenkins!" said the deputy. "You know damn well her feelings are clouding her judgment. Look at her." His face distorted with anger, he stood up to add effect to his statement.

This time she was seriously pissed. The pain in her head ceased. Standing up, she clenched her hands into fists, trying to control her anger, but the words flowed out of her mouth like venom. "Fuck you, asshole! I'm doing my job, and yes, I knew them, which makes me work even harder to find out who this person is who's killing my friends!"

The deputy leaned over the desk, sneering at her, his voice pitched higher, "Oh yeah, so what do you have on the suspect anything?"

"I have my leads," she retorted.

"Yeah, right!" Gathering the papers into a pile in front of him, he continued challenging her. "The only thing you possibly would deduct from Susan's murder would be that a drunk killed her, not that there is a real murderer out there. Why don't you let the real detectives do the investigation instead of wasting everyone's time, little girl!"

She walked quickly over to the deputy. All reasoning had left her. She slapped the deputy across the face not once, but twice. "You arrogant jerk! Susan was my best friend and like a sister to me. And as for Scott Kemp, Deputy Thomas, we've been friends for several years. I care about both of these people very much, just as I do all my friends. Just because I have feelings, you quickly make deductions that I can't do any reasoning. Well, go to hell, you chauvinistic asshole! And as for my leads, I do have them, and it'll be a cold day in hell before I tell you about them." By this time, she had leaned into the surprised deputy, invading his personal space.

"Come on, Jade." Her sergeant had both hands on her shoulders, pulling her away.

Picking up his paperwork, Deputy Thomas stormed out of the office with her handprint still left on his cheek.

"Well there goes any cooperation between our departments out the window." Sergeant Jenkins walked back into his office, mumbling under his breath.

She turned walking toward the window rubbing her temples again. The pain had erupted again in her head, giving her a tremendous headache. Thoughts of what had just happened rolled through her mind, and the fact that Scott was still alive sunk in. She had been so distracted by the deputy bringing up Susan's death, that she forgot about her other friend. Please God let him recover, she thought.

Walking back to her desk, she grabbed her stuff and proceeded into her sergeant's office. He looked up with stress written across his aged face. "Yeah?"

"You stated earlier that I was handling Scott's case. Don't you mean Trooper Hernandez?" Being thorough, she wanted clarification on what she had heard.

"No, I stated correctly that you're handling the deputy's case. You are officially informed that this case is now yours." He smirked and then turned back around in his chair, picking up his phone. "Now, if you don't mind, I need to call Sheriff Franklin and try to clear up what happened in our office before the deputy turns it around and makes us the bad guys."

"Thanks, Sarge, for not being a chauvinistic jerk like that guy was. And need I say, he was more than that?" She knew he was having problems with the narrow-minded, chauvinistic coworkers in the building in regards to her working in traffic homicide. It was typical male chauvinistic thinking that women either should be at home raising kids or employed in a job other than law enforcement. There were a few left in the building who still thought women were hired to fill a quota, but she knew if she was going to stay employed, she would have to both ignore those people and learn to work with them. She chose to keep her job.

"All right, get out of here, and keep me informed on Deputy Kemp's health." He handed her the deputy's case folder.

"No problem." Grabbing it, she turned and left.

Chapter 29

THE YOUNG MALE deputy was sitting next to Scott's hospital room door, eyeing her as she entered his room. The room was dark, with only a light from a nightstand. She pulled the curtain back, and Scott came into full view, laying still on the bed in a deep sleep. She listened as a machine hissed with each breath forced into Scott. Next to him, she observed an intravenous bag hanging from a hook, dripping medicines into his veins. The top of his head was wrapped with a large white bandage and his face was swollen. He also had a broken right arm, and his left leg was in traction from being broken in several places.

She proceeded to do her job and took a couple of pictures of him lying in his hospital bed before one of his nurses entered the room. After gathering the data she needed from his nurse, she left the hospital and proceeded to the crash scene. There she took digital photographs of where the crash had happened. Trooper Hernandez had marked the road where the deputy had been at the area of collision and final rest. He had also marked where the patrol car had been parked. Thank you, Enrique, for listening to me about marking the roadways at scene, she thought to herself.

After documenting the scene, she proceeded to interview the witness.

When she knocked on the first door, a short stout old man wearing a thin cotton robe answered. "Can I help you officer?"

"Yes, sir, I am Corporal Davis, with the patrol out of Deland. I am here in regards to the crash with the deputy last night that you witnessed. Do you remember that crash?"

"Yes ma'am. Come on in. I've been expecting someone from your department." He opened the front door for her.

⋄⟫═◈═⟪⋄

Over an hour later, the interview ended. She had obtained pertinent information from her witness. A full-size sedan four-door had steered toward Scott and run him over. Her witness felt strongly that it was definitely intentional. He couldn't see who the driver was, but with the silhouette in the vehicle, he thought it was possibly a male. Her witness also saw the brake lights come on after the crash, the vehicle slowed down to almost a stop, and then it took off heading north. As for the license plate, he couldn't see it from the window.

A male. Somewhat of a lead so far, she thought.

Jade drove back to the station, letting the information from her interview sink in. Lost in her thoughts, she failed to notice Jason's patrol car as she parked next to it. She walked into the traffic homicide room, and placed her stuff onto her desk. Looking up, new and unexpected warmth surged through her as she saw Jason sitting at his desk.

He made no attempt to hide the fact that he was watching her intently. The look in his eyes held a maddening hint of arrogance, causing a ripple of excitement to pulse through her.

She didn't want to tear her attention away from him, but the sound of a person walking into the room brought her back to her senses.

Tom Jenkins ran his hands through his hair as he walked toward her desk. "So, how was Deputy Kemp?" His voice sounded tired as he casually sat down on the desk next to hers, waiting for her response.

Jason leaned back in his chair, still watching her closely.

Unconsciously her brows furrowed, as unspoken sorrow reflected in her eyes. "He's unconscious. He has bruises all over him, and he's also intubated. Fortunately his doctor says he'll make it." Clearing her voice, she gathered her composure. She had to focus. "The injury pattern on him is consistent to a car striking him on his left side. He sustained dislocated hips and a fracture to his left leg. He also had abrasions and head injuries. Other than that, they are just waiting for him to wake up."

"Who are we talking about? What deputy?" said Jason. There was an edge to his voice as he sat there. His eyes narrowed, and his back became ramrod straight.

"I don't know if you remember Scott. He was at my surprise birthday party." Dread started to make its way into her thoughts. She realized Jason might not have approved of Scott's actions.

Turning, Jason asked, "He was the one who gave you a kiss at your party causing your other male friend to act jealous, right?"

"Yes." Her mouth curved into a smile as she recalled the incident like it was yesterday.

Seeing her reactions aroused old fears, uncertainties Jason hadn't felt in many years and it scared him. Before he could stop himself, he blurted out "Oh, really," in a cool, disappointed tone.

Both pair of eyes turned to him.

"Yeah, really." Sergeant Jenkins didn't want to question why Jason was acting out of character, but he had his suspicions. Standing up, he walked back into his office, where a pile of reports were waiting on him to review. Barking over his shoulder one last order for both of them to get to work, he sat down and concentrated on reading the reports.

The call came in minutes after her sergeant fell silent.

Baffled by the sudden change in mood from Jason, she answered the telephone. "Traffic Homicide."

"It's dispatch. We have two confirmed for you."

She grabbed a sticky note prepared for the information. "Go ahead with it."

"It's going to be U.S. 17 at Spring Garden Ranch Road. It's a car verses a motorcycle two confirmed dead on scene. We already have a trooper on scene, and he advised there's roadblock."

"OK show me and nine-eight-four en-route."

"Ten-four."

She hung up and quickly gathered her stuff. Jason hurried also following Jade out of the office. Walking by her sergeant's door, she informed him of the double homicide. Her department's policy stated that if two or more people died due to a traffic crash, a supervisor had to be notified. She did her job and left.

Twenty minutes later, she arrived on scene, with Jason trailing behind. The fog was incredibly thick in the northwest section of Volusia County. Visibility was very limited.

After parking in a safe area, she walked through the scene first before speaking to anyone. She observed where the collision had occurred and noticed there were no skid marks prior to collision for the northbound vehicle. After analyzing where the other vehicle came out from, she observed there was no indication of breaking by that vehicle either. Blood was everywhere. The salty, tangy, metallic smell was strong. The body of the motorcycle rider emitted most of the smell, partially because of the head injury. Walking over to the other vehicle, she could also smell a strong odor of blood. The driver was lying prone on his right side across the front seat. She noticed the leg injury the driver sustained; he didn't have a chance of surviving with an injury so critical. Hoping neither of the drivers felt any pain, she said a quick silent prayer for both men.

Signal seven echoed in her head. Within the last two months, since Susan's death, Jade had her share of dead people. Still deep down inside she felt a loss for the deceased loved ones.

Finally, she signaled for the zone trooper to come to her.

"Trooper Applegate how are you doing?" she politely asked.

He smiled quickly at her, "Good, good."

"OK, what do you have?" She knew what had caused the crash; she wanted to hear if there was anything she could had missed.

"It's simple. Car pulled out in front of oncoming traffic. The motorcyclist was traveling north on U.S. 17, and I'm guessing traveling faster than he should have for the weather conditions. The driver in the car is old, didn't see the motorcyclist, pulled out, and probably didn't even hear him coming either."

"Oh, really?" She answered in a challenging tone.

"Yeah, the driver's window was shattered so I'm guessing he must not have heard the motorcyclist coming."

"Good job. Now did you get the names of the fire personnel, whoever called their deaths, and the times?" She would have been most impressed if the Trooper did.

"No, not yet," he answered frowning.

"I'll need that, along with the front page of the crash report. Have you been able to identify the drivers yet?" Her matter-of-fact tone was cool and commanding.

"No, but I'm on it." The zone trooper turned and walked back to his patrol car.

Jason walked up with his camera on a tripod and looked at her with a spark of some undefined emotion in his brilliant blue eyes.

"Let's get to work," he said tersely.

Confused by his demeanor, Jade went back to her patrol car to get her gear.

Chapter 30

THE SUN HAD burned off the fog from the scene completely by the time they were done with their evidence collection at the crash scene. The humidity had slowly seeped into the hot early spring afternoon. Wiping sweat from her forehead, she stole some glances at Jason as they worked. He seemed tense, like something was bothering him.

She walked up to him, and he turned with a frown on his face. "Are you done?" Her voice echoed in her ears as traffic slowly streamed by their scene. She had let one lane open on US 17 after Jason was able to photograph the scene and she was able to get her scene measurements. The semi-trucks rattled with their diesel engines as they crawled past her.

Nodding, he placed the last bit of his equipment in his trunk.

She placed her hand on his shoulder to stop him from just leaving without speaking to her. She could feel him stiffen under his uniform as he turned around to face her.

Jason's expression stilled and grew serious as his blue eyes focused on hers.

Somehow, she felt she had done something wrong, but for the life of her, she had no idea what. A tumble of confused thoughts and emotions rode through her like a wave. Focus - focus on what's wrong., she told herself. "Jason are you OK?"

The tense lines in his face relaxed when he looked at her. He realized she could read him, and at that moment, he felt foolish - foolish for letting jealousy peek its ugly head out when she was concerned about the deputy. Silently cursing himself, he mumbled, "I'm fine. I'll see you at the station."

She watched his broad back as he turned and opened the driver's door and got into his patrol car. He left her standing, watching him leave. She walked back to the zone trooper and gave him the OK to open the roadway completely.

Driving back to the station, she couldn't figure out why Jason was acting the way he was. Her head swirled with doubts as she drove. One minute, everything started to make sense, then the next minute all hell had broken loose. Her day had started out well, and then she'd learned Scott was almost killed last night. Of course, she couldn't leave out the fight with the deputy, what was his name? And now fighting with Jason, why? Could I just start my day over again? she silently wished.

Ten minutes later, she pulled into the patrol station's parking lot.

Jason wasn't there.

What was going on?

Walking inside, she placed her equipment on her desk and started inputting the data into the computer.

Fifteen minutes went by. A noise at the door caught her attention. She saw that it was Jason.

Signaling her to be quiet and follow him, he hid something behind his back, away from her view. There were only a few people in the station, mostly up in the administrative section of the building, which was up front. He pulled her into the dark office near the back of the building, and captured her lips with his so suddenly it startled her.

He tasted her, letting his tongue explore the recesses of her mouth. Holding her snugly against his frame, his lips lightly touched her with tantalizing persuasion.

Her heart thudded quickly from his expressive behavior. She could feel how she affected him, his manhood pressed against her pelvis rousing her passion. If anyone came into the office now, Jason wouldn't be able to hide his erection.

Just as quickly as he'd captured her in his embrace, he released her. She saw the heart-rending tenderness in his gaze mixed with desire. It was so easy to get lost in the way he looked at her. She grinned mischievously at him wondering what his next move would be.

The arm hidden behind his back came around. He was holding a single rose, bloomed, with the thorns taken off. He handed it to her, smiling as she reached out to take it. Inhaling the fragrance of the rose, she never took her eyes off of him. She was confused - not sure why he was acting the way he was. One minute he was cold at the homicide scene, the next, he pulled her into a dark office to give her a kiss and then this rose. She wasn't complaining, she just didn't understand his behavior.

"This rose is for you. I've been acting somewhat like a jerk today. Please accept my apologies."

Frowning, she cocked her head to one side considering his words. "I don't understand."

Looking down at the rose, his voice was smooth but insistent. "Just take it from me - I was a jerk."

"OK, I won't argue with you. I shall accept this beautiful rose as your gesture of apology." She purred those words as she pulled him down toward her and returned a quick kiss. Releasing him, she walked out of the office and back into her office, knowing he would need a few minutes of privacy before he could come out. Chuckling to herself, she recalled how lucky it was to be a female in situations like this.

No sooner had she sat down at her desk than her phone rang. The ring indicated an inter-departmental call. The name of Lieutenant Jeremy Mason appeared in the small screen on the phone. She answered, "Yes, sir?"

The voice was heavy with sarcasm. "Are you having a nice day, Corporal Davis?"

Confused she answered, "No, not really."

"Well I suggest you come into my office. I'm going to need to talk to you."

"OK." She headed directly to his office, and her head spun with several possibilities of why her lieutenant needed to speak with her. What weighed the most on her mind was her behavior with the deputy that morning.

It would be just my luck that guy complained on me, she thought.

Her steps were filled with confidence as she approached the closed office door. She knocked and waited for his response.

"Come in," he answered.

She hesitated before going in. The hair on the back of her neck rose, indicating to her that her intuition was correct about a complaint. It had to have been from the deputy, she reasoned. Shit!

Opening the door, she entered.

"Shut the door, please."

She did as instructed, turned, and waited.

"Sit down." His voice was rough with anxiety as he sat behind his desk with his hands intertwined.

She sat rigid, back straight, waiting for the accusations to fly. Unfortunately, her lieutenant was one of the old fashion breed of law enforcement officers who felt no women should be cops. But then again, he was going through a nasty divorce, and most of the female staff were his targets whenever he had a chance to project his anger.

Leaning toward her, his eyes were cold. "I received a phone call this morning while you were out on your homicide scene." His tone was disapproving.

Common sense told her to remain quiet until he was done.

"You apparently aren't cooperating with the Sheriff's Department and had the audacity to strike a deputy in the face." He continued, and his voice hardened ruthlessly, "What the hell were you thinking?"

She took a deep breath in her attempt to remain calm, and it wasn't easy for her.

"All the Sheriff's Department wanted was cooperation, but like always, women like you feel you're superior to everyone else."

Her temper flared as she spoke loudly in her defense. "Excuse me, lieutenant?"

"You heard me!" he shouted.

She stood up, hands on her hips, and she concentrated on her breathing. When she was taunted, like now, she would normally say what was on her mind without any thought. This time, she didn't want to give him an excuse to suspend her. Her voice was low and controlled as she rebutted his remarks through gritted teeth. "Lieutenant, the deputy was rude and insinuated I wasn't getting anywhere with my case. As you know, gathering evidence takes time, and unfortunately, our department is at the mercy of another agency to assist us. I am doing my job, but I am not a miracle worker. I can't produce a suspect without enough evidence."

He sat very still. His eyes narrowed as he watched her, analyzing with what she said.

She waited, wondering if he was baiting her.

"Sit down, Corporal," he ordered.

She sat like an obedient employee, yet she continued to concentrate on her breathing. Emotionally, she was hanging by a thread.

"The big question here, Corporal, is if you have any leads. By your statement just now, it sounds like you have no leads. Am I correct?" He crinkled his nose at her with that last statement as he leaned forward in a challenging posture.

Realization struck her. He was trying to pry information out of her. There was no way she was going to tell him anything. Call it pride or ego, but he was going to fail. This time she chose her words carefully, knowing his temper would fail him. "I do have leads, and this case is still under investigation. With all due respect, lieutenant, are you trying to get information on this case out of me? Because if you are, and you leak this information to the Sheriff's Department, you will then be interfering in my investigation, and I would have to charge you for interfering. Now with regards to this deputy accusing me of striking him, if he isn't pressing charges, then, lieutenant, I suggest you need to speak to my immediate supervisor regarding my behavior." She stood up, ready to leave.

"You sit your ass down right now. I am not done with you!" he yelled in a nasty tone. Standing up quickly, he pointed at her and then to the chair in front of his desk. "Sit down, dammit!"

With an air of confidence, she stated in a cool tone of voice, "Lieutenant, your attitude is aggressive and unprofessional. The correct chain of command is for you to speak directly to my sergeant, so let me go get him." Turning, she opened the door and started to walk out, but she felt a hand on her shoulder holding her back.

"Little lady, if you don't get back in here, I'll charge you with insubordinate behavior, and I'll convince Deputy Thomas to press charges against you for your irrational behavior." His fingers dug into her soft flesh, keeping her from leaving. His body trembled from his anger, and his grip on her shoulder tightened. He spun her around to face him.

A disturbing look moved across his face. His mouth took an unpleasant twist in his anger and prejudice for the female officer.

For the first time, a rush of fear rose up, choking her. His surprise behavior and sudden anger toward her was stunning. This was a first in her experience of unprofessional and unbridled anger from a supervisor. Uncertainty washed over her as the lieutenant released his grip, turning his attention to the approaching person.

The sound of footsteps to her right broke her attention away from her lieutenant. She turned to see who it was. Relief spread through her as Sergeant Jenkins walked purposely toward them. In an authoritative voice he spoke, but continued to keep eye contact with her. "Corporal Davis, you're needed in our office. Lieutenant, we need to talk *now*!" Jenkins guided her away in the direction he wanted her to go. He turned, walked into Lieutenant Mason office, and slammed the door behind him.

The yelling match began. Their voices roared behind the closed door. Walking back to her office, she unconsciously rubbed her sore shoulder where Lieutenant Mason had grabbed her. Replaying the incident in her mind, she just couldn't believe his behavior toward her.

Walking through the hallway, she ran into Jason. He placed both of his hands on her shoulders.

The pain in her right shoulder caused her to wince and pull back from his grip.

A look of alarm clouded his face. "Are you OK?"

The sounds of loud arguing voices echoed in the hallway. He turned in the direction momentarily listening.

Reaching up, she gently rubbed her shoulder, kneading the pain out of it. Her voice cracked in her reply. "Yeah." Turning, she just wanted to get out of the hallway, away from the yelling voices. The accusations seeped into her, causing guilt to eat at her. If only there were more information, she would have better leads into the suspect who killed her best friend.

If only.

She could feel Jason behind her. His presence was like a warm glow.

He leaned over, placing a kiss on her head.

"Please tell me what is going on?" When he spoke, his voice was tender almost a whisper.

His strong supportive hands gently massaged the tension in her neck and left shoulder. At this moment, even with the pain subsiding in her shoulder, she was utterly confused. Too much had gone wrong since the moment she had woken up this morning with her sergeant's phone call.

What next? she thought.

A beeping sound came from Jason's gun belt. He looked at the front of the Nextel cell phone and walked away from her, taking a few steps toward the window.

"Go ahead," his voice sounded resigned.

"Jason?" He quickly pressed the phone button for private mode, then placed it back on his ear.

Jade noticed the voice on the other end was female and upset. Nope, she wasn't going to let jealousy seep into her already confused state, so she filed it away for later to find out who that was.

He continued facing the window with his back toward her.

The arguing voices in the office subsided. Footsteps caught her attention, echoing in the hallway. Her sergeant walked into the office red-faced, fist clenched. He turned toward her. He completely ignored Jason as he gathered his thoughts before he spoke.

Her stomach tightened. Unconsciously she crossed her arms, covering her stomach in a protective posture as she waited.

He let out a long audible breath and straightened himself like a towering spruce. He cleared his throat. "Jade, I want you to know…" He stopped mid-sentence and shut the homicide room door for privacy.

Her attention was quickly diverted back to Jason. He stiffened turning back away from her stare as he finished his conversation with the unknown woman.

"Crystal, look I'll be right over," Jason said. "Talking about it to me on the phone while I'm still at work isn't helping matters. I'll be there soon." He quickly closed the phone and placed it back onto its clip that was attached to his gun belt. Turning back around, he realized his Sergeant had shut the door and had a serious look on his face. He stood there and watched, waiting to see what was going to happen.

"OK that…" he pointed toward the closed door. "That was absolutely unprofessional and… and… wrong! He is not allowed to talk to you about any cases unless directed by the captain and if I am there. Do you understand?"

"Yes, but."

"I know he called you into his office, and you did what was right."

She nodded in agreement.

"He made remarks that he can't take back. You know the man is going through a nasty divorce, and that is no excuse, but, I guess what I am trying to say… is … do you want to file a complaint against him?"

She thought about it. If she complained, her lieutenant would be coming after her, making her the only target of the mess he was in. And other people she worked with would call her a complainer, not that she cared much what they thought in this particular situation. "No, no." She shook her head.

"Are you sure? He did grab you. That is grounds for assault. He could lose his job for his actions." Concern clouded his eyes as he stood there in disbelief at her answer.

"Is he filing charges against me regarding Deputy Thomas?" If he was then she would definitely reconsider her decision.

"No, that's going to be dropped."

Relieved she answered, "Then my answer again is no."

In disbelief, he reached across, gently placing his hand on her right shoulder. Quickly, she pulled away wincing.

"What the hell?" said Jason.

Her stomach was still clenched tight, gnawing away her last bit of confidence. Looking at Jason, she stood up, opened the door and walked out in one quick motion.

Jason followed behind her.

Pushing the back door open, she walked out under the overhang, taking deep breaths in her attempt to relax.

Jason stopped watching her as his anger built.

She began to paced back and forth, and the silence loomed between them like a heavy mist.

His patience was gone. "What the hell just happened back there? I obviously must have missed something." He spat the words out impatiently as he stood there waiting.

Her eyes reflected her pain and confusion. Right now, what she needed was to be alone with her thoughts. Jason's sudden demand of her caught her by surprise but also irked her. "You sure did." There was defiance in her tone as she turned her back to him.

He took a step toward her. "What is that supposed to mean?"

Anger vibrated through his voice as he stood there.

She continued to hold her silence, not willing to overwhelm him with her problems. She had learned when she was younger silence was golden, hopefully at this moment it would prevail. A warning voice whispered in her head that it wouldn't.

His phone beeped. The sound of his disapproving sigh at the interruption caused her to look over her shoulder for a quick glance.

His steady gaze bore into her face and searched her eyes as he quietly listened to the person on the cell phone. He wanted to help her, but she wouldn't let him.

"Just wait, I'm on my way", he said and he hung up the phone, placing it back onto his gun belt. Glancing at watch, he took note of the time, knowing he had only a few minutes before he really had to leave.

Jade turned her back, gathering her wits before they continued with their conversation.

Jason stepped in front of her and cupped her face gently with his large hands. Tilting her chin up and forcing her to look up at him, he saw the unspoken pain glowing from her eyes and knew she wouldn't let him into her world. Their intimacy had just begun; he had not earned enough of her trust to let him in. "I don't know what had happened in there, but when I hear our sergeant asking you if you want to file a complaint on the lieutenant, I'm concerned. Then when I see the sergeant touching your shoulder and you pull back, obviously in pain, I'm now involved. I'm not going to let anyone hurt you, do you understand? You mean a lot to me, Jade, and I'm sure as hell not going to stand here and let that bastard get away with his behavior." His eyes blazed with anger.

Her expression grew serious. "If you care for me, you will not interfere. Just let me handle this."

"No way." His voice rang with disbelief at her response.

She took a step back away from him, and a warning cloud settled on her features. She fired back, "I'm serious Jason. Do not interfere."

Even before her husband was murdered, he recalled how she built herself up, acting strong in times of crisis. He had watched her at different crime scenes and saw her reactions to the victims young and old. She held herself strong. Still Jade had the extra patience most other officers didn't, to listen-really listen to what the violators and the victims' families had to say. Some of the officers called her too sympathetic; others saw her as being too soft. He didn't.

What he had for her was respect, incredible desire, and an overwhelming urge to protect her like now at this moment. "You know how hard it is to just stand by and let that go?" His voice faded, losing the steely edge it had moments ago.

"Please," she begged. Raising her chin, she assumed all the dignity she could muster. "For over a year, I've managed." Her voice held a faint tremor.

Jason's cell phone beeped, and he looked at the caller ID. He cursed when he saw the name on the screen. In his haste, he accidentally pressed the speaker button as a woman's voice broke the silence. "Jason...Jason are you there?"

He quickly changed from speaker to private mode as he looked back to her. There was a spark of indefinable emotion that crossed her face. Jade took another step back further away from him.

Without really listening to the woman on the cell phone, he studied Jade. Knowing the woman's voice coming from his phone had upset her, he watched her walk around him in silence. "I'm leaving now," he hung up the phone, watching Jade walk into the station without looking back. How fragile she looked, yet she fought hard to keep her composure. Convinced Jade wouldn't let him comfort her, he sighed and headed toward his patrol car to leave.

Chapter 31

THE POUNDING ON the door continued until she answered it. Relieved he was finally there, she threw herself into his unsuspecting arms.

"Crystal what the…" His tone was coolly disapproving.

She withdrew her arms reluctantly as he pushed her off of him gently. "What took you so long?" she inquired.

"Look, you have to understand that I have a life too. You cannot expect me to be here at any given moment," he said bluntly.

"I know, but your son needs you…and so do I." Her voice trailed off as she turned away.

Shutting the front door, he followed her down the hallway to their son's room. The door was open. He could hear cartoons in the background coming from the small television he had bought him last Christmas. When he entered the room, his son's eyes grew large, as he lay so small and fragile under the Spiderman blanket.

Sitting down next to his son, Jason placed his hand on the small damp forehead, checking his temperature. Junior was hot. "When was the last time you checked his temperature?" he asked.

"Just before you came. He was 101 degrees."

"Then why do you have a blanket on him?" His patience was wearing thin.

The child placed a hand on his chest, getting his attention.

"Daddy, me cold. No mad at Mommy," he begged in a throaty whisper.

His tight expression relaxed into a smile as he looked down at his son. Tendrils of hair were matted on Junior's forehead. He gently brushed them to the side. "Son, I'm not mad at anyone, I'm just concerned for your health," he said softly. Turning around, he asked, "Crystal, how long did you say Junior's been sick?"

"Well, since yesterday. He's had a fever and was vomiting. As of today, he only has a fever." Her voice quivered slightly.

"What have you been giving him for the fever?"

"Tylenol, like you said, every six hours." Nervously she started fiddling with her hands.

He turned back to his son. He didn't want to make the child afraid. Placing a kiss on his son's forehead, he stood up. He walked to his ex-wife and stood towering next to her. "Have you called his doctor yet?"

Her eyes darted up. "Yes. He has a four o'clock appointment, but I can't take him." Not meeting his gaze, she continued. "I took work off yesterday, and I have to show up today. Can you take him?"

He quickly glanced at his watch and noticed the time two forty-five. Frustrated from the sudden momentary notice, he raked his fingers through his hair. "Yeah, sure it's no problem. Do you work tomorrow too?"

She nodded.

"All right, I'll call in sick and take him to my place for a couple days until he's better. Pack his things, and I'll be right back to pick him up."

A smile spread across her face. "Thank you. I knew I could rely on you."

With that, he left.

⊷⊨◎ ◎⊨⊶

Jade replayed the earlier events of that day in her mind as she drove home from work. Her captain had called her into his office along with her sergeant to tell her side of the story of what had happened with her lieutenant. This time, her sergeant heard all the events, not just their lieutenant's version. Again, she was asked if she wanted to file a complaint against Lieutenant Mason. She refused.

Sergeant Jenkins brought up the injury to her shoulder; she had no choice but to show it to them. Lieutenant Mason had gripped her shoulder so hard when he reached out to make her stay that he had left her bruised. The evidence on her shoulder proved where he had grabbed her; there was an injury pattern of his fingers where he had gripped her. The captain ordered her to let her sergeant take pictures of the bruises while they were in his office. The scenario played repeatedly in her mind, bothering her.

She went by her mother's first and picked up Gracie. Then she drove home. Remembering she had a problem, she parked on the side of the house. The stranger who was bothering her daughter could possibly be stalking them at this moment. Hesitating, she wondered what to do next.

What I'm going to have to do is protect my family and go check out the house first, she thought. "Gracie, darling, stay here in the car until I come get you, OK?" Her voice was stern as she watched her daughter looking so helpless in the backseat holding her stuffed Barney doll.

"Ok Mommy.," she answered.

Locking her patrol car door, she shut it and proceeded toward the back door. She pulled her weapon out, and silently prayed as she unlocked the door and entered slowly. Despite her fear, she knew she could only rely on herself and no one else. Tension crept through her body as she checked each room, each closet and the every hiding place.

Nothing, thank God.

She went back to the car and gathered her daughter and took her inside. Tonight she was going to have Gracie sleep in her bed with her. She couldn't shake the fear that had already seeped inside her, knowing the night was soon to come. She also couldn't figure out what had happened to Jason. He left and she hadn't heard from him since their last conversation.

Just when I thought I could finally start to care about someone, she thought.

She used to be able to rely on Bob until he started becoming possessive of her. Recalling the last embarrassing moment with him, her cheeks burned. He had taken advantage of her and just about forced himself on her. He had been a good friend, someone to trust, someone to rely on. It had been several weeks since she saw him last, and she felt uneasy about it. Somehow, he had misunderstood her behavior for something else. This man was her daughter's therapist and confidant. Gracie loves him and trusts him, she use to trust him. Not now. All she could do was be his friend, nothing more. There were no feelings of desire she could find for Bob, only friendship. Damn complications. If only Chuck hadn't died.

If only.

Walking over to the portable phone, she picked it up and dialed Jason's cell phone number. She walked into the family room, where Gracie was watching cartoons. She couldn't let her pride interfere with their relationship. She would help him understand why. She waited for him to answer.

"Hello?" The woman's voice was hesitant.

Jade hung up abruptly, confused, thinking she must have dialed the wrong number. She dialed Jason's cell phone number again, making sure she dialed correctly this time.

"Hello." Again, the same woman's voice answered.

Her heartbeat started to quicken. "Can I speak to Jason?"

"He's busy at the moment taking care of my needs. Who is this?" the woman inquired, her tone coolly disapproving.

A tumble of confused thoughts assailed Jade as she fought the urge to insult this woman. "My name is Jade, and you are?"

The woman giggled and then let out a low seductive moan before answering in a purring voice, emphasizing each word, "His every desire."

Jade hung up. She fought back the tears but lost. Warm tears flowed down her cheeks as she silently cried behind a pillow. Burying her face, she hid her emotions from her daughter, who was sitting in front of her, fully enthralled with a purple dinosaur singing on the television.

What have I done? she asked herself. Silently, she chastised herself for letting down the guard around her heart.

I should have opened up to him.

She replayed their last conversation and began blaming herself. She had really liked Jason for a long time and finally let herself have an intimate moment. Now because she had to pick up all the responsibility of raising her child, paying all the bills and facing her husband's death, she had put up a protective wall around her. Because of this, she had pushed away a good man. A man she felt she could have loved.

There was a noise at the front door.

She put the light on and peered through the glass pane three quarters to the top of the door. Her heartbeat became irregular when she recognized who it was. The sound of footsteps caught her attention, and she turned and watched her daughter come into the room.

"Mommy who's that?" Her voice sounded so childish.

A man's voice was heard coming from the other side of the door. "Jade's it's OK, it's me, Bob."

"Ooh Mommy, let him in!" Gracie's voice shrilled as she jumped up and down in excitement. Clapping her hands, her ever-so-trusting daughter waited for the man on the other side of the door to come in.

Unlocking the front door, she opened it slowly, making sure he was alone. Satisfied, she opened the door further.

"Bob, how can I help you?" She stood at the door, not letting him in. Her voice carried authority surprising even to her. A warning echoed in her head telling her not to let him in. Gracie squirmed, making a space for herself at the door so she could see.

Bob saw his favorite little girl making room next to her protective mother. His heart melted watching such an innocent face that obviously loved him. Bringing his attention back up to the one woman he vowed to love, he saw the hesitation in her body language. She refused to move her foot from behind the door, while her daughter attempted to push her mother aside.

"Mommy, let him in!" her tiny little voice demanded as she glared up at her mother.

"Look, Jade, I didn't come over here to start anything. I realized what a fool I've been." He sighed heavily. "And I wanted to apologize for my irrational behavior." There, he said it.

"Do you realize you over-stepped your bounds?" she said in an accusing tone.

"Yes, I do realize that. Again, Jade, please forgive me. I've been so caught up with what has been going on the whole year. I guess my hormones clouded my best judgment." He shrugged. "You and Gracie are the most important people in my life. I don't want to lose you two." He stood outside, looking defeated and feeling it. He needed Jade to listen to him.

She pondered what he had said. Gracie tugged at her clothes, wanting her attention.

Her daughter's little face was beaming an incredible smile at her. Her childish voice begged, "Mommy, Mr. Bob be good now. Mommy, please."

Glancing back at Bob, she couldn't push away the feelings of missing him. "Look, Bob, I want you to know you made me feel really uncomfortable around you since our last encounter. I keep going over and over it in my mind and wondering how it might have been if things were different, but they're not. I can say for both Gracie and I that, yes, we have missed you. But, Bob, I want to set the record straight. I care for you very much as a friend and only a friend. If you want to be a part of our family, the rules are that we remain just friends. Deal?"

He sighed in relief. Oh, thank you, God! he thought. The word rolled off his tongue so fast he couldn't stop himself. "Deal!"

Leaning through the screen door, she reached out her hand. He shook it. "Definitely a deal."

Gracie jumped up and down, clapping her hands and cheering.

Bob looked at Jade for approval to hug the little girl. Jade nodded to him. Opening his arms while bending down, he waited for the only child that felt like his. "Come here, Gracie."

The small child pushed her mother aside and dashed out of the house and into his arms. Hugging her tightly, he felt relief flow through him as Gracie's love poured into him with and she squealed with delight.

"Mr. Bob, you here 'moral?"

Her enunciation of her words needed more practice, he realized.

"Honey, you'll see Mr. Bob at school tomorrow. Come on back in, please."

Smiling at the child, he reemphasized to her in a slightly stern voice, "Gracie, listen to your mother. Go on inside."

She reluctantly let go of him, frowning. "OK". She kissed him on his cheek and quickly turned and entered the house. There she stood behind her mother.

He stood up smiling, feeling better than he could remember feeling in the past several weeks. "Thank you."

Her intuition told her to beware of him. "Good night, Bob."

"Goodnight." He took his cue, turned, and left. He heard the front door shut and the lock set in place. He didn't question Jade about why she had been crying before she answered the door. He accomplished his first plan apologize and get accepted back into her life. He'll give her a couple more weeks and if she didn't accept him as more than just a friend, then, well she'll lose the best thing that she has in her life. His beautiful Gracie would just have to adjust without her mother. But first thing is first, his plan. He drove away plotting his next move.

Chapter 32

"COME IN!" SAID the lieutenant in response to the knock at the door. He was trying to organize the clutter of paperwork on his desk. Looking up, he noticed the captain was his visitor. "Good morning, sir. You're here early."

The captain frowned and nodded.

"Lieutenant, I am here to inform you at this moment you are under investigation for your behavior yesterday with Corporal Davis."

"What?" He stood up abruptly, fury spreading across his face.

"Lieutenant, it has been brought to my attention that you grabbed Corporal Davis roughly on her right shoulder when she was attempting to leave your office. You left bruises."

"That bitch! What the hell was she thinking!" His anger was about to explode as he stood there trembling, trying to keep it under control.

"Lieutenant it wasn't Corporal Davis who made the complaint."

Confused, the lieutenant waited for him to elaborate.

"Sergeant Jenkins brought it to my attention. Corporal Davis does not want to file a complaint."

"Are you kidding me?" His voice began to elevate.

"Lieutenant, don't forget who I am. You better lower your voice," he barked. "As for the bruises you left, pictures were taken and a report was made. Investigations will be in touch with you in the near future. As for right now, you are suspended with pay and will not report back here until this investigation is finalized."

His face turned a bright red. "This is bull-shit and you know it!" he said through gritted teeth.

"As for your anger problems, I suggest, lieutenant, that you find some counseling for it." He walked out of the office and immediately dialed up the major of his district to inform him of lieutenant's suspension.

⋙ ◉ ⋘

Jason looked at the clock. The red illuminated numbers read seven fifteen. Reaching across toward his sleeping son, he felt the child's forehead. Finally, he was cooling off, meaning the fever was breaking. His eyelids were heavy as he fought to stay awake long enough to give his son the last dose of Tylenol before he closed his eyes. The night had flown as he fought to keep Junior's fever at bay. The morning sun wouldn't come through the blinds; he had remembered to close them and the curtains too.

He wanted to call Jade last night, but when he remembered, he knew it was too late, she would be asleep. He couldn't believe how time had slipped by with him attending his sick son. He reminded himself he would call to check on her after he got some sleep.

He gave his son the medicine and the boy quickly went back to sleep. Placing the little cup on the nightstand, Jason finally let sleep take him into oblivion.

⋙ ◉ ⋘

"Gracie it's time to wake up." Jade kissed her daughter, trying to wake her up.

The child opened her eyes and smiled up at her mother. "Morning Mommy." Throwing the covers off, she wrapped her arms around her mother's neck.

"Sweetie, I have to go to work early today, so I need you to hurry and get dressed for me, OK?" She lifted her daughter down to the floor.

"OK, Mommy." Obediently, Gracie went to her room to get dressed.

Worry had kept Jade up most of the night. The woman's voice kept ringing in her head as she repeated the conversation silently over and over. As for Jason, she wasn't sure, but he had a lot of explaining to do. What also bothered her was the fact Lieutenant Mason would be confronted by the captain today about yesterday's incident.

Damn, damn, damn! she thought.

The fingerprint bruises were turning a yellowish-brown on her shoulder when she checked in the mirror this morning before her shower.

Oh, Jason, of all times, I need you now! she thought.

Thirty minutes later, after dropping her daughter off at her mother's, she pulled into the station's parking lot. What caught her attention was the lieutenant's unmarked patrol car. Next to his was the captain's unmarked patrol car. Exiting her vehicle, she gathered her brief-case and headed toward the back entrance, hoping she wouldn't run into Lieutenant Mason. She wasn't in the mood for any confrontations, especially after her night of tossing and turning due to her insecure thoughts concerning Jason.

As she turned the corner to the back entrance, she walked straight into Lieutenant Mason as he was hurrying out of the station in her direction. His body felt like a brick wall as she bounced off of him in complete surprise. Both of them grunted as they collected their bearings.

He was surprised by their sudden encounter, but his expression swiftly changed to arrogance.

"Watch where you're going!" he growled.

"Excuse me. I didn't see you." she mumbled. She proceeded to walk around him.

He step to the side blocking her way. "Figures. A typical woman too conceded and always expecting men to get out of her way." His tone became sterner as he continued his assault. "So you think you're so tough, but you're not! Look how easily you get hurt with me just trying to hold you back. All I wanted to do was finish our conversation, but you go running to your sergeant to complain about me hurting you. Like I always said, law enforcement is no place for females. You are all too fragile, but of course you have to act like you're not - you little bitch!"

That was all she could take. "Bitch? What gives you the right to call me a bitch? That's funny, coming from a crusty, old-fashion, backward, inbred bastard like you. Closed-minded people like you are what give our agency a bad name." She took a step into him as he stood there trying to be intimidating. "Women have a lot to offer this department and all the other law enforcement agencies, but of course, you're so narrow minded and determined to think otherwise."

His eyes narrowed, and he stared down at her with his fists clenched at his sides. Through clenched teeth he said, "Go to hell!"

"Funny thing is, lieutenant, I've been there with the loss of my husband. Even though you're being more of a bastard lately, I hope your life gets straighten out so you can actually have a clearer mind and realize what you're doing to yourself and to your career." Clenching her car keys through her fingers like brass knuckles, she pulled her arm back and downwards ready to throw a punch. In a nasty tone she said, "Now get out of my way before I use my keys to stab your balls."

He jumped back, covering his manhood and giving her room. Her shoulder smacking into his deliberately, and she continued, opening the back door and leaving him puzzled. She hated having to prove herself and behave dominantly around her male coworkers. It made her feel less female, but at this moment, an aggressive behavior was needed.

Her captain was standing with his hands on his hip and a disapproving look on his aged face. "He's being an ass isn't he?"

She stopped to answer him. "Yes he is, but it's been handled." She continued to her office.

"You don't want to press a complaint with what just happened out there?" he inquired.

Placing her brief-case down at her office door, she turned to answer. "Look captain I am a grown woman and can handle myself. If you're asking me if I want to press a complaint and I am assuming for unprofessional and prejudice behavior, the answer is no. He obviously has more on his plate with his home problems than he needs."

He shook his head in disagreement. He couldn't figure her out. "Corporal, I don't understand why not. If the situation was changed, he would have pressed charges against you. I don't condone his behavior, and he has already been warned for his unprofessional attitude."

"Captain, I'm not like him. I don't agree with the 'tit-for-tat' approach, and I refuse to be like that. People like him who work for our agency expect women to act like that, so I won't."

"You're more professional than he is, and I appreciate that." He laughed. "It means less paperwork for me, thank you."

She nodded and unlocked the homicide room door. Sighing heavily, she entered, placing her brief case down on her desk and proceeded to work.

An hour later, Sergeant Jenkins arrived and appeared even more fatigued than she felt. Poking his head into the office, he said, "Jason reported in sick so you'll be solo today. If anything comes up, I'll help. Let's just pray it stays quiet."

She was puzzled, she couldn't recall Jason looking or acting sick. A bad feeling started to grow inside her as she recalled the woman's voice answering Jason's phone last night.

Her phone rang.

"Corporal Davis speaking." She tried to concentrate on the call, but was still wondering about Jason.

"Hello, my name is Amy. I'm a nurse on the intensive care ward at Halifax Hospital, and in Scott Kemp's chart, it reads to contact you if he wakes up. This morning, approximately an hour ago, Mr. Kemp woke up. I would have called sooner, but the doctor wanted to run some tests on him before we called anyone." The nurse sounded calm and reassuring.

"Thank you, Amy. Will the doctor let me see him in about forty-five minutes?" Her voice was excited about her friend's awaken condition.

"Yes, he'll let you talk to him if Mr. Kemp is still awake. Unfortunately, if the amount of visitors he's getting keeps growing, his doctor will have to put a stop to it. He isn't supposed to be overly excited."

Puzzled, she questioned the nurse. "What do you mean visitors? He already has visitors there?"

"A lot, unfortunately, and they're all co-workers of his."

"I'm on my way. Just inform the doctor if he has to limit the visitors do so, but I need to speak to him. He was involved in an attempted homicide, and I need to question him about it."

"Yes ma'am, I'll inform him." The nurse hung up abruptly.

Jade quickly gathered her stuff and informed her sergeant of the good news.

Finally, something good happens today! she throught.

She drove east on International Speedway Boulevard toward Daytona Beach in a hurry.

Chapter 33

WONDERING WHAT THE excitement was all about, Bob sat down closer to the jabbering nurses as he ate his sandwich. There was no one outside in the designated break area for employees except for him and the two nurses, who were smoking their cigarettes and chatting away like two nervous canaries.

"It's a miracle he's alive. This morning he finally woke up from a coma and seems to be OK." The young blonde nurse took a long drag from her cigarette.

The older nurse put her cigarette out and turned her attention to the younger nurse. "So who is this guy and what's his story?"

"Well, he was hit by a car while working. It was some weirdo who left the scene. Can you believe that? And he's a cop!"

Alarms went off in his head as the information he was listening to sunk in.

Damn, he's was alive.

It was just his luck he was working with a patient at the hospital today when he found out the important news. He thought the deputy was going to die, but now he's awake, and oh, hell no, he thought, he couldn't get caught. Not now, Jade just let him back into her world.

He had to get up there and finish the deputy off. He threw the rest of the sandwich into the trash and proceeded to the deputy's room.

Within minutes, he was on the intensive care floor. Wearing his white coat for the therapy work with his clients today helped him blend in with the rest of the hospital staff. All he had to do was walk by the deputy's room without being identified by him. He proceeded and scanned the deputy's room quickly as he walked by. A doctor was telling the remaining visitors to leave. Good.

He walked around the corner. No one was in sight as he grabbed a chart from the door of an unknown patient. He stopped where he had a good view of the deputy's room and pretended he was evaluating the chart. Actually, he was watching for his chance to make his move.

Another few minutes went by. He saw no one. He walked to the nurses' station, which was abandoned at the moment. He turned off the monitor alarms for the deputy's room.

The nurses were buzzing around in the other rooms, checking on their patients and doing their rounds. Before he left the nurse's station, he grabbed a surgical mask put it on. Looking at the clock, he knew he had about five to ten minutes before the nurses would head back in this direction.

Now he made his move.

His heart race suddenly, and his adrenaline kicked in. Knowing he was going to attempt to kill a person excited him. Perspiration started beading on his forehead.

He went to the deputy's room, and pulled his knife from his pocket. He always kept it for protection, and now he opened it and concealed it in his sleeve. He walked by one more time, scanning the room. No one was inside the room. The deputy had his eyes closed and was resting.

Bob had to wipe the sweat from his forehead as he proceeded into the room, quietly shutting his door. Softly walking toward the deputy, he reached the side of the bed. His victim continued to rest. He listened for any possible intruders for a few seconds. There was no noise. He turned off the alarms to his machine, and still the deputy rested. Realizing stabbing his victim would be too messy, he opened the disposable used sharps container. Then he went to the deputy's intravenous line. After pulling back on the syringe to let it fill with air, he injected the needle into the intravenous line pushing the air in. He withdrew the syringe and watched as the air bubble made its way closer to the deputy's injection site. Just as the air bubble made its way into the deputy's vein, he turned and placed the syringe back into the used sharp's container, and then he left. He could hear the deputy groan as he left, pulling the door almost shut. Without a nurse in site, he left knowing he'd succeeded in finally killing his victim.

Chapter 34

EXITING DOWN THE stairway, he became suddenly overwhelmed from the rush of his adrenaline. His heart raced pounding like drums in his ears as a coppery taste developed in his mouth. The sweat was pouring down his face; he untied the mask and took it off breathing in fresh air. There was no time he had to keep walking down stairs to get away. He tucked the mask into his work jacket pocket and proceeded quickly down the stairs to the exit.

Once Jade fines out about the deputy, I'm sure she'll need my comfort, he thought.

⊷⊨⊙ ⊙⊨⊷

The elevator bell chimed when the steel doors opened to the intensive care floor. As she stepped out, Jade heard the nurse yelling for assistance down the hall. Hurrying her walk, she watched the other nurses come running into Scott's room along with a doctor. Dread started seeping into her bones. She hoped it wasn't what she thought it was, Scott coding.

Silently she prayed for him, hoping God would at least grant this one prayer of all the others she had asked for and been denied. Patiently, she waited until the dreaded words came echoing out of the room. "We've done all we can, I'm calling it." The voice was a male and she assumed it was the doctor who ran into the room last. He said, "Time is eleven forty-eight." Several nurses came walking out wide-eyed. One had tears falling as she silently held her emotions in.

No! thought Jade.

No!

No, no!

She stopped one of the nurses. "Please don't tell me Scott Kemp just, just…" She couldn't say the words; her mouth shut, waiting for acknowledgement.

The middle-aged nurse nodded her head. In a tight voice, she said, "Yes ma'am."

Tears swelled up quickly and started falling as Jade placed her stuff down on the counter top. "Can I go in for a moment, please?" she asked in a trembling voice.

The nurse grabbed the chart to jot down the information. "Go ahead, Corporal. I take it you knew him?"

She nodded and walked into his room. He lay with his chest exposed on the bed. He looked so vulnerable, like he was sleeping, but she knew better. There was no rise or fall to his chest. Death is inevitable, even for someone so young. She let out a trembling breath as her tears continued falling, obscuring her vision of her friend. She walked quickly up to him and kissed his forehead. Then she left, wiping away the tears. A nurse handed her a tissue, and Jade began to wipe the tears away. She had to leave. Notifying the Sheriff's Department of Scott's death was not on her agenda today or ever.

Gathering her stuff, she headed toward the waiting room, where coworkers and friends waited for their turns to visit. With utmost regret, she notified the crowd of Scott's death, her voice trembling. Several of the women started crying. A sergeant proceeded to call their shift commander to notify him of the death.

Now it was a homicide.

She was the one in charge of Scott's homicide, and the knowledge that the Sheriff's Department was not in agreement with her investigation seeped into her skin.

She returned to the Deland Station to notify her sergeant.

Chapter 35

"Daddy, I better now." The child shook Jason awake.

Slowly opening his eyes, he squinted to adjust to the light in the room. His son had put the bathroom light on and left the door wide open beaming the light onto his face.

"What's the matter, son?" he asked in a groggy voice while stretching in bed.

"I better now." He smiled his toothless grin at his father.

Grabbing his son, he gave him a quick kiss on his forehead. The child was cool. Relief spread through him, knowing the worse was over. The clock on the nightstand read three thirty-five. He had slept the day away, unfortunately, and hadn't called Jade.

He took a shower and dressed before making breakfast for the both of them. He called Crystal and was waiting on her arrival to pick Junior up. An hour later, Junior in his mother's care, he left to find Jade. He had miss placed his cell phone and assumed he left it at work.

At the station, he failed to find his cell phone. The sergeant was still in his office.

"Hey, Sarge, I miss placed my cell phone, so if you see it, put it in my desk drawer. Why do you look like someone took your best toy away from you?" The frown on his sergeant's face would not cease.

"Well, the deputy that was run over, Kemp is his name. He died at the hospital a couple hours ago while Jade was there." He shook his head. "She was there when he coded. He died before she could talk to him."

"I thought he was in a coma?"

"Yeah, he was, but the hospital called and informed us he woke up, so Jade went over there to talk to him. I guess the reaper had his number first."

"Oh, shit! Not another one dead. That makes two police officers in less than two months. And another friend of Jade's. How did she handle it?" He stood staring sternly at his supervisor, waiting anxiously for his answer.

"I can only imagine how she was at the hospital, but she looked like she had cried a lot on her way here. I told her to go home and take the rest of the day off. By the way how's your son?"

"He's better thanks. I got to go." He exited the office in a hurry. He had to go see Jade he just knew she needed him. When her other friend Susan was murdered, he held her for hours comforting her. He could only imagine now with another friend of hers being murdered. Quickly he drove to her house.

⌁⊶⊷⌁

"OK, Gracie, go ahead and finish watching your movie, and I'll be done cooking here," said Bob. Don't forget to leave your mother alone, she's sleeping and doesn't want to be disturbed." He pulled the pan out of the oven placing the food on the stove to cool and replaced the pan with cheesy bread back in to cook.

He was very content with himself knowing his plan was working. He had called Jade after he left the hospital and the deputy to see if she would let him come over after school. She was distraught over from her friend's death, just as he planned, so he offered to bring Gracie home after school and watch her until she was feeling better.

He smiled. He felt at home in her kitchen, cooking for her and Gracie. The dinner was just about done; he was going to surprise her with it after he woke her. Setting the table, he placed the dinner on the table and knocked on Jade's bedroom door.

The door slowly opened, Jade stood there looking vulnerable, her hair flowing down, her eyes swollen and red. "Yeah?" she mumbled.

He could barely hear her. "Jade, I took the liberty of cooking dinner for you and Gracie. It's late. Come on out and eat so Gracie doesn't start to worry about you." He gave her a smile as he took a step back, offering her his hand.

She took his hand, wishing it was Jason's.

Where are you, Jason? she thought. And who is this woman who is answering your phone?

She sat down at the dinner table, and the aroma of the food became overwhelming, causing her stomach to lurch. Jumping up quickly, she ran to the bathroom and vomited.

Gracie looked at Bob for reassurance.

Realizing the child understood her mother was upset, he tried to comfort her. "Honey she'll be OK. She heard one of her friends had passed on today."

Puzzled, she cocked her head, "Passed on?"

"That means the person is gone forever, Gracie, like your daddy." He knew she would understand that.

Nodding, she looked down at her food and waited.

Bob walked to the bathroom door and gently knocked on it.

"Just a minute," said Jade.

He waited patiently for her to come out.

The bathroom door opened. She looked terrible. Protectively, she covered her stomach with both of her arms as she looked up. Silent tears threatened to fall. She covered her mouth and started to cry. She felt defeated. She was losing her friends to a murderer, and she couldn't do anything about it.

Bob took a step toward her, placing his hands on her shoulders. Jade walked into his arms as he comforted her. "Jade, it'll be OK. Shhhhh, it'll be OK." This was what he planned on, to be there when she needed a man's arms to protect her and comfort her.

Neither heard the kitchen door open when Jason walked in. He took two steps into the dining room and saw Jade in another man's arms. Standing in shock, he watched Bob whisper in her ear as he held her, stroking her hair in a soothing manner. Jade was crying, and he had failed to be there for her. He had failed to call her yesterday to tell her he had to leave because of Junior's ill health. Realizing he should be the one holding her, not Bob, he cleared his throat to let everyone know of his presence.

Bob immediately turned. His look of surprise quickly turned to one of hate.

Jade felt the tenseness in Bob's body and lifted her head to see who was there. Feeling suddenly as if she had just cheated on Jason, she took a quick step backward, leaving Bob's embrace. "J-Jason, -" she stuttered.

Gracie turned and clapped her hands together, blurting out, "Junior here?" She looked around turning in her chair looking to see her little friend.

Looking down at Gracie, Jason was able to answer her. "No honey." He looked at Jade again. He felt betrayed, seeing Bob there not leaving her side and Jade standing wide-eyed wearing a T-shirt untucked, not wearing a bra, in boxer shorts, with her hair down, making her look sexy as hell. His heart felt like someone was squeezing it, and he wished like hell he had been here for her. However, Bob had taken his place. Taking a step backward, he turned and quickly blurted out, "I should have called, I'm sorry."

He left.

Stepping around Bob, Jade quickly followed Jason, calling out, "Jason, wait!"

A jealous rage roared in Bob's head as he watched his woman run after another man. He saw Gracie watching him. Her innocent expression caught him off guard as fear started to show on her face. As quickly as the rage came, it left as his over protective nature for Gracie brought him to his senses. He walked over to her and sat down giving her a reassuring smile. "Honey its OK, let's eat before the food gets cold. Your mother will be in after she talks to that man, OK?" He studied her facial expressions making sure the child wasn't afraid of him.

Nodding her little head, she picked up her plate holding it to him. "Food, please."

He took her plate and filled it along with his and they proceeded to eat. He wouldn't forget the incident, that guy was going to pay for the interruption.

Jade shut the utility room door calling out to him, "Wait Jason, please."

He stopped but didn't turn around. He waited as he fought the urge to just leave. It was easier for him to leave than face her so she could experience the confusion he was feeling.

She stood in front of him, arms crossed in her defense, but unknowingly sexy as hell. "Jason, what happened to you?"

Looking down at her, he couldn't find his voice and stood staring down at her with a hurt expression in his eyes.

She wasn't sure where to start, but she knew if she didn't say something he would leave. "I… I've been wondering what happened to you since you left the other day. Now….now…" She knew she was stuttering, but how could she come right out and act as a jealous girlfriend when they hadn't even spoke of a relationship. She felt defeated and at loss for words. Her emotions were in turmoil with her friend's death and the knowledge of another woman, besides herself, in Jason's life. Life was too complicated now; she didn't want anything else to happen.

Closing his eyes, Jason concentrated on controlling the lump that developed in his throat causing him not to be able to talk. He had a habit of forcing his feelings deep down inside, but being around Jade, he had a difficult time controlling himself and his emotions. If only he didn't cross that line with her and slept with her, he would have been able to respond better to walking in on her being in another man's arms.

"Jason, I don't know what to say. You disappeared, and Bob came over last night and apologized. Then… then…" Her voice cracked from emotions. She stopped and took several deep breaths trying not to cry again, but failed miserably. She returned her gaze at the one man she finally found she could love, and saw a single tear escape falling down his face slowly. Reaching up on tippy toes, she responded instinctively pulling him downward and gently kissed his lips as she cupped his face. Afterward, she leaned her forehead on his, looking at him.

Slowly, he opened his eyes.

She kissed him again, longer this time. He responded back hesitantly whispering, "I didn't call you because…" He kissed her back again, this time longer. "My son was sick." Another kiss. "But why him?" He took a step back with a hurt look on his face.

She hesitated, not sure what to say. "You weren't there, Jason. I called and called, but -"

He suddenly clenched his fists in his anger. "So you call him over. So are you two an item now?"

"What?"

"You heard me. Are you or are you not seeing him?" He sputtered the words out as if they were burning his tongue.

She frowned, responding quickly to his misunderstanding of Bob's relationship with her and Gracie, "No! He's just a friend of the family, Jason, that's all." She watched his facial expressions change turning softer. "What? Do you think just because I couldn't get a hold of you that I would find a replacement for you?"

Ashamed, he looked down not able to answer her honestly.

"Jason, that's not going to happen. But I am confused. Do you honestly think I'm that shallow as to run to the first guy I know for emotional support?"

Looking up quickly, he realized he was stepping into dangerous grounds if he didn't answer her. "No, Jade. It's just pretty damn hard for a guy to walk in on what I just witnessed and not be jealous and wondering." He sighed heavily not wanting to open himself up to her, but if he didn't he knew this would be his last chance to be a part of her life. "Look, I've known you for several years. I watched you grow from a fresh green investigator, to an experienced one who actually enjoys working and is good at it. I've also grown very fond of you. Trust me, watching you through the years around your male friends; it's hard for any guy to handle, because I know those guys aren't thinking anything of friendship when they are around you. Yeah call me a jealous ass, but you are one hell of a woman and beautiful too and I don't believe in sharing." He shoved his hands into his front pockets of his jeans not sure what to do at that moment.

Her insides were screaming for joy. She just couldn't believe he actually said that. Reaching up she tugged at his front buttons of his shirt, suddenly curious what he would look like with his shirt off and her running her fingers over his bare chest. Feeling like a freshman in high school, she leaned in closer to him laying her head gently on his chest. Looking up with a wide grin, she exclaimed seductively, "So you like me, huh?" She batted her eyes at him still grinning devilishly.

His body reacted to her nearness. Pulling his hands from out of his pockets, he pulled her hips closer into his hips letting her feel his manhood. "What do you think?" He returned a smile back and waited for her response.

Stepping out of his embrace, she tugged him toward the wall of the house. Away from any curious eyes, the house at her back, she reached up on tippy-toes and kissed him with every ounce of lust she felt suddenly flowing through her.

Groaning softly, he stepped closer returning passionate kisses back. Their tongues danced against each other as their lips met hungrily. His hand cupped her breast instinctively as he teased her nipple through the material.

She reached up under his shirt, exploring his muscular chest. Slowly she massaged her hands toward his back enjoying his hardness while fighting to keep her control from his arousing torment to her breast.

He chuckled, "Woman, you're driving me crazy."

Laying her hands on the front of his jeans, she hesitated. Biting her lower lip, her mouth watered to savor him, but not just his mouth, everywhere. Now she could devour him. A crazy lust was taking over her logical thinking clouding her sense of good judgment. A primal need was fighting its way out, wanting to take Jason right there against the wall. Her palms started to sweat, her heartbeat began racing while her overwhelming lust reflected in her eyes.

Sensing her needs, he was amazed how their bodies would ignite when they were together. Even with their clothes on, his body would react leaving him a slave to his attraction to her. The problem was that he wanted, with every ounce of his being, to make love to her right there out in the open. Taking a deep breath for control, he closed his eyes trying to tame the flame she had already ignited.

Watching him, she knew what he was doing, but her sudden sense of desire assisted her to reach down and rub his swollen groin until he growled at her.

"Woman, please, I'm trying to calm myself down, and that's not helping." Opening his eyes, he took a sudden intake of air noticing her beauty as she looked seductively at him with her devilish smirk.

Whimpering, she hugged him tightly attempting to gain control of her over-whelming rise of primal need. What am I doing? she thought. I can't believe I was trying to seduce him!

"Jason, I need you to understand Bob is a friend to Gracie and me. He has been there for the last several years through the good times and bad times. Gracie looks up to him even more so since her father died. Yeah, Bob and I have had our differences, but we've worked through them. He is only a friend and will never be anything else. I have absolutely no desire for the man and when you walked in on us, he was only consoling me." The memories flooded back causing her desires to melt away. Her smile faded as she continued. "Bob came back to apologize last night and we compromised our differences. I can't hold that against him, I'm not like that."

"I just don't like the way he touches you. I can see in his body language that he wants more from you." He was frustrated with her statements and took a step backward shoving his hands back into his front pockets.

"I don't see it, and I've known him a lot longer than you. We are only friends Jason. I need you to be able to accept that without feeling jealous every time I'm around him."

"I can't guarantee you that." The words slipped out before he could stop them.

"I'm sorry you feel that way. Especially now, since everything we've been through. And you know that's not fair when you are seeing someone at the moment besides me."

A surprised look crossed his face as he stood there looking at her wide-eyed and confused.

She continued. "I haven't placed any rules on us since I really don't know what claim I even have on you. So when you're ready to behave more maturely about this, then let me know." Turning, she walked into the utility room shutting the door behind her.

He stood there not sure, if he heard her right or not. Did she just say I was seeing someone else at the same time I've been with her? he thought. Thoughts flooded through him, then a realization formed. One minute he wanted to leave to get away from her because she was in Bob's arms. Next, she ready to rip his clothes off of him and have sex outside while her kid and Bob were inside waiting on her. Now, she said he was seeing another woman and tells him when he matures to talk to her, and then finally she wasn't going to give up her friendship with Bob. "What is she, nuts? This is bullshit!" He turned and walked briskly to his vehicle as he cursed under his breath.

Chapter 36

HE WATCHED THROUGH the kitchen window at the scene he was witnessing. Clenching his fists, he wanted to strike anything. It didn't matter what. But he controlled his fury because of the little angel that sat at the kitchen table eating and watching him. Shaking his head in disgust, he witnessed Jade acting like a harlot and engaging in foreplay in front of anyone's view.

Damn her, she's mine! he thought.

That thought repeated in his head as he continued watching the show. An overwhelming feeling of wanting to go out there and tell both of them off raced through his veins, but he restrained himself with the most self-control he had ever possessed.

Jason suddenly walked off, and Bob heard the utility door shut. Turning quickly, he went back into the dining room, sat down, and started eating. Gracie giggled as she continued eating and watching him.

Jade was frowning when she entered the room. Looking at her daughter and her friend sitting there waiting on her, she felt like she had a family again suddenly. Sighing, she walked to her chair and sat down and began eating her meal.

"Bob…" She chewed her food for a moment. "This is really good. Thank you for everything." Her smile found its way to her eyes as her expression showed sincerity.

She was a lovely site sitting there beaming him a smile that melted him to his bones leaving him feeling suddenly like an inexperienced teenager in love. The feelings of anger he had boiling to overflow, simmered to level of coolness that for a moment caused him to forget why he was even irritated with her. His body reacted to her giving him a flushed face and an instant erection.

They ate their dinner in silence. He continued watching her as Gracie continued watching both of them. Afterward, she cleared the table and told her daughter to get ready for a bath.

Turning to Bob, she reached for his hand. She looked into his surprised eyes and said, "Thank you for helping me today and for dinner. You've been a great friend and we appreciate it." She looked at her daughter then turned her attention back to him. "It's getting late, and I need to get Gracie ready for a bath." She lowered his hand, grabbed his keys and handed them to him.

"Jade, you know if you need anything, just let me know, and I'll be there. I won't disappoint you, I promise." His serious look told her he meant what he said.

"I know, and I appreciate it." She openned the front door, and waited for him to leave.

Taking the hint, he turned and walked through the door. He took his last view of her before they said their goodbyes.

The door shut as he walked to his car. Back at his house, he changed into blue jeans and a black shirt that would help conceal him in the darkness. Parking in the woods across from Jade's house, he exited the car and proceeded walking toward her house.

⊷⊷⊙ ⊙⊷⊷

After bathing her daughter, she took a shower. Standing in the shower longer than usual, the stress of the day washed down the drain. The loss of her friend Scott slithered its way back into her thoughts as she focused trying to put the puzzle together. Who is this person killing cops? First her friend Susan. Now Scott. What is the connection? There were only two connections she could think of. One was they're both cops, and second was they were her friends. She knew that tomorrow she needed to go over Susan's reports for the past year and Scott's too.

There has to be a connection somehow, she thought. My only leads are the hair found with Susan, a sedan with a male driver; the killer used a knife to kill Susan, but a car with Scott. That's it, a car! I need to call around to find out how many people had their windshields replaced with hood damage. Tomorrow I will call Jack I definitely will need his help.

Turning off the water, she dried herself off and then slipped on her robe. She could hear the *Barney* video her daughter was watching, with Barney singing "I love you." Chuckling, she started to shut the windows she had left open. The weather had been wonderful to where she could turn off the air conditioner and open the windows to air out the house. Pulling the shades open, she stopped realizing someone was standing in front of her right outside her window. A scream tore out of her mouth as she let go of the blind cords. The blinds lowered in a rush and she stepped back, in her frightened state, causing a thumping sound. Her heart threatened to jump out of her body as it thundered in her ears. Realization struck her as she remembered the rest of the windows were open and she needed her service weapon for protection.

She grabbed her service weapon from its holster, gripping it firmly.

"Gracie come here now!" she yelled in panic.

The child scrambled to her feet and ran into the room with her eyes wide in fright with tears threatening to fall.

Instinctively she hugged her daughter tightly. Tucking her daughter's hair behind her ears, she whispered for her to lock the bathroom door and stay in there until she told her to open up. "Everything is going to be OK. Just do what I say" she attempted to reassure her scared child, but she needed to protect them both. This required her to finish what she had started and close all the windows, and then she would call Jason.

She finished shutting and locking the windows in her room and proceeded into Gracie's room. In each room, she scanned for any intruders, locked the windows, and proceeded to the next room. After what seemed like forever to her, as her adrenaline rushed through her veins, she finally secured the house. They were finally safe.

Silently she thanked God and went back to her room to get her daughter.

As she approached, she saw that the phone line led under and behind the locked bathroom door. Knocking on the bathroom door, she tried opening it. "Gracie, its OK. Open the door honey." She could hear her daughter's voice mumbling behind the door.

"Now Gracie, unlock the door." Her irritation was evident in her voice.

The sound of the door being unlocked helped ease her stress as the doorknob opened. Gracie had the phone to her ear still. Her little voice answered whoever was on the other end of the line. "Yes, it's Mommy."

"Honey, who are you talking to?" She took the phone from her daughter and placing it to her ear. "Hello?"

"Jade, it's me. I am almost there. Is everything OK?" she could hear a bit of panic in Jason's voice. Relief started to spread through her, knowing he was coming over to protect her and Gracie.

"Yes, we're OK." She couldn't help the trembling in her voice.

"Don't worry. I'm here, I'm here." He hung up as he turned onto her property.

She could see his car headlights as he approached, in her fear she realized she still had her service weapon gripped tightly in her right hand, pointing downward. She turned to her daughter and, bent down eye level to her. "Honey, that was a really brave thing to do calling Junior's dad. Thank you, honey." She placed a kiss on her daughter's forehead and hugged her tightly. Standing up, she took Gracie's hand and walked into the living room and turned on the television.

"*Barney*, Mommy, please?" The child tugged gently on her mother's robe in her plea.

"Sure why not. You saved the night." Smiling at her daughter, she hugged her one more time. Quickly she found a Barney movie and played it for her daughter.

Content, the child sat down on the couch, hugging the pillow and sucking her thumb.

Looking through the blinds, Jade searched for Jason. She didn't want to put her service weapon up yet, just in case. Switching to another window, she looked through the blinds again and caught a glimpse of Jason jogging around her house with a handgun out. Ten minutes later, he knocked on the front door.

"Jade, it's me, open up." His voice was stern as he waited in the darkness as the humidity enclosed around his skin like a blanket.

The door opened. Opening the screen door, he walked in. Before the door shut, he heard a car engine turn on nearby. "Wait." He held the door open and listened. The sound wasn't far. "Wait here, I'll be right back." Exiting the house, he ran in the direction of the sound of the car. He stopped at the front gate looking for headlights, but there were none.

What the hell is going on?

The sound of the engine was to his left, and he started jogging in that direction. A refection of the neighbor's yard light glimmered off the chrome of the car in the woods.

Shit the car does not have any headlights on. It must be him! he thought.

The suspicious car came barreling out of the woods in a rush and turned abruptly to the right, away from him. He quickened his pace to a full out sprint. The car took off as the driver gunned the engine, causing the car to fish tail on the dirt road. It took off, leaving him in a dust bowl. He stopped trying to catch his breath and continued watching the car until it was out of view. He was too far from his car to run back and try to catch the person.

Damn it!

He went back to Jade and Gracie. Sweat was soaked through his clothes. Tonight it would rain, and another cool front would be coming through during the early morning. He knocked on the front door again, and Jade let him in.

Without looking in her direction, he told her of his findings. "Someone was parked in the woods across the street. He walked down from there and spied on you two. I heard the car start up the first time I came in here, so I went to find out where it was coming from. As I turned and started heading in the direction of your neighbors, the car came barreling out with no headlights on. It's a late model car with chrome bumpers. I think it was four-door, but I couldn't say what make." He raked his hand through his hair. Relieved to see that everything seemed to be in place, he turned his attention to her. He involuntarily sucked in some air as he stood looking at her. She was a site to see, with her service weapon gripped firmly in one hand wearing a silk robe with her long hair flowing. He captured every bit of her with his eyes watching her in front of him.

Curiosity overwhelmed him, he had to know. "Right before you saw this person in the window, did you just come out of the shower?" His eyes betrayed his arousing interests as they reflected his desire.

Embarrassed, she crossed her arms across her chest and looked away from him. Her face flushed, at the moment she did not want to answer him. Clearing her throat, she answered, "Yes."

Hands on his hips, he continued his questioning. "Do you have anything on underneath the robe?" His desire began to ignite, as she stood there, captivating in her embarrassment.

She shook her head. He wanted to make love to her right there. Before he took a step, Gracie came running in, throwing herself against his legs. "You saved us!" Her voice boomed in excitement.

The sudden pain exploding from his groin caused him to bend over in pain. "Gracie, you need to be careful what you do." His voice echoed his pain.

"Sorry." She stepped back and ran to her mother.

Embracing her child, she kissed her on top of the Gracie's head. "Honey, its OK, he'll live."

She frowned, "Mommy, what happened?"

She laughed and explained to her daughter what she just did.

Gracie's eyes grew wide in understanding, "I sorry."

The pain started to slowly subside. He felt bad about what had just happened. If Gracie hadn't come out of the room at the particular moment, he would have been embarrassed at fondling her mother in front of her. He completely forgot about Gracie when he saw Jade in her silk robe, radiating beauty. The child brought him to his senses, thank God. "Gracie don't worry about it. It was just an accident." He gave her a quick smile and went to the living room to sit down.

Thirty minutes later, Gracie finally lay safely tucked away in bed after they both read her *Sleeping Beauty*. Walking out of her room, he slipped his hand over Jade's, giving her a slight gentle squeeze.

She flashed him a quick smile. They both walked down the hallway and into the family room closing the French doors almost completely. She did not want her daughter to have an excuse to wake up.

He let go of her hand as he sat down on her couch facing her. She sat down as eloquently as she could manage wearing the robe. She knew tonight was not going as planned.

Chapter 37

ONCE HE WAS finished securing the house, he felt better. His need to stay and protect the two females set in. He wasn't going to leave, no matter what.

Confused about her feelings for Jason, she tried to understand why she was feeling so indecisive with him. One part of her wanted to throw herself into his arms; the other wanted him to leave, because she knew there was another woman in his life. She did not want to share him with anyone, but again, she reminded herself, that she had no claims on him. He still to this day hadn't mentioned wanting a relationship with her or speak about not seeing other people. If only, if only –

He was not hers; she had to face the facts. She silently scolded herself. Watching him across from her, she couldn't help but watch his every move. Her body was reacting to him being in the same room with her, and with her wearing scarcely any clothing. What the hell was she thinking?

She went to her bedroom to put on more clothes. Jason stood, blocking her way.

Gently cupping her chin in his palm, he leaned down claiming her lips with his. A spark ignited between them with that simple act. Possessively, he pulled her into his embrace feeling her soft body envelope into his. Her body fit his like a glove. Breathing became rapid as his kisses fevered. Cupping her firm behind into his groin, his desire over took him.

A moan escaped her lips as she caressed him under his shirt, wishing it was off of him. His muscles rippled under her soft small hands, causing his skin to respond. Rubbing her breast against his chest unconsciously, as she reached up on tippy-toe to kiss him, was causing her nipples to harden.

The touch of her breasts caressing his chest caused his thoughts to go haywire. He couldn't think rationally. The only thought was to rip her robe off and make love to her standing up near the hallway. Turning her around, he leaned her against the wall as one hand untied her robe quickly. Once the robe opened, his hand dove downward to her womanhood in one swooping caress. She spread her legs bracing herself as he gingerly massaged her vulva as another finger slid its way into her warm moist folds. Her hips rocked slowly against his hand as he mastered her rhythm. Kissing down her neck, he gently suckled her earlobe and then kissing further downward to her breasts. One hand fondled her right breast as his mouth enveloped her harden nipple.

A whimper escaped her lips as her hands raked against his back and through his hair while lost in sweet desire.

His hand was moist from her excitement as he slowly pulled his fingers out of her. Quickly he unbuttoned his pants freeing his inflamed erection. A sigh escape his lips when her hands assisted him pushing his pants further down to his ankles. Stepping out of his pants quickly, he tore his shirt off. He kissed her again, his lips demanding more of her as their tongues danced against each other's. Stepping closer toward her once again, his erection pressed against her stomach. His breathing quicken as she folded her arms around his neck placing one leg up against his hips. Holding both of her hips, he picked her up holding her directly above his shaft. Slowly he lowered her onto the top of his swollen member as she wiggled herself against him causing him to lose his mind with desire. Her moistness assisted his insertion easily as she rocked on top of him. His heart was beating so strongly he thought it was going to burst out of his chest from his excitement.

She bucked against him as he continued to hold her hips controlling the rhythm. Her kisses devoured him, as her body tormented his in her continued arousing rhythm against him. He wouldn't be able to take much more of their sudden passion, but he held on forcing himself to wait. He slowly walked toward the table focusing on anything to help him to not blow his load too fast. Reaching the table, he laid her on it and he continued pumping into her.

He massaged her breasts, then caressed slowly down her body as she lost herself in the spiral of ecstasy. His hands gripping her hips not letting go, his manhood swelled even bigger. She could feel every inch of him entered her again and again. Arching her back upward, she felt the tingling start from her belly downwards to her sex. A moan escaped as the tingling exploded, shooting to every inch of her. Her breasts swelled even more, causing her nipples to tighten during her climax.

His manhood felt her inner folds tighten, then spasm in her orgasm. She looked incredibly sexy. Her body glistened in a light sheen of sweat as it arched towards him. Losing all train of thought, his excitement overtook him. Her orgasmic contractions sent his manhood to oblivion as he pumped into her velvety tight moistness. His orgasm shook his soul as he poured his seed into her over and over. Time slowed and his breathing became erratic as each thrust slowly emptied him. Pulling the chair out, he sat down carefully with Jade still straddled on top of him. Beads of sweat rolled down the side of his face. Slowly he opened his eyes. The light, any light, hurt his eyes for a short period of time after his orgasm. He wouldn't trade anything in the world for this strange but heavenly moment.

Their eyes met and both were afraid to say anything for fear of the unknown. Brushing the hair away from her cheeks, he cupped the side of her face, gazing lovingly at her.

A sudden knock at the door brought both of them back to reality. Her eyes widen with sudden realization. Standing up carefully, she attempted to situate her robe in a more modest wrap.

Before she finished he had already pulled his pants up. "Go get cleaned up," he whispered. "I'll take care of it."

Nodding, she quickly turned and exited down the hall to her bedroom. After pulling his shirt back on, he answered the door. There in front of him was the deputy that was dispatched for Jade when he called earlier. Inviting him in, he proceeded in telling the story to him.

Chapter 38

THE DEPUTY AND his zone partner checked the property before leaving. Watching through the front window, Jade saw both patrol cars leave. She turned her attention to Jason. He was standing behind her with his arms wrapped around her protectively. Sighing, she knew she could get use to this with him here watching over her and Gracie. As for the love making, guilt nagged at her. The only way to describe her life now would be to say it was at its best only when she was with Jason. She never felt this with anyone.

Turning, she hugged him, enjoying the luxury of his strong arms holding her snug to him.

Kissing the top of her head he said, "Jade, I can't leave the two of you alone with that weirdo watching." He sighed heavily, "If you don't mind, I'm staying tonight."

The seriousness to his voice caused her to look up at him.

His brows furrowed as he stood there waiting for her to reply. She memorized his handsome face, his strong jaw and deep sapphire blue eyes that drew her into his causing her to drown if she looked too long. The beating of her heart thundered in her ears as she envisioned how they could spend tonight together. Here I am, acting like a teenager, she thought. Thinking about sex all the time when I'm around him. I have to stop it.

"We don't mind at all." She couldn't help herself, and she smiled mischievously.

His body reacted to her incredible seductive smile. Grinning back at her, he knew it was going to be a long night. He couldn't help himself and chuckled at the way both of them were acting. Standing up he held his hand out, "Let's go to bed." That last statement held many promises.

⋆⊷◉ ◉⊷⋆

The next day came. They both barely had slept from their all night lovemaking. Quickly he dressed knowing he had to go home so he could get ready for work. He hated being away from her, especially with a strange person watching her. If he hadn't responded so quickly, coming to their rescue, he wondered what that guy had in mind to do. His chest-constricted and he felt a heavy weight of guilt at the thought of Jade or Gracie getting hurt. Bending down, he kissed her forehead before leaving. It was early; the sun was starting to rise as he started up his car. Thoughts of how strong his feelings are for Jade weighed heavily on his mind as he left.

⋆⊷◉ ◉⊷⋆

The buzzer went off, waking Jade up. She turned it off and peeked out from under the bed covers. She looked at the clock to see what time it was. Six o'clock. She had an hour to get Gracie ready for school leaving very little time for herself to get ready for work. Stretching she smiled as she recalled how the night went. She couldn't recall feeling this happy in a long time. Getting out of bed, she went to wake her daughter up.

Half an hour later, she had both herself and her daughter dressed. The phone rang in the middle of her making them breakfast.

"Hello?"

"Well, good morning. How are you and Gracie this morning?" Bob's voice was cheerful.

"Good morning, Bob. We're both doing fine, thank you," her voice was reserved as she answered.

"Well, I called to see if you don't mind me participating with Gracie in her field trip today?" He knew she had been very busy and probably had forgotten about the child's field trip to Sugar Mill Plantation today.

"Damn. I forgot about that. Is it today? Are you sure, Bob?" She normally went on the field trips with her daughter due to her daughter's poor vision. She wanted to be there to help her.

"I'm sure. I reconfirmed it yesterday." His voice held the air of confidence as he answered her.

"I normally go, but since I can't take today off, would you mind going and being there for Gracie?" Disappointment hung heavily in the tone of her voice.

Smiling to himself, he continued, "No I don't mind at all. I called because I figured you've been really busy with work that you probably had forgotten."

"Yeah, I have. Bob, thank you."

"Do you mind if I pick her up and take her to school? I bought some doughnuts for the faculty and would like Gracie to have the first pick."

"Sure. Come on over. We'll be outside waiting."

"See you ladies in a few minutes." He hung up, smug with himself. He had to know if Jade had any idea it was him last night at her window. If she didn't say anything, then Gracie would fill him in. Knowing how to question the child was easy for him.

He locked the garage door that hid the rented vehicle he used last night. Getting into his car, he drove down the street to pick up his sweet innocent child.

Arriving five minutes later at Jade's house, he opened the back passenger door for the child. Gracie had given him a big hug before climbing into the backseat. Once she was seat belted, he drove down the street to her school. The smell of fresh doughnuts clung heavily in the vehicle.

⋄⊱⊷◉ ◉⊶⊰⋄

Relieved that Bob would fill in for her for the field trip, she gathered her workbag and went to her patrol car. Dark clouds hung heavily in the sky in a threatening manner. Starting her patrol car up, thunder rumbled in the distance. As she spoke on the radio calling in for the day, the dispatcher immediately responded back with a call.

"The signal seven occurred on A1A in Ormond Beach just south of the Flagler County line in Volusia. There is a wildlife officer on scene confirming two possibly three fatalities with roadblock."

"Ten-four, Orlando, I'll be enroute." She put the car in gear and headed north. A few minutes later, she heard Jason call in for duty and then dispatched to the traffic fatality. Immediately after, her cell phone began ringing.

"I heard, and I should be there in about one hour or less. How about you?" She knew the answer but waited for his response.

"Well, good morning to you too." His voice purred from desire. He couldn't shake the feelings he had for her. They were highly arousing and caused a strong desire to touch her in her most intimate places. The soft murmurs she moaned when he aroused her close to a climax gave him a semi-hard-on as he drove.

"It's definitely a good morning, except for these darn rain clouds. Is it raining where you are?" her voice gave away her stress of the upcoming down pour of rain.

"No, it's not. I called because I just wanted to hear your voice. Now that I heard it, why are you stressing so much about the rain?"

"It's Gracie. She's going on a field trip today. I forgot to take the day off to go with her, but Bob called to remind me and wanted to fill in for my absence. Can you believe that since I let him back into our family, he already wants to be the responsible protector for her? I don't know if that is a good thing or not." Exasperated, she sighed.

A twinge of envy edged its way into his heart causing a deep engrained feel of over protectiveness and territorial when it came to Jade and Gracie. He didn't like it at all. "Well to be honest with you, I don't like it at all."

Biting her upper lip, she thought about what he just said she needed more time to think about their situation. Could it be he wants more? She wasn't sure at all. "And what also bothers me is this rain. For some reason I have this bad feeling."

"What kind of bad feeling?" He was genuinely concerned. Bad feelings about something that had yet to occur left him feeling as if he had no control of the situation. Jade had a really good sense of intuition, the best that he ever encountered in any person. This wasn't good that she was feeling something inevitable was going to occur.

"I don't know yet. Maybe I'm just over reacting when it comes to Gracie. I don't know."

"Honey, listen to me, if for any chance, anything bad ever occurs from this point on, I'm here for you guys. I'm serious anything at all." His voice was stern reinforcing how he felt.

"Thank you, Jason." The rain started to down pour, leaving dread sinking in. "Jason, I'm going to hang up now. It's raining, and I need both of my hands to drive. I'll see you there." She hung up not waiting for a response as stress shook her nerves with the curtain of rain pouring down.

An hour past, they both arrived safely despite the heavy rain down pour. The display of emergency lights from law enforcement, fire trucks, and ambulances filled the area, causing a brilliantly lit scene. Reporters were placing their camera stands up as both her and Jason walked the scene looking for evidence of the crash. Feeling the strong sexual magnetism between them, he stared quietly at her several times during their walk through. Every time his gaze met hers, her heart turned over in response. This day is going to be a very challenging one, she thought.

Even though Jason distracted her, she documented the evidence they both found on a pad of paper while awkwardly holding an umbrella. The initial responding trooper assigned to the crash approached her. The campaign hat that he wore fit snug, tilted downward giving the short trooper more of a drill sergeant persona, demanding respect. Walking over he stopped in front of her waiting for her to acknowledge him. She had won over from some of her coworkers this respect.

Smiling, she acknowledged him. "Good morning trooper. What do you have for me?"

Nodding at her, he started his explanation of the crash. "Morning. Officer Lovell over there…" He pointed to a wildlife officer standing by a patrol car looking distraught, "He was enroute to his house when he came upon this crash. As you can see, it involves three cars with three fatalities, and which all the victims are still on scene. I have all the passengers' names from all three cars listed on this paper." He handed the paper to her. "And all the passengers were transported to Halifax Hospital." Pointing to the other side of the paper, he said., "Those are the names of the witnesses, and I have them waiting at their cars over there." He pointed behind the scene in a north direction.

Reading only two witness names on the paper, she closed the trunk, knowing witness statements needed to come first, before they decided to talk to each other or leave. "Thank you. I need you to assist Jason with the measurements and tell him I'm going to interview the witnesses. Just… before you go, come with me and point out the witnesses for me please."

"Sure thing." They both walked north, leaving Jason watching after them. The morning was definitely going to be a long busy one.

The morning at the scene went slow. The rain caused several more crashes to occur making it more difficult to clearing the scene. A foreboding continued to nag at Jade as she worked at the scene. This morning when she checked in for work, it started. Quite possibly the rain might have brought it on, but the nagging feeling would not stop. Finally, after five hours at the scene and assisting with two other minor crashes, they were all able to leave. Waving at Jason, signaling him to leave, she sat back in her patrol car and proceeded to drive south on A1A.

Driving back, she found her towel and started wiping off the rain from her arms and face. While doing this, she knocked some papers out from her visor above her head.

Buried between the loose papers was a photograph of a group of her friends at a barbeque, sitting around on a picnic table. It was Susan, Bob, Scott, Jason, Jack, her sergeant, and a few other law enforcement officers who had all posed at that moment. Gracie had taken the picture of them as her daughter played with her camera last year. It was surprisingly a good picture, and she kept it as a reminder of that fun day. Gently rubbing her thumb across the picture, her chest tightened up with sadness remembering her recently deceased friends. She had been keeping her feelings in check, but she hadn't had time to really mourn her friends. Suddenly a strong overwhelming feeling gripped her returning the feeling of dread as she held the picture. She couldn't control the spasmodic trembling that took control of her. The picture brought back feelings she tried to bury down so she wouldn't lose her mind from her losses. A knot formed in her stomach as she struggled with her uncertainties.

Thankfully, the drive back to the Halifax Hospital was a long one due to the traffic and the continued downpour of rain. She had laid the picture down a couple times, and each time she picked it up, the feeling of dread would return. She wasn't sure why, but her instincts caused her to keep coming back to looking at her friends from that single picture as if something kept drawing her back to it. She couldn't shake the feeling away nor ignore it. Something about the picture caused her to react to it. It was more than knowing her friends were all on it. There was something about it she couldn't pinpoint.

Parking her patrol car, she gathered her notes and equipment. She put the picture in her pocket and went inside the hospital, running from the rain. Jason followed right behind her. Both were drenched from the rain even with their rain gear on.

Looking at the list of names, she went on to say who she would interview first. "I'll try John Polatty." She handed the sheet of paper over to him. His large hand closed around it.

Reading the names, he paused. "OK, so I have Javier Rodriguez. Let's go find them." Even in the hospital, his presence was compelling. People he passed would stare at him. The women would smile, but the men stared at him with stone faces.

Three hours later, with exception of two people on the list who were missing, the interviews were completed. Tired and hungry, they both agreed to eat out. Ten minutes later, they both drove into a Denny's Restaurant and parked. A few minutes later, they sat down at their table and ordered off the menu.

Both of them sat quietly gathering their thoughts. Jade looked up at Jason. He searched her face, sizing her up. His eyebrows raised he said, "Jade are you all right?"

Her eyes were filled with intense emotions. "I found this in my car on my way back." She pulled the folded picture from her pocket and handed it to him.

He looked at the image intently. "I remember this. Gracie took the picture, right?"

"Yes, she did." Her voice was almost a whisper.

Quickly he looked back at her, realizing something was definitely wrong. "Honey, what is it?" His voice was low and filled with concern.

Sighing, she buried the feelings down deep again as she attempted to maintain her professional composure. "You're going to think I'm crazy, but every time I touch the picture, I get a feeling of something terrible. I can't explain it; it's just if I put it away, the feeling isn't strong. When I touch it, I feel an intense feeling every time. I don't know. Maybe I am losing it." Her voice was stifled and unnatural.

He recognized the sadness in her voice. He gently covered her small hands with his in an affectionate manner.

A look of tired sadness passed over her face as she sat in silence. The picture lay on the table, folded in half, but she stared at it as if afraid to touch it.

Attempting to take away the awkward moment, he chatted about the interviews he had conducted at the hospital. Next was the case. He had formulated by the evidence and partially from the statements what had actually caused the fatal crash. She sat in silence listening, absorbing what he was saying. The food came and they ate as he continued with his premature hypothesis. When he was done, he asked, "Jade, what do you think?"

She contemplated his theory and then answered, "If I were you, I would calculate the first driver's critical speed to make sure it backs up what you're saying." Crunching the numbers really told the story. People tended to fill in the gaps between what their brains had comprehended and what had occurred. Making a case involved measuring crush damage and skid marks, evaluating the vehicles involved, along with the medical examiner's report on the injuries and, yes, statements did help, but not all the time. The totality of all the evidence told the story. She didn't like to guess ahead of time.

The glow of his smile warmed her and echoed in his voice. "That's my Jade always calculating."

Resting her chin on her hand, a bemused smile spread across her face echoing his words in her mind. Several times she played over the term he had used when referring to her "his Jade." Suddenly feeling like a teenager at his remarks, happiness seeped in, taking away the sadness she was feeling.

Watching her, he took in her wet appearance. They were both drenched, but no matter what she looked like, he was extremely attracted to her. She had found her way into his heart when he thought no one could. He wanted to be there and protect her from the stalker. He also wanted to discover every inch of her body and taste every part of her. What had he turned into? Every time he was near her, she quickly conquered his normally clear thinking and turned him into a hungry teenage boy again that desired to have sex. The only catch though was he only wanted to have sex with Jade. Ashamed of how his body was responding to her nearness, he fought to push away his arousing thoughts.

After lunch, they drove to the station in Deland. Jade called Jack, realizing she was going to be late picking him up to work some extra overtime with her. She continued to drive to the patrol station; she had to take care of a few things before she was done. On the third ring, Jack answered. "Hello?"

"Jack, it's me. I'm running late. We had a triple fatal up in Ormond-by-the-Sea area and I still have a few things to do at the station." She sneezed.

"OK honey, don't worry about it. If you need me to meet you somewhere to make your drive easier, I will." His tone held concern for her.

"Well, it'll take me about an hour to take care of a few things, but I'm drenched, and I need to change into another uniform before I catch a cold. Can you meet me at my house?" She sneezed again.

"Sure thing, honey." He hung up.

Relieved, she dialed Bob's cell phone number. He answered after the second ring. "Jade, is everything OK?" His voice was calm.

"Yeah, we had a triple first thing this morning and then additional crashes occurred, keeping all of us there longer. I'm running late. Do you have any plans today?"

"Matter of fact I do. I'm here at your place, entertaining Gracie. I promised to watch *Barney's Adventure* with her after dinner, if that's OK with you?" He knew she would be perfectly fine with it. Smiling, he was sure of his rightful place in Jade's house. She needed him. Now, if she could realize that, they're relationship could start.

Relief filled her, knowing Bob was a good friend. "Absolutely. Thank you, Bob. I'll bring dinner home once I'm done here."

"Take your time. We'll see you later." He hung up, smug with himself. He now had the opportunity he wanted, with Jade arriving late, to satisfy his curiosity.

Chapter 39

JACK PULLED INTO the backyard of Jade's property and parked. Exiting his vehicle, he noticed Jade's patrol car wasn't there and decided to go inside to check on Gracie. He recognized Bob's vehicle parked in front. He did not like Bob, even though the man helped Jade out with Gracie. He had his doubts about the intentions this man had.

Looking at his watch, he knew he was early. Jade wouldn't be home at least for another forty-five minutes. He quietly walked inside.

The sound of music was echoing down the hall as he looked around for everyone. Walking down the hall, he realized Gracie was in her room watching television. He also noticed the door to Jade's room was open. He peeked into the bedroom and saw Bob next to the dresser drawer. It was open, and he was perusing Jade's under garments. Disgust boiled up inside him as he watched Bob pick up a pair of Jade's sheer panties and rubbed them on his face. Damn pervert! He seethed with fury. Before he said something, he turned and left the house.

Once outside, he cursed aloud vehemently. Pulling out a cigarette, he smoked it as he contemplated what to do.

Anger hardened his expression. He knew Bob was hiding something. Pacing back and forth as he smoked, he decided what he had to do. He took one last drag, tossed his cigarette on the ground, and stepped on it. Looking at his watch, he saw he had thirty minutes before Jade should arrive. He drove down the driveway and turned left onto the roadway.

Within five minutes, he pulled into the driveway of Bob's house. Before exiting his car, he looked around to see if he was being watched. There was no one out. Good. He went up to the front door and pressed the doorbell, just to make sure no one was home. He waited and pressed the doorbell again. Nothing. No sound came from the house. He tried the door, it was locked. He had to see if Bob had left any of the doors open. Walking around the house, he opened the metal fence gate while still looking around to see if he was being watched. No one was outside. Confident, he tried the back door, but it was locked. Damn! Peeking through the cracks in the curtain that blocked the public's view into his home, he didn't see anything out of the ordinary. He walked by windows that had no access for viewing inside, and then he decided to give up. Still leery about any curious watchers, he continued to scan for anybody. As he walked by the side garage door, he noticed the outside utility door had a window. "Ahh, what the hell." He peeked inside the garage. He saw a car with windshield damage, but the car was new. He saw nothing else. "How many cars that son of a bitch have?" he asked himself. Taking out his note pad from his front pocket, he wrote down the description of the car and the damage it sustained before heading to his car.

Getting into his car, he looked at the time. It was almost four o'clock, about the time Jade should be arriving at her house. Not sure, how to bring this up to her, he drove to her house. A few minutes later, he drove onto the property, parking again in the backyard. Jade wasn't there yet. He decided not to go in. He pulled out another cigarette to smoke.

As he finished his cigarette, Jade pulled into her driveway. Walking up to her driver's door, he helped her with the takeout food she had bought.

"Hi, Jack, sorry I'm late." She sounded tired.

"Hi, honey, we need to talk in private when you get a chance." There was an edge to his voice that caused her to look at him.

His expression was serious as he stood there with the fast food bags in his hands. A quick and disturbing thought flashed through her mind, and her eyes widened in alarm.

Seeing her expression, he quickly tried to reassure her it was not what she thought. "Honey, everyone is just fine. I need to talk to you about your friend Bob. That's all."

Relief washed over her face as she closed her patrol car door. "Let's get inside and hand off the food. Bob is here, in case you didn't know."

"Sure, honey, I know. I'll help with the food. You just get changed."

"OK, Jack. I'll hurry." She opened the back door for him, and they entered the house.

Fifteen minutes later, she was changed and ready to go. They both left the house, with her mother on her way to relieve Bob. He promised to eat dinner and watch a Barney movie with Gracie before he left. Jade was relieved, but Bob's presence there longer bothered her.

She clocked back on at work as she pulled onto the roadway. "OK, Jack, fire away."

He sighed, uncomfortable at what he was about to say to her. Knowing she might not believe his story, he hesitated, measuring her for a moment. "Look, what I'm about to say to you, you're probably not going to believe. Now, all I ask is that you hear me out, OK?"

She started to feel uncomfortable. She stole a glance at him. There was an arrested expression on his face as he waited for her response. Awkwardly, she cleared her throat. "Ok, Jack, I'm listening." Unconsciously she held her breath as she waited.

"I'm starting to have an idea of who the cop killer you're investigating is." He said the words as if testing them.

Jade let out the breath she'd been holding. "Who?"

"OK, baby doll, let's get this straight. You're the smart investigator and you're really good at what you do." He hesitated, watching her expression.

She raised her eyebrows. She shifted her eyes from the road to him for a moment, then focused on the road. "OK, Jack, this has to be good, because you're complimenting me. Now I know there is a 'but' coming."

"Well give me a chance, sweetheart, and I'll get to it. I'm old and cantankerous, so give me a chance to say this right."

"Fair enough. You'll need to get to the point, Jackie boy, before I find a violation on someone," she said in a teasing tone.

Frustrated now, he contemplated how he should tell her that the one man who Gracie trusted and loved who helped her and who she trusted that might be the killer. "OK, I've been thinking about the victims and how you knew them. It didn't dawn on me who it might be until I came here earlier to wait for you.

I walked into your house looking for everyone, heard some music coming from the hallway, from your daughter's room..." His voice trailed off as the vision became alive in his mind's eye.

Tension formed like a ball in Jade's stomach tightening at each word he was forming. Oh, God please don't let it be what I'm thinking, she thought.

"I heard some sounds in your room, so I looked in there first. I saw your friend Bob in your dresser drawer, bathing his face with your under garments." His tone became angry as he spit out those last words.

Frowning she asked, "That's it?"

"No, it gets worse. It dawned on me that this guy is nuts. I left and went to his house on a hunch. Nobody was there and I couldn't get in, except one thing."

Her body stiffened waiting in anticipation of his last discovery.

"Honey, I looked through the side utility door to the garage and saw something. I don't know how many cars Bob has, but parked inside is a vehicle with windshield damage. Now when I say damage, I'm not talking about a crack or anything like that." His voice hardened as he continued. "It looked like someone or something had struck the front windshield. Your Bob looks like he had been involved in a crash, and he's hiding the car in his garage."

Gripping the steering wheel and taking it all in, she contemplated what her old friend had said. She turned back onto Beresford Avenue and, drove to Bob's house. Of all people, she trusted Jack; he had nothing to gain or lose from telling her what he'd seen. "OK, Jack, lets go check out this car."

"I reckon we have enough time before Bob arrives, right?" He had some uncertainties, knowing Bob could be the killer.

"Yeah, at least fifteen more minutes." Parking the patrol car on the driveway, they both exited and walked around the house to the side utility door to the garage.

Stopping, he peeked inside and then stepped aside to let her look in as he watched for any visitors or nosey neighbors.

Looking inside, she saw the vehicle and the damage to the front windshield. It looked just like how Jack described, like someone or something had struck and flew into the windshield. Warning spasms of alarm erupted within her at the same time realization started to sink in. She turned away in uncertainty, not wanting to believe, but the facts were there. Not wanting to run into Bob, she turned to leave. "Come on, Jack, let's go." She heard her voice, and it sounded stifled and unnatural.

They both sat back into the patrol car. Putting the gear into reverse, she pulled out and drove away. Her brain shifted into high gear analyzing the information she had to the possibilities of Bob's vehicle parked in the garage. "You know, Jack, I never saw that vehicle before, and Bob only owns one car. Wait a minute." She flipped open her mobile laptop and entered the FCIC system. Inputting Bob's name and date of birth, his driver license information came up on the screen, along with the vehicles he owned. She confirmed her worries. "He only has one vehicle, Jack. He never talks about having another one, but then again, Bob wasn't in my life for a while, since the bad episode him and I had a while ago."

"I know, honey, but do you really know a lot about your friend Bob?" His voice was calm and low.

She clenched the steering wheel tight, causing her knuckles to whiten. Her face clouded with uneasiness with the fact that he spoke what she had suspected earlier, but couldn't prove it. She had a suspicion the killer was possibly someone she knew, but she couldn't think of who. This was a good lead. She knew what needed to be done. "Jack, I had a bad feeling it was someone I knew, but it's really hard for me to accept that it could possibly be Bob. I'm taking in consideration the vehicle in the garage and the fact that Bob hasn't mentioned anything about it. What I'm going to need to really convince me that it's him is some pieces of his windshield for comparison."

He lounged casually against the doorframe listening to her. "I understand, Jade, but face it. With the odd behavior he was displaying with you, the second car hidden in the garage, and the mere fact he wants to be involved your life so much, he's a prime candidate." The memory of him rubbing her under garments on his face and inhaling deeply came rushing back. His tongue was heavy with sarcasm as he continued. "And don't forget about him going through your drawers earlier. That pig!" His expression grew hard with loathing.

She stole a glance at him and then returned her focus back onto the road. Rubbing her face, she was frustrated. This was complicated. The man she trusted with her daughter's life, the same man who has been a friend to her family for over several years, could also be the cop killer.

Damn!

In a resigned voice, she said, "Jack, let me think about this. Please don't go around telling everyone what you think until I get back with you. Remember rumor doesn't solve crimes, evidence does. For now, let's just get this evening done by finding some activity. Tickets Jack, let's keep our eyes open so I can write some tickets. OK with you?"

Realizing this is a lot for her to digest he didn't push it. "OK, honey, I'll keep a lid on it and wait for your approval. Now let's get some tickets. You know I-95 is the easiest fishing spot. You want to go there?"

Her brows shot up in surprise at his suggestion. "Oh, yeah, that's right. On I-95 between Daytona Beach and LPGA Boulevard exits definitely an easy fishing spot. That's where we're going." Turning the patrol car northward, they headed for I-95.

Chapter 40

JACK DROVE FROM the patrol station back to Bob's neighborhood and parked several houses down from his. He waited. Jade had told him when she dropped him off this evening that Bob would have to be under surveillance at all times until he drives the car that he has parked in the garage.

Jade specifically told him she needed a sample of the windshield from that car. So he waited. Bob pulled into his driveway and parked at around ten thirty. He watched as Bob went into the house and did not come out for the night.

Eleven thirty passed. Jack looked at his watch noticing the time. He had nodded off, he couldn't help it as the years passed by the older he became. Sleep would evade his waking thoughts easily and he would nod off. Bob's car was still parked in the driveway. No way had the car in the garage driven out. He continued to wait.

One forty-five displayed on his watch. He had nodded off again. The car remained parked in the driveway blocking the way for the car parked in the garage. Irritated, he exited the vehicle quietly and looked around for any curious eyes watching. Jack continued his way silently toward Bob's house, making his way to the side utility door. Standing outside the door, he peered in. The car remained parked in the dark, with the front windshield still intact. Pacing back and forth, he debated about trying the door to see if it was locked. The grass had worn down near the door from his pacing. It was obvious he noticed that he had been there at the door. With all the courage he could muster up, he attempted to open the door.

It was locked.

Cursing quietly under his breath, he gave up and walked back to his car. He sat in the car and waited. As the time passed, he couldn't keep his eyes open and fell into a deep sleep.

⋆⊨◉ ◉⊨⋆

Stiff from his uncomfortable posture sleeping in his car, Jack checked his watch again. It was five thirty-eight. The night was over and the sun was going to rise soon. Looking back at Bob's house, the car still remained parked. It hadn't moved. Turning the key in the ignition, he started the car and drove home. He reminded himself when he got home, he'd have to call Jade and let her know Bob stayed home all night long.

⋆⊨◉ ◉⊨⋆

Jade's phone rang twice before she picked it up. Suddenly awake, she looked at the time displayed on the cable box. Good. She wasn't late, but someone was calling her very early.

"Hello?"

"Jade, honey, it's me Jack. Look, darling, I watched Bob's house all night and he didn't go anywhere. I'm going to bed, and after lunch, I'll head back there. I'm sorry it's early, but I wanted to check in with you. Talk to you later." He hung up the phone without waiting for a reply from her.

Surprised that he didn't wait for her response, she turned her alarm off. It was just a few minutes before she had to get up anyway, so she decided to get ready. While in the shower, she went over in her head what Jack had told her. She had to talk to Jason to see if she could get him to watch Bob until Jack could return. She was disappointed that he hadn't called or let her know what was going on. It would have been very nice if he stood over night.

She recalled her last conversation with him, and he knew she was going to do extra work last night. She didn't know what to do; over and over, her brain would focus on Jason. Just thinking about him her body felt heavy and warm. He radiated a vitality that drew her to him like a flame. Her body ached for his touch. Each day without him near her, she missed him miserably.

Drying off, she put her robe on and picked up the portable telephone and dialed Jason's number.

"Hello?" he said with quiet emphasis.

"I missed you last night," she said in a silky voice.

"Did you?" His voice was low and purposely seductive.

She fought to control her swirling emotions. Her heart ached for him. "Yes, I did."

"I dreamt about you last night." His body definitely responded as he thought about her and listened to her voice. His throbbing erection ached with need.

"Hmm. If I ask what the dream was about, we would be talking a lot longer, and I unfortunately need to get ready for work. Maybe you could find sometime in your schedule to come by and tell me more about the dream."

"Definitely. How about tonight?"

"OK, but I need to ask you a favor." She waited as he groaned on the other end.

"Ah, you need something. What can I do for you?"

"I need you to follow Bob today until Jack can relieve you."

"And why, may I ask, do you want your friend Bob to be followed?" His curiosity sprang up.

"I think possibly he might have something to do with my case, and I need him watched. Apparently, he has a car in his garage that's not his, and it has a busted windshield that looks like he struck a pedestrian with it. I need a piece of that windshield to compare with my evidence. How's that in a nutshell?"

He whistled aloud. "OK, I'll just take your word for it and ask later. Let me get dressed, and I'll head over there."

"Thank you."

"For you, anything" he said, and he meant it.

⊷⊶◉ ◉⊷⊶

An hour later, Jason parked several houses away from Bob's house waiting to see what would happen next. It was early and the sun was rising. People streamed out of their houses picking up their newspapers in their pajamas and then made their way back into their homes. An older male walked his dog near his car as he slumped down in his seat. Thankfully, he had tinted his car windows very dark, and he hoped no one came any closer to him.

Thirty minutes later, he watched Bob come out of his house with a bag of trash in his hand. Jason watched him lower the bag of trash into the trashcan on the side of his house. Then Bob stopped and began looking down.

What are you doing? Jason thought.

He watched as Bob continued analyzing the ground near the side utility door. Then he watched as Bob stood up in one fluid motion looking around and then into the window of the door. He watched as Bob's mouth turned with an unpleasant twist when he scanned the area. Then he turned quickly retreated back into his house.

What the hell was that?

Thirty minutes later, he watched Bob drive past him. He documented the times and followed Bob, leaving several car lengths between them. They didn't drive far. He watched as Bob drove into Woodward Elementary School parking lot and parked. He drove up the side of the parking lot slowly, watching Bob exit his vehicle and walked toward the main building. Parking, he documented everything and waited.

Auxiliary Jack Spry relieved him from the surveillance after lunchtime. Jason drove to his house, switched cars, and changed into his uniform. An hour later, he drove up to the patrol station and parked.

Walking into the traffic homicide room, he saw Jade typing away at her laptop. Placing his workbag down, he sat next to her lounging casually as he waited.

The tantalizing smell of his aftershave caused her to divert her attention to Jason. He seemed to be peering at her intently as he sat across from her.

Her cheeks colored under the heat of his gaze. Anticipation crossed her face while he studied her features. He began to tell her of his eventful day following her friend.

"Well, nothing exciting happened. He got up, threw his trash out, and drove directly to work."

Irritated that nothing happened, she asked "Anything unusual in his actions at all?"

Pondering for a moment, he only recalled one thing, but that wouldn't really be considered unusual. "OK, maybe this would be considered an unusual thing. When he put his garbage out, he stopped next to the side utility door and examined the ground. That would be the only thing unusual."

She considered what he said and jotted it down in her notes. Bringing her attention back to Jason, she said, "Thank you for doing this at the last minute I know this sounds a bit crazy, asking out of the blue for you to do go around watching people for me." She gave him an incredible smile.

The power of her smile was overwhelming. His body reacted immediately leaving him uncomfortable sitting across from her with a semi hard-on.

Jack followed Bob as he drove early away from the school traveling north. A few minutes later, he followed Bob back to his residence as he drove onto his driveway. Not thinking Bob would drive back to his house, Jack past his house and circled the block. He pulled onto the shoulder of the road at the same spot he parked last night and waited. Ten minutes later, he watched Bob come out of the side utility door with a white sheet wrapped around something that was bunched in the middle. The shape of the item was oblong. Bob walked to the back of his car and opened the trunk. Bob tossed the wrapped item into the trunk and shut the door, while looking around suspiciously.

A smile spread across Jack's face as he realized what Bob was doing.

Hide the evidence you son of a bitch that's it. That's it, he thought.

Bob walked back into the garage through the side utility door and locked it. A minute later, he exited his house walking to his car. Looking around suspiciously at his neighbors, he cursed under his breath and sat back down into the driver's seat shutting the door. Shifting the car into reverse, he backed out of his driveway and shoved the gear shifter into drive traveling north in a hurry. He knew where he was going to throw the evidence away at, but he had to make sure no one was following him.

His pulse racing in his aged body, sweat beaded on his forehead as his excitement poured through his body like a volcano erupting. The chase was on. He let Bob have a good distance as he followed, determined not to lose him. Reaching for his cell phone on his belt, he dialed Jade's cell phone number.

"Hello, Jack."

"Darling, I'm following your boy around town. He put something into his trunk, and I think it's the windshield." His voice held a rasp of excitement.

"Jack, it's early. He should still be at school. Where are you?"

"I'm following your boy. We're traveling north on the truck route passing State Road 44 right as we speak."

"OK, don't lose him. When he dumps the item, call me. Don't be a hero here, Jack. I don't want you getting hurt. Oh, God, Jack, if he realizes you're following him and he's the killer, he'll…" A warning voice whispered in her head at the realization that Bob really could be the killer. "Jack, just be careful." Her hand hurt from clenching the phone receiver so hard.

"Darling, I will. You know me. Just be ready for my phone call." With that, he hung up the phone.

She hung up slowly as the case came rushing through her mind. Pieces of evidence she found of how the bodies were damaged from their injuries and of the scene. It all came rushing through her mind as she held her head leaning onto the table with her elbows. It was all too much, too much for her.

Jason watched the emotions cross Jade's face, and he knew it wasn't good. Quickly, in one fluid motion, he stood up from his desk across from her and walked over. Placing his hands on her shoulders, he rubbed gently, trying to ease the stress she obviously had building up.

She moaned with the touch of Jason's strong hands.

Leaning down close to her ear, he whispered, "Honey, what's wrong? Talk to me." His voice was low, but it was hypnotic to her already sensitive ears.

Mumbling through her covered face, she forced the words out. "I think I know who the killer is."

Leaning over, he spoke close to her ear. "Who is it?"

She mumbled something under her breath, but he couldn't quite make out.

"I need you to repeat that. I couldn't understand you."

"Jason, I think it's Bob," she muttered hastily.

He froze momentarily, knowing what the consequences were if it was Bob. "Are you sure?" He said the words tentatively, as if testing the idea.

The anxious look on her face told him she knew.

She placed her hand on his forearm, needing to feel his comfort at this moment.

Her touch tugged at his heart. He knew if this information was true, her friend and daughter's mentor had deceived everyone. That would make Bob a very dangerous individual, especially with the trust of Gracie who he knew loved the man unconditionally. How would they explain that to Gracie? The mere thought tugged at his mind demanding an explanation for the child. Another realization dawned on him a second time, Jade. She trusted the man with her child, with her life. Jealousy suddenly crept up inching its way inside him; he wanted to be that man in Jade's life. That sudden realization shook him like a wave. He knew deep down in his heart he was in love with Jade, but he never realized how much until now.

Looking down, he watched her trying to gain her composure. The woman he loved was hurting right now, and there was not a damn thing he could do to take that pain away. His emotions weighed heavily on his heart, as he debated on what to do next. He gently kissed the side of her face then whispered in her ear, "Jade, no matter what happens, I will be here for you. We'll do this together." He laid his cheek against hers and hugged her.

She turned her head toward him. Searching her eyes he could see the knowledge of what she had just learned was tearing at her. Clearing her throat she replied, "Thank you, Jason. I will need your help in this case, if you don't mind?"

"Whatever you need anything."

When her phone rang, she grabbed it out of reflect. "Traffic Homicide. Corporal Davis speaking."

"Honey, it's me. He just left. I'm behind the businesses located at the intersection of Plymouth Avenue and the truck route," Jack spoke breathlessly.

"All right, Jack, I'm on my way," she answered. Hanging up the telephone, she started gathering her equipment together.

Jason stood back, astonished. "Don't you mean we are on our way?"

"I'm sorry," she said. "I meant, we are on our way." And gave him what resembled a small quick smile.

"OK, good." He turned and quickly gathered his equipment together. Within two minutes, they were ready and heading out the door.

Knowing she didn't want a lot of suspicion going on from any on lookers, she blurted out to Jason, "Put your stuff in your car and then I'm going to need you to ride with me."

He nodded.

Chapter 41

Within ten minutes, they parked next to Jack. Jason and her both exited and walked up to Jack. Jason nodded at him and waited patiently for the story. Jade didn't hesitate. "OK, where is it?"

Pointing to the trash bin, Jack smiled like the Cheshire Cat.

They all walked over to the trash bin and looked in. Lying inside was an oblong shaped item wrapped in a sheet.

Jade walked back to her patrol car and grabbed her camera. Walking back, she took photographs of the bin and the item inside the bin as it lay in its original placement.

Finished, she asked, "Can you guys lift that out without hurting yourselves?"

Jason grunted and began climbing up the side of the trash bin, knowing the old auxiliary trooper wouldn't be able to do it. Lifting the item carefully, he could hear crunching of whatever it was wrapped inside as he handed it to Jack. Jack took it and laid it on the ground. Jason quickly jumped out of the trash bin brushing off his uniform.

Putting on gloves, Jason carefully pulled the sheet open. It was evident the item was a destroyed windshield. Jade took pictures of it. Next, she took as evidence four small pieces of the windshield that contained a red stain on it and placed it in an envelope.

"OK, guys, wrap it back up. I need it as evidence."

After they'd placed the wrapped windshield into the back of Jade's patrol car, Jade turned to Jack with a digital recorder and paper in her hand.

He looked down at what she was holding, and understood what she was going to ask. "I know what you want, Darling, your car or mine?"

"Yours will be fine." They both walked over to Jack's car and sat down getting comfortable. Within minutes, Jade had the digital recorder ready and the paperwork filled out.

"OK, Jack, just to fill you in, this interview will start when you told me what you thought yesterday about Bob. Be honest and say everything. Just watch your language and know this will be, if the windshield comes back positive with Scott's blood, placed into the report. Judge what you say wisely. Are you ready?"

He nodded.

"OK, here we go."

Jason watched the interview take place knowing this investigation is not going the way Jade would prefer. Knowing how damaging this will be to little Gracie, he shook his head. He loved the little girl with all her disabilities. Gracie is beautiful and a wonderful little girl that his son loves to be with. He recalled his son wishing Gracie was his sister. That thought had been weaving its way into his head for the past several months. Now that his relationship with Jade has changed, he could envision easily all of them as a family.

He stood frozen, realizing what he had just thought a family with Jade and Gracie. He stared, wordlessly at Jade as the thought sunk in.

Jade suddenly felt she was being watched, looking up she realized her instincts were right. Realizing it was Jason, she beamed him a dazzling smile.

At that moment, he knew his answer. His smile broadened in approval.

Ten minutes later, the interview was done.

"Jack, thank you for your help." She leaned over and kissed him on his cheek.

"Anything for you, honey. You know you're like a daughter to me. I'll take care of you." His southern accent was thick in his happiness.

"See you later, Jack." She winked at him and then exited his vehicle with her equipment.

Jason walked over taking the recorder out of her hands as she fumbled to keep the items in her grasp.

"Thank you." Her clear blue eyes swept over him approvingly.

He studied her thoughtfully for a moment before answering, "You're welcome."

Within minutes, they were heading back to the station with their evidence.

⊷⊫⊜ ⊜⊰⊶

The rest of her shift, Jade placed the windshield into evidence and wrote down in her notes the incident. Next, she called the Florida Department of Law Enforcement in Orlando, requested the lab to analyze her evidence and requesting a rush on it. Jade emphasized the importance of her case to the lab technician on the pieces of windshield and then thanked them for their assistance.

"Corporal Davis, if you drive here today and drop off the evidence, I'll have your stuff done by the end of this week."

Jade's heart dropped. She knew that once the evidence came back with Scott's blood she had her suspect. The only problem was that Gracie would not understand why she had to arrest Bob. The worst part is that now Bob is with her daughter now treating her like his own. She cared about Bob, but only like a friend, nothing more. If she only could redo the last year and not let Bob become so close to Gracie, but she knew that was only foolish thinking on her part. Bob had been like a pillar for Gracie, a male figure she learned from and loved greatly. He also had been a good friend to her when she was feeling the tremendous loss of her deceased husband. A part of her wanted to preserve the idea that Bob was innocent, but her instincts for the last several months had warned her of Bob's change in his behavior toward her. On her birthday, he acted like a jealous boyfriend, and for a short time, he became possessive of her. She just couldn't see him as a murderer, especially how Susan was murdered.

Returning to her senses, she answered, "OK, I'm on my way." Her nerves tensed immediately as she hung up the phone.

Jason noticed her sudden mood change. Looking at his watch, he suddenly realized why she became increasingly uneasy under his scrutiny. His paternal instincts kicked in. He stood up in one fluid motion and walked over to Jade.

When he placed his large strong hand on her small uniformed shoulder, she stopped in mid-motion, looking up at him.

"Look, I know the shift is almost over. I'll take the evidence over to the lab for you. I don't want Bob being around Gracie more than is necessary."

Her nervousness suddenly lifted, and some of the tension eased away from her body. Placing her hand on his and patting it, she beamed him a dazzling smile that would melt even the meanest man's heart.

"You would do this for me?" she asked.

"Of course if you trust me enough with this, I will." His eyes were even darker than sapphires as he towered next to her with an irresistible grin.

A sudden impulsive feeling overwhelmed her as she stepped in hugging Jason.

He was momentarily speechless in his surprise, but he returned her hug savoring the feel of her small body fitting snugly against his. Inhaling her scent, he felt a stirring starting to develop as erotic images started to form in his mind eye.

She pulled out of the embrace first, looking up into his waiting face. "Thank you. If you only knew how much this means to me," she blurted out, scarcely aware of the nervousness in her voice.

A devilish look appeared on his face as he lifted her chin up. "You can make it up to me tonight when I get back."

A blush crimsoned her face. She understood what the suggestion meant.

Slowly and seductively, his gaze slid downward over her body.

The mere unspoken suggestion his eyes displayed, caused her body to ache for his touch. Aware of their surroundings, she cleared her throat while stepping away in order for her to gain her composure at the same time.

Chuckling, he took the evidence and paperwork from her then exited the room. There was a maddening hint of arrogance about him that drew her to him like a moth to a flame. Gathering her equipment, she left the station heading home.

Chapter 42

PULLING INTO HER driveway, Jade tried to calm herself down from the adrenaline rush flowing through her. Looking at her hands on the steering wheel, she watched how they trembled. Sadness enveloped her as she continued rationalizing her feelings for Bob. And she knew her and Gracie's lives would be forever changed if the results came back positive with Scott's blood. At the same time if she did solve the murders, she would finally have peace knowing it was over. Most importantly, the rest of her friends would remain alive.

Placing the patrol car into park, she radioed to dispatch the end of her shift. The feeling of being watched over rode her senses again. Looking up at the back of her house, she saw Bob watching her through the kitchen window with a frown on his face. Not wanting to give him any reasons for suspicion, she said a short prayer for strength, gathered her equipment, and walked into her house through the back door.

OK, act cool, she thought.

Walking through the kitchen into the living room, she placed her equipment down and pulled Gracie into her arms. Bob was standing in the living room next to Gracie.

"Hi, Gracie. You had a good day at school?" She avoided looking up at Bob.

"Yes, Mommy." The child squirmed in her arms, wanting to be released.

Releasing her, Jade stood up. giving Bob her attention finally. Reading the expression on his stern face, she presumed he was either mad or upset about something.

"Bob, are you OK?"

"Yeah."

He paused and watched her.

"What's with the serious look suddenly?" Placing her hands on her hips, she waited for his reply.

Her mother walked in from the family room. "Well, hello, honey. How was work?" Her mother looked every bit of her age at seventy-two. She walked with a limp and took smaller steps to compensate for the arthritis that ached in her hips. Her white hair flowed down her shoulders as her mother winked at her.

"I picked Gracie up, and Bob asked to stay to help with her homework. I didn't think you would mind. He's such a helpful fella."

"Thanks, Mom. You feel all right?" The distraction of her mother helped with her adrenaline high. Relief knowing her mother was there, even though she didn't feel any of them were in danger at this point in time from Bob.

"I noticed you're limping a little, that's all. You are staying for dinner right?"

"Yes, dear." She turned and started walking back into the family room. "I'll leave you three. Opera's on."

Looking back at Bob, she saw that the stern look he had earlier had soften a bit.

"I hope you didn't mind me being here," he said.

"No, not at all." She turned away from him and walked down the hallway to her room. She hoped that he would leave.

Taking the hint, he realized he wasn't wanted here now, so he decided to leave. He was suspicious of her behavior. She never gave him the cold shoulder the way she just did. Wondering if she might know something about his involvement in the murders, he debated about how he was going to question her about it.

A few minutes later, Jade walked back into the living room dressed in shorts and a T-shirt. He sucked in his breath of how sexy she looked with her hair hanging down her back and her T-shirt clinging to her body. His imagination raced standing there quietly.

She stopped, abruptly looking at him.

"What?"

Clearing his throat, he answered, "Nothing."

"So why are you looking at me like that?" Pausing for a brief second, she continued. "And what was with the serious look when I first walked in?"

"I...I," he stuttered, caught off guard of her confrontation.

"What?"

"I was just wondering how to ask you about the big case you're on."

Her heart started hammering in her chest. Oh, God, no, she thought. Taking a breath, she said, "It's going slowly."

He hesitated, reading her face. "Any leads yet on who's murdering all these people?"

She looked away. She was having a hard time lying to him. "No, nothing yet."

Liar!

Watching her eyes shift back and forth as she avoided looking at him, he was convinced that she was absolutely lying to him. Damn it!

Not sure what he was going to do, he excused himself and left her house.

Uncertainty nagged at him as he drove out of Jade's driveway. He couldn't understand why she was suddenly lying to him.

A quick and disturbing thought sunk in as beads of perspiration formed on his forehead and upper lip.

Maybe she knows, he thought.

Shit!

Driving his car in the direction where he was not long earlier, fear enveloped him like a welcoming child.

Within five minutes, he arrived at the medical complex and drove around back slowly looking for any unwanted visitors. Convinced no one was around, he drove around the complex again. Stopping in front of the familiar dumpster, he looked around for anyone who might see him. There was no one. Getting out of his car slowly, he continued to look around suspiciously. Wiping his forehead from the sweat, he walked over and lifted the dumpster's lid. Looking down into it, he couldn't see the sheet. He scanned the area quickly before jumping into the dumpster. He moved the trash around, searching intently. The longer he searched, the more cold fear ran its course through his veins. Damn it, where was it?

Frustration and fear overwhelmed him as he started flinging trash out of the dumpster in search of the item. Puffing from exertion, he had thrown most of the trash out of the dumpster before stopping. He wiped his face clean with his shirtsleeve and, took a minute to calm himself down. Blood pumped through him rapidly.

Taking one last look down, small bits of broken glass on the floor, but no windshield wrapped in his sheet.

Damn! She had to have found it, but how?

Climbing out of the dumpster, he replaced the trash bags that he had thrown out. The last thing he needed was someone to report him to the police for attacking a dumpster. It would be ironic.

He drove toward his house, building a plan in his head for his next move.

Chapter 43

THE UTILITY DOOR opened; in walked Jason dressed in jeans and a T-shirt. The tantalizing smell of his after-shave caught Jade's attention. Looking up from the couch she was laying on, she saw Jason standing in the shadows of the doorway staring intently at her.

"Hi," she said with a small smile.

Walking toward her, he could see the pain in her eyes that flickered there. "Jade, are you OK?" His voice was tender, filled with concern.

She ached with an inner pain that squeezed at her heart. Tears threatened to fall as memories of her dead friends continued to flood her thoughts. She had tried very hard not to be a basket case with the loss of her friends. Since the victims were her friends, this added insecurity about her abilities as an investigator, because she couldn't solve the cases immediately.

Jade had the evidence of a person with dark hair, along with the DNA from the hair and skin cells found at Susan's scene. She had concluded the murderer was a male that fit the profile of someone who had a deep-rooted hate that he used to kill with. Susan's murder was with a knife and the killer had her friend caught off guard. This meant Susan had her guard down because she knew the killer. As for Susan being over-powered, that meant the killer had to be a male stronger than Susan. She knew Susan was very strong and a definite challenge for any male. As for Scott's murder, the windshield from Bob's car will determine if Bob was involved.

Jason saw the distraught look on Jade's beautiful face. She was fighting her emotions and didn't hear his question. He repeated his question, this time squatting down in front of her. Lifting her chin gently up, he asked, "Jade, are you OK?"

A tear slid down her face as he waited for her answer. She shook her head no, and he gathered Jade in one fluid motion into his embrace. The over-due release of tears and emotions racked her body, and Jade cried in Jason's arms. Holding her gently, he rocked her back and forth while whispering in her ear his promises that everything would be OK. She buried her face into his shoulder until the last of her sobs subsided.

Pulling away reluctantly, she wiped the tears from her face.

Jason pulled his shirt off quickly and used it to gently clear the remaining tears from Jade's face.

A stab of guilt weighed heavily on her heart with the thought that Bob might be the actual killer. This is the same man she trusted with her daughter. Damn! If this is true, how am I going to break the news to Gracie?

"Jade, talk to me, maybe I can help." His voice was smooth, but insistent.

"The man who's killing my friends could be the same man that cares for my daughter. Gracie loves him a lot and... and... how would I explain this to her?" Her voice still shaky, she sighed with exasperation.

Exhaling a long audible breath, he considered what to say.

"If Bob is the killer, then we will sit Gracie down and explain to her the best way we can."

Looking up she gave him a small smile. "I just hope he isn't the one I hope you understand."

"Definitely." He lean over and kissed her tenderly.

⋄⊱══◉ ◉══⊰⋄

In the shadows under the dinner table, clutching a teddy bear, Gracie listened. She listened with bewilderment, but remembered some of the words she did not understand. Tears slid down her face as she watched her mother cry.

⋄⊱══◉ ◉══⊰⋄

Pacing back and forth and tapping his forehead, Bob reflected on his earlier mission. He'd planned everything right! What happened to the windshield? He continued pacing back and forth wondering.

Realization struck him dead cold as he suddenly stopped in his tracks.

She knows! he thought. She has to know. How else did the windshield disappear?

Recalling when she'd came home acting strange and then lied to him, he cursed. But maybe she took the windshield trying to protect him? He thought about how Jade had been treating him and her behavior toward the other guy, Jason. He knew Jason would be too hard to kill and decided not to even try. He decided to go back and watch her.

⊷═◉ ◉═⊷

Nighttime came early due to the dark clouds. Parking in the woods across from Jade's property, Bob stood outside his vehicle listening for anything out of the ordinary. He looked around with his night vision binoculars. There was no sign of anyone around. He walked the short distance over the hill that faced the house he intended to watch.

Crouching behind brush, he scanned Jade's property for anyone walking outside. This time he wanted to make sure no one saw him. He had already thought out his plan of action repeatedly in his head knowing everything in his world was fixing to change. The property was clear. He placed the binoculars down and quickly went down the hill and over to the property line of Jade's.

Using the tree on the right of way, he jumped the wire fence and went around back. Peering through the windows, he had trouble looking into the house. Frustrated he walked around to the north end of the house and peeked through the blinds catching two people inside.

He recognized Jason and saw Jade in his arms.

His mood veered swiftly into anger. Clenching his teeth, he held back from cursing aloud.

As Jason and Jade talked, their voices were muffled and unclear. Leaning closer, he placed his ear on the window. He could hear clearly what was being said.

⟶▢◉ ◉▢⟵

Tilting her chin up Jason said, "Jade, you're not responsible for Bob's actions. If he really is the killer, we'll know when the results come in."

"I know, but it's just hard for me to believe he could be like that. He is so wonderful with Gracie." She paused trying to conceive the thought of Bob being as ruthless as the one murdering her friends. "Jason, he has been there for me and Gracie for several years, and I couldn't forget the way he stood by me when my husband past on." She wiped the tears away from her eyes.

"Jade, you know better. If the evidence comes back verifying Bob as the killer, its over. I won't let you and Gracie become his next victims, you hear me?"

Nodding her head, she hugged him tightly.

An urge of protection so strong flowed through him. He knew he would do whatever it took to protect the two women he loved.

He captured her lips with his, gently kissing her.

⟶▢◉ ◉▢⟵

Curiosity over took Bob as the sudden quiet grew longer. Looking through the opening of the blinds, his breath caught in his throat.

He stood there watching amazed and very upset.

How could she?

Watching her return his kisses with passion, he felt his heart burst with humiliation. No!

Suddenly all the emotions pumping through him stopped. A floodgate opened inside him and out flowed cold hatred for the woman he thought he loved. The coldness soared through his veins leaving emptiness behind. No feelings. Nothing.

He continued to watch both of them kissing for a few more minutes. He had to make sure of what he felt. Absolute coldness absorbed him as he took his last look at Jade, no love, no desire. Nothing.

A shadow caught his attention near the French doors. Something small moved. Squinting he could make out a figure moving through the darkness.

Gracie. His poor darling, shouldn't have to see that.

Moving away from the window, he went around the house to the child's bedroom window. Waiting a few minutes more he heard complete quietness. He tapped gently on the glass.

Waiting for a full minute, he gently tapped again on the window.

Whispering, he called out to the child, "Gracie, come to the window."

The blinds moved slightly.

He whispered again, "Gracie, it's me Bob. Don't be afraid."

The blinds opened. Gracie's smile broadly as she stood in the window.

In a low voice he said, "I need you to be quiet, OK?"

The child nodded her head.

"Good. Now, unlock the window, honey."

The child reached up and pulled at the latch. It took her three times and she finally unlocked the window.

Pulling the screen out, he slowly pushed the window open.

"Shhh, Gracie, be quiet." He opened the window completely, and hugged the child that stood clasping her hands in anticipation.

"OK, now you need to follow my directions and be quiet at the same time. OK?"

Nodding, she hugged him again.

His heart opened up to the sweet child's behavior. He knew he couldn't leave Gracie behind. She was going with him. "OK, I'm coming in."

Five minutes later, he had Gracie's things together and her shoes on. Exiting through the bedroom window, he turned and placed the backpack with her things down and gently pulled her through. Gingerly, he placed her next to him as he then closed the window quietly.

"OK, let's go," he whispered.

Taking the child's hand into his, he grabbed the backpack. They both walked away into the night and toward the woods without being discovered.

Chapter 44

Searching the darkness of the bedroom, Jade checked on her daughter. As a nightly ritual right before going to bed, she would tuck her daughter in again while placing a kiss on the child's forehead. Blinking several more times to adjust to the darkness, she searched for Gracie in her bed. There was no-body there.

Where is she?

She went into her own room, searching for her daughter. Sometimes Gracie would crawl into her bed to sleep with her. She realized Gracie wasn't there either. Icy fear enveloped her heart as the search for her daughter began. This wasn't normal of her daughter to be missing from her bed or hers.

Walking up behind her, Jason stopped. The anxious look on her face told him that something was wrong. "Jade, what's going on?" He saw her face fill with panic, and a quick disturbing thought took hold of him. Something was dreadfully wrong.

Her voice trembled as she blurted out, "Gracie is missing!"

Pushing him out of her way, she continued searching for her daughter.

"No." The thought of the small child gone missing gripped his heart. Walking quickly back to Gracie's room, he turned on the bedroom light. The child was gone.

He stopped and took a good look of the bedroom and how the items in her room were arranged. Her pajamas tossed on her chair. Looking around for her shoes, he noticed they were gone too. He didn't go any further into the room knowing Gracie all too well. The child would never leave the house, especially in the dark by herself. Gracie had poor vision and she had a very strong instinct not to get herself hurt. Going outside in the dark by herself, she wouldn't be able to see much and hurt herself. This left one thing. She was taken, but how? He scanned the room quickly looking for any clues something that would give him an idea of the kidnapper.

Jade's voice echoed in the house as she continued calling for Gracie in her search. One by one, she searched frantically each room in every spot that Gracie would and could hide in. Her name called from the other side of the house brought her back to her senses momentarily. She turned and ran to Jason. A pulsing knot in her chest grew as her fear turned in to panic. A fear so strong her maternal instincts continued to override her rational thoughts. All she could think about was Gracie and the overwhelming need to have her in her arms safe.

Pulling Jade into his arms, he knew how upset she was and wanted to help her anyway he could. "I need you not to go in Gracie's room anymore until we can get prints pulled."

Her eyes filled with acknowledgement of what had happened to her daughter. Hot tears blinded her, and she tore herself away with a choking cry. "No! Jason, I have to look for her." Deep sobs racked her insides as she turned and went outside in the darkness searching.

Biting back his own emotions, he dialed 911. A few minutes later, several patrol cars pulled up into the yard as the sheriff's helicopter flew overhead assisting in the search for Gracie. Once all the information was given to the deputies, they called in the Florida Department of Law Enforcement evidence technicians to search Gracie's room.

Jason's first priority was to take care of Jade. She is the only parent he knew that went through hell in order to save her daughter's life when Gracie was born. With the disabilities Gracie had, he had watched Jade become determined to assist her daughter in the child's long journey in life. He knew Gracie's disappearance would slowly destroy the woman he loved. He found her around back, crying as a deputy attempted to comfort her. Taking over, he gathered her into his embrace, trying to reassure her the best way he could.

Two hours later, with Gracie safely tucked away, asleep in the spare room, Bob waited.

When the phone rang, he knew who was calling him. He waited until it rang again.

"Hello," he said in a nasty tone.

Panic rioted within Jade as she fought to keep herself under control. Finding her voice she said, "Bob it's me. Have you seen or heard from Gracie within the last couple of hours?"

"No, why?" There was a cold edge of irony in his voice.

She answered over her choking, beating heart. "She's missing!" Sobbing, she handed the phone to Jason.

"Hello, Bob?"

"What?"

Jason had not missed the flare of temper in his voice. "Look, I know it's late, but we can't find Gracie. Has she contacted you or came by within the last few hours?"

"If she did, I sure as hell wouldn't let her walk home by herself." His voice was heavy with sarcasm.

Restraining his own emotions at Bob's behavior, he hurried the conversation on. "Thanks, sorry to bother you."

The phone went dead.

"Asshole!" Bob yelled into the receiver.

Pacing back and forth, he had to get his anger under control for Gracie's sake. He wanted Jade to hurt as much as he did, and taking Gracie was the best idea yet. It was only a matter of time before they would figure it out that he had the child. He knew what he had to do next.

⋯⊷⊷⊶⊶⋯

The next day, he called a company to replace the windshield of the rented vehicle he used to run over the deputy. He wasn't scheduled for work today, and his only priority was entertaining Gracie. By two o'clock, he called Enterprise Rental Car Agency to have their vehicle picked up from his residence. By three forty-five, the evidence was gone. A male driver from the agency had driven the vehicle away.

His plan was working well. Smug with himself, he pulled his luggage from under the bed and started packing his clothes. Next, he was going on leave from work to get away from Jade. Gracie was going with him. The lies he invented for the naïve child were believed with no questions asked. He knew it was only a matter of time before Gracie's interest would wane, and she would start inquiring about her mother.

He had to get away and fast. Jade's mother would come over and inquire soon.

Before the sun had set, he'd packed food and some clothes. Again peeking through the blinds, he continued to look for any possible surveillance that could be set up around his house. Earlier on the television Gracie's picture was displayed as law enforcement displayed their Amber Alert for her. Fully aware of how law enforcement officers behave when you take one of their own, he knew the hunt for the missing child had become even more intense. The officers would act like bloodhounds, checking everything twice over until the evidence was found. Disgusted with himself, he shook his head as realization sunk in. He wasn't careful when he took Gracie. No gloves, nothing for protection, and it'd be very soon when Jade and her friends would be knocking on his door. Then with them knowing he was the cop killer, he wouldn't stand a chance against them. Peeking through the blinds again, sunset had arrived as darkness began. He had to pack and get Gracie ready for their road trip. Lying to the child was easy, but it hurt knowing how much she trusted him.

Chapter 45

"WHAT? GRACIE'S MISSING?" Jack's southern accent was thick from his surprise.

Choking on her sobs, Jade wiped her eyes clear again as she continued. "Yeah, Jack. When I went to check on her last night before I went to bed, she had already been taken from her room." Her heart felt like it was torn out from her pain. She had lost her husband over a year ago leaving her a widow and now Gracie was missing. She felt helpless.

There was silence on the phone as Jack considered what had happened to Gracie. Realization struck him hard like a sledgehammer, it was him! "That son of a bitch took her!" he growled.

"What?" She was mentally exhausted and trying to figure out her old friend's logic was too much for her.

"You know that Bob fellow!" he sighed with exasperation.

A wave of apprehension went through her as she considered what he said.

"Don't take this the wrong way, but who else would try to get to you by taking Gracie." His voice faded, losing its steely edge.

A new anguish seared her heart as his logic unfolded. He was right.

"Jade, darling, to him, we crossed the line when we took the windshield. He knows, I'm sure, and he's trying to save his ass the only way he thinks he can. Your daughter she's his ticket to not being caught, or so he thinks."

Her mood veered sharply toward anger now. Jack was right. If Bob were the killer, he would have taken Gracie for his ace card.

"Gracie's his bargaining chip Jack."

Damn him!

"Let me get dressed and head over there to help you."

The phone was dead before she could protest. Hanging up, she walked over to Jason, who was watching her from her family room.

"Jack's coming over. He wants to help."

His blue eyes met hers as she continued.

"It has to be Bob who took her."

⊷⊜ ⊜⊶

Several hours later, nighttime fell across the city, and the temperature dropped twenty degrees. Looking out his windows, Bob continually checked for unwanted visitors. Only one car had passed. Pulling one of his jackets over Gracie and fitting her into it snug, he put his own jacket on and placed the child into his car securely. Once he was satisfied she was safe, he opened his garage door, and that was when he noticed he was being watched.

Jack sat in his vehicle for the last fifteen minutes waiting for Bob to leave. He sat cursing under his breath when he saw the garage door open. He planned to give the man a piece of his mind and get the child from him. His Beretta .40 caliber laid on his lap with his hand firmly gripping it. If he had to shoot the man, he would.

Bob recognized the car and the man in it. Irritated, he approached the vehicle, watching every move the old man made as he came closer.

Jack's anger ignited as his patience for the man left him. Screw it, he thought. I'll just shoot him. Lifting the gun slowly up, he held it pointed at Bob.

Walking up to the driver's door, he noticed the gun pointing at him and stopped dead in his tracks. He stared speechless at the old man, wondering if he would actually shoot him or not.

"You bastard!" said Jack. "I knew you were up to no good the first time I met you." He spat out the words impatiently.

Expressionless, Bob stood like a statue, waiting for the right moment to strike if the old man didn't shoot him within the next few minutes.

"Jack, I don't know what you mean." His voice was low and smooth.

"Bob you took Gracie, trying to scare Jade, you son of a bitch!" His voice rose an octave as his anger mounted.

A familiar childish voice echoed in the distance, distracting Jack's attention. Turning his head toward the house, Jack saw Gracie in the backseat, waving. Raising the gun, he started to turn back when a hard blow to the face radiated through is head. The gun fell from his grip to the floorboard as he fell into unconsciousness. Before he completely blacked out, Jack honked his horn and then fell on top of the steering wheel.

A rush of adrenaline ran through Bob when he punched the old man out. It felt good. The only problem was that the gun fell beyond his reach. As he reached into the car, the horn startled him, causing him to yank himself back out of the driver's window. "Shit!" Panic took hold of him, and he jerked his head back and forth looking for any witnesses. Realizing he only had moments before his nosey neighbors looked out their windows, he ran back to his car.

⊷═◉ ◉═⊷

Looking at her watch, Jade realized it had been an hour and a half since she last spoke to Jack. She was exhausted. She hadn't slept since the night before. Her chest felt like a weight was left on it from her sadness. Anxiety seeped through her every pore as each minute away from her daughter passed slowly by. She had to find Gracie.

Where was Jack? He never took this long.

Jason woke up and pulled her into his arms, gently hugging the woman he loved. Kissing the top of her head, he inquired about Jack. "Has he called back?"

"No, this isn't like him. I tried calling his cell and home phone, but his wife told me he left over an hour ago. I'm worried about him."

In the distance, the sound of sirens sang through the air and was getting closer.

Jade, Jason, and two deputies standing nearby stopped what they were doing. One of the deputies leaned his ear down, listening to his shoulder mic that was turned down only for him to hear. The sirens were only a block away, and suddenly they stopped.

Jason stood frozen, waiting for the deputy to tell him what was going on.

The deputy looked up, shaking his head. "Don't worry, it's a medical call. About a block away, an old man was found unconscious in his car." The deputy quickly leaned his ear back down to listen again. Several seconds later, he said, "It looks like the old man was beaten up too."

The color drained from Jade's face as an unwelcome thought developed. Her instincts flared up. She knew it had to be Jack. It was impossible to keep her panic from rising, knowing deep down inside her friend was hurt. "Jason, let's go." Her voice trembled, giving away her fear.

Hearing the fear in her voice, he looked down at her. Reading her expressions, he would do anything to help her, but he had to know what was bothering her at this moment. "What's the matter?"

Meeting his gaze, she said in a choked voice, "It's Jack, it has to be."

He grabbed her hand, and they quickly walked to his vehicle and drove off, looking for the ambulance. A couple minutes later, they found the ambulance parked in front of Bob's house. The crew was lifting the gurney up into the vehicle.

Jade recognized the vehicle as Jack's. Half in anticipation and half in dread she approached the back door of the ambulance. "Is he going to be OK?"

A young female paramedic looked up from her paperwork. "You know this man?"

"Yes, I'm a traffic homicide investigator, and Jack works with me. Is he going to be OK?"

She frowned as she looked at her patient and then looked back at Jade. "He was struck pretty hard on his head. Once we get a CAT scan completed for his head, the doctor will be able to determine from that. Do you know of any medical conditions your friend has?"

"I'll tell you anything you need to know, but can I look at him real quick?" She had to see him.

"Quickly, and then I need his information." The young paramedic stepped out letting Jade in.

"Hurry up, Jade, they need to go." Jason turned to the fire personnel who always responded with the paramedics. Showing his badge, he informed the fire fighter he would take care of the vehicle.

A deputy pulled up and exited his vehicle. Jason turned and spoke to him as Jade assisted the paramedic with Jack's information. Jason knew this had to be related to Bob and hoped that the man didn't hurt Gracie.

Chapter 46

"MR. BOB, WHERE we go?" the young child asked while looking out the window.

Looking in his rearview mirror, he saw Gracie returning his stare. Smiling, he responded in an even smooth voice. "Sweetie, we're going to Disney World. What do you think about that?" He knew if he distracted her, she wouldn't ask about her mother.

Gracie beamed me a big toothless smile.

He knew there were no witnesses to his assault on Jack and his departure. He had driven to Orlando and gotten a room near the attractions so he would be able to blend in better. There would be no questions as to why he was alone with a small child. Furthermore, no one would be asking if Gracie's was his. This particular Central Florida location contained approximately fifty percent tourist. The night went quickly. The episode was publicized on the television, but there was no word as to who the attacker was. Good.

Today his plan was to go to Disney World, give Gracie a wonderful time, and distract her from thoughts of her mother.

He knew it was only a matter of time before Jade received the information on the windshield. The woman he loved would inevitably hate him for what he did, but if he couldn't have her, then she would pay for it. Gracie was his to keep and he was going to do his best to make sure that would happen. The only problem is that why was he still hurting from seeing Jade making out with Jason?

Disney World property came into view as he drove up to the parking toll-gates. A squeal in the backseat gave him another smile. Looking in the rearview mirror, he saw Gracie was beaming with a huge smile and clapping her hands. He was fulfilling one of her biggest wishes.

⊷⊨◉ ◉⊨⊶

Hours later, Jason drove with Jade to visit Jack at Halifax Hospital. Both dressed in their work uniforms, they were able to visit the fourth floor with no questions asked. A few minutes later, they walked into Jack's room. He looked so fragile lying in the hospital bed hooked up with wires and an oxygen mask.

Crossing her arms across her chest, Jade felt the pain weave its way into her as she watched her old friend, who was like a father, lying so fragile in a deep sleep. Reaching out, she touched his shoulder gently. "Jack?"

There was no movement or change to the monitor that beeped with every heartbeat. Jade tried again, nudging a little harder at Jack's shoulder. "Jack, it's me. Wake up, please." Her voice trembled as she stood over him.

Reaching out and placing his large hand on Jade's shoulder, Jason tried to reassure her. "Jade, I think it's too soon. We can come back later. Let him sleep."

Stepping back into Jason's embrace, she turned and laid her head on his chest.

He gently hugged her giving Jade what she needed. As he kissed the top of Jade's head, a nurse walked in with a chart in her hands. "Can I help you two?"

Jade turned around. "Hi we're wondering what his condition is?"

The older nurse sized them up quickly and knew they were close to her patient and cared about him. She scanned the chart again quickly and looked back up, "He's been given a shot to relax. He was struck pretty hard in the side of his face." She pointed to the bruise on his face. "See here. His CAT scan showed he received trauma. No blood clots detected, but he did suffer some brain damage from the injury. We really won't know how much this has affected him until he wakes up. For now, he needs his rest." She smiled briefly and waited for them to leave.

Taking the hint, Jason pulled Jade away. "Lets go, we'll come back later."

"OK."

⊷⊨◉ ◉⊨⊶

Watching Jade stare at the page she was working on, Jason called to check on the status of the windshield. Finally getting a hold of the evidence technician, Quinten Farrell, he inquired.

The sound of paper being handled was heard on his end. "OK, Corporal Lance, I have the request in my hands right now. This will be simple to do. All I need is your case number to compare the blood to what we have on file. Do you have that?"

When he read the case number to Mr. Farrell, Jade looked up. They were both anxious to find out if the blood matched the dead deputy's blood.

"OK, I have it. This shouldn't take long. Under the circumstances, we would normally handle this first come first serve. Could you let Corporal Davis know we're praying for her and her daughter?"

"I'll let her know."

"Thanks, I'll get to this right now. I'll call you back in a little bit with the results."

Relief washed over him. He knew they'd know soon enough if Bob was the cop killer. However, if the blood did come back positive, logically Bob would be the one who would have kidnapped Gracie, but why?

Jade could see Jason was in deep thought. Clearing her throat, she said, "And?"

"They're on it now. Oh, by the way, they're hoping everything clears up soon. I was told to tell you that Gracie and you are in their prayers." He gave her a thoughtful smile.

A little smile played at the corners of her mouth for a brief couple of seconds, and then it was gone. Her hands were hidden from sight as they twisted nervously in her lap. Insecure with doubts and fear since Gracie's disappearance, her mind continued to play scenarios taunting her. Fighting exhaustion continually, she refused to give in to sleep until she finds her daughter. Leaning her elbows on the table, she rested her forehead in her hands contemplating.

He settled back in his chair disappointed as he continued watching her. Knowing there was nothing he could say to reassure her, his inadequacy gnawed at him.

At the sound of someone walking down the hallway and stopping at the traffic homicide room, Jason turned. He gave the approaching man an angry look.

There stood Lieutenant Mason in civilian clothes, looking haggard but determined. He only gave Jason a quick look and focused on Jade, as she ignored her surroundings.

"Corporal Davis." His voice cut the silence.

Recognizing the voice, she looked up.

There stood Lieutenant Mason with his hands down by his side and a soften look on his face.

She leaned back in her chair, confused as to why he was here. "Yes, Lieutenant?"

"I heard what happened with your child, and I can't sit still and not do anything to help."

A surprised look crossed both Jade's and Jason's faces as he continued. "I know I'm not supposed to be around you, but I would like to put our differences aside and help, and I won't take no for an answer." His hands automatically went to rest on his hips as he waited for a defiant answer.

Her brows shot up in surprise as he continued to stand in the doorway waiting. Recovering, she answered. "Lieutenant, I don't know what to say?"

His voice was courteous, but patronizing. "You can say, thank you."

Surprised again by this unpredictable man, she said, "Thank you."

Walking into the office, his appearance commanded respect. He stopped at the edge of the desks, turned around and continued. "I know this isn't going to sound right, but let me finish before you reply. First off, you're the victim in this and your decisions will be clouded with emotions and not logical."

Her eyes narrowed with anger but he didn't give her a chance to answer. "As a victim, Jade, you need to be where your child will need you when we find her, which is at home. Our agency doesn't need an outraged mother carrying a loaded gun to shoot any potential suspects."

Jason rose to his feet as fury crossed his face.

Realizing Corporal Lance's demeanor, the lieutenant addressed him immediately. "Corporal, sit down and let me finish," he barked.

Sitting back down, he waited to hear what the lieutenant had to say.

"You've had this case for several months. By now you have to know who the possible cop killer is, correct?" Looking at her, he waited.

Nodding in response too angry to say anything, she sat with her arms crossed.

"OK, now, would you say this suspect would go after you for any reasons?"

"Yes." Her tone had become chilly.

"The big question is why? Why would this suspect want to make you the next victim? Why did this suspect kill the Daytona cop, the deputy, injure your auxiliary partner, and now snatch your child?"

Sitting quietly, she considered what the lieutenant said. Why would Bob do this? Thinking of Susan, she recalled Bob's and her friend's demeanors around each other. It was as if they were jealous of one another. Then Scott he was her friend. They didn't date, but at her birthday party, he did kiss her, which made Bob very upset. Now Jack. He must have confronted Bob with his accusations. Why else would he be injured? And her daughter, Gracie. Who else but Bob would take her in order to make her feel his pain? But why? Realization dawned on her as the memories of Bob making his advances and confronting her with his feelings concerning them. That's why he took her daughter; it was to make her pay for not being with him.

Barely able to grasp the idea, but it all made sense. She took a deep breath and released it slowly as she looked back up at the two men. "OK, I know now why this person would take Gracie, but to make this case air-tight, we need the results of the blood test from the windshield."

The lieutenant's eyes flashed in a familiar display of impatience as he stood watching her. "What windshield?" he asked.

An expression of satisfaction showed in her eyes as she explained. "The windshield we found in a dumpster. This windshield was from the suspect's vehicle that I had my auxiliary man conducting surveillance on."

Surprise showed on his face as it took several seconds for him to adjust. His prejudices of women, particularly this one, started to lift as respect settled in. "Good job. Now, if one of you will give me the case number so I can inquire about the results, we should have an answer quickly enough."

The man's smugness irritated her, but putting her feelings aside, she wrote the case number down on a sticky note and handed it to him.

"Lieutenant, I called up there right before you came in and they were just getting started," Jason said tersely.

"Son, you'll soon learn that rank has its advantages." The lieutenant walked confidently out of the room and down the hall to his office.

The feeling of wanting to reach out and strike the man for his arrogance was overwhelming to Jason as he sat clenching his fists. Disgust crossed his face as he continued watching his supervisor walk away. What bothered him even more was the way his supervisor spoke to Jade, disrespectfully. One day he'll get what's coming to him.

Chapter 47

"Mr. Farrell, I'm Lieutenant Mason with the…"

"Sir, I know who you are. Can I help you?" Farrell asked with an edge to his voice. He had little patience with the lieutenant who acted as if he walked on water.

Irritated at the interruption, he continued. "I'm inquiring about Corporal Davis's case the one in which you're comparing the blood on a windshield. Are you done yet?" He ripped out the words impatiently.

Farrell knew if he didn't give the lieutenant the information he asked for, the irritating man would continue to bother him for the results. Looking at his watch, he saw that it hadn't been too long ago when the corporal from the same agency had called. "Boy, you people are impatient. Give me some time and I'll call you with the results personally, OK?" He retorted sarcastically.

Sighing deeply the lieutenant replied, "Mr. Farrell, I'll be expecting your phone call." With that, he hung up.

⊶⊙ ⊙⊷

The evening blanketed the sky with dark threatening rain clouds. Grabbing Gracie's little hand, Bob walked quickly back to their car that was parked among the thousands in the Disney World's parking lot. Making the child wear a hat and dark sun glasses cover over her prescription glasses was a brilliant idea. No one suspected anything especially after the Amber Alerts were displayed continually.

Pictures of Gracie were even in the security officers possession as they glanced at the picture and then each child as each person walked by them into the park.

Smug with himself, he continued his journey to find his car.

Squealing with delight, Gracie asked, "Mr. Bob, tomorrow we go to other park?" She had the pass in her hand and held it up close to her glasses.

He smiled at the child. He was exhausted, and tomorrow would be another day of fun at Islands of Adventure. Thankfully, having bought their park hopper pass, he was able to afford it. He needed to let time pass, and entertaining Gracie at the parks wasn't such a bad idea. At least for her. She has no idea what was really going on. My precious child, Jade doesn't deserve you, he thought.

→≡◉ ◉≡←

Jason escorted Jade to Halifax Hospital. He wouldn't leave her alone knowing how distraught she was feeling. She had lost two of her friends and Jack who was like her father is injured and now Gracie kidnapped. There was no way he would leave her side.

Holding her hand, they walked into Jack's room. The old man lay motionless and was wearing an oxygen mask as he slept. Jade walked up and placed a kiss on Jack's forehead. The monitor above Jack's bed started beeping quickly. Both of them looked up at it and then down at the man.

When Jade reached out and placed her hand in Jack's, the old man woke up. "Jack, it's me Jade."

His dark eyes looked out from his sun-toughened face. He took in his surroundings. Squinting from the pain in his head, he gently rubbed his face.

Her voice broke miserably. "Jack, say something, please." Tears were threatening to fall as she waited for his response.

"Honey…" his voice was raspy and low. " I need some water please."

Pouring the water into the foam cup, Jason handed it to Jade. She gave the cup of water to Jack, who was pushing the buttons on the remote that lay on his bed. The front of the bed rose slowly up to a forty-five degree angle. Jack took the cup and drank. Clearing his throat, he tried again to speak.

"Thank you."

She smiled and nodded.

"Why am I here?" he asked.

Jason started. "Old man, you got your ass kicked. What the hell were you doing parked across from Bob's house and not driving to meet us?"

The man frowned and took a deep breath as the headache disappeared due to the elevation of his bed. Looking himself over curiously, he lifted the sheets to make sure he had both of his legs. Patting himself down there, he felt no pain and no evidence of bandages. Finally, he touched his head and realized he wore a bandage there on his head. "What the..?"

Taking his hand in hers, Jade answered, "Jack you were struck on the side of your face. You have a big bruise on your face, and I have no clue what's under the bandage."

He was too surprised to do anything more than nod.

"We were worried about you because the doctor said he couldn't say anything about the extent of the injury to your head until you wake up. How do you feel?"

"Since I elevated the bed, the headache I had disappeared. Otherwise, I don't feel hurt."

With his swollen face and bloodshot left eye, he looked terrible. Jade smoothed his hair back away from this face, and relief washed over her. She couldn't lose Jack. She considered him like a father and loved him very much. Looking at him, she knew he only had a limited time on this earth due to his age. She kissed him again on his forehead. "Jack, I need to ask you who did this to you?" The worried look on her face was evident as she sighed.

Taking her hand in his old one, he kissed it. "Darling, I couldn't just sit there and not do something to help," he snarled. I waited for that son of a bitch to come out of his house, and when he did I was going to kill him if I saw Gracie." The machine on top of the bed beeped quicker, indicating his elevated heart rate.

"Oh, Jack, what were you thinking?" she asked while patting his chest with the hand he had covered with his.

"Darling, that's just it. I wasn't at the moment. However, I did see Gracie. She's the one who distracted me when I was talking with Bob. Then the lights went out, and I felt a terrible pain on the side of my face. I knew that man was going to kill me after he hit me, so I honked my horn, hoping someone would come out. I'm assuming somebody did, otherwise why would I be laying here?"

Jason felt a deep respect for the man. "Jack, one of the neighbors heard a horn. Thinking it was UPS, he came out and saw you slumped over your steering wheel."

"Oh."

"And you're right. If you hadn't done what you did, I'm certain Bob would have done something a lot worse to you. Are you certain it was Bob who struck you?"

"Yes," he snapped as anger lit up his eyes.

"And as you spoke to Bob. You said you saw Gracie. Where? And what was she doing?" He stood very still behind Jade as he waited for an answer.

Quietly thinking about the incident, he answered, "She was in the backseat of his car that was parked in his garage. I heard Gracie's voice so I turned and saw her. Then the rest is history." His blood pressure was up as his face turned red.

"Jack, I have one last question, and I won't be the only one asking you this. I found your service weapon on the floorboard. Why did you have it out of the holster?"

Jade turned and looked at Jason before turning back to Jack.

"Honestly, I had to protect myself from him, and if the situation was right, I think I would have shot him." His voice grated harshly. Shaking his fist, he continued. "That son of a bitch stole Gracie, and God only knows what his intentions are. I was stupid when I looked too long away from him. Damn him!" The monitor above his bed started to beep loudly and make a dinging sound.

Less than a minute later, an older female nurse walked in to check on her patient. Seeing him angered, the nurse barked, "What are you two doing to my patient? Don't you want him to recover?" Defiantly she stood with her arms crossed, waiting.

The noise of the monitor became annoying as Jason answered, "Yes, but this is official business we're conducting."

"Oh, really? Well so am I, and you two need to leave now," she barked.

Shrugging he said, "OK, we're leaving, but not before you call security over. We need this man guarded, his life is in danger and either we stay with him, or you have security come over until we can get another officer over to relieve him." He was smug with himself when the nurse turned and was gone.

"Hey, young man, don't piss off my help, OK?" Jack begged.

"Look old man, we're going to make sure you're not the next victim. Do you have a problem with that?" He stood like a statute, powerful and yet striking as he made his point.

"OK, you win." Jack kissed the top of Jade's hand again, trying to give her reassurance. "Darling, I'll be all right. Don't focus your attention on me. Just find Gracie and bring her home, OK?"

She nodded and attempted a feeble smile as a security officer walked in with the nurse. This was her cue to leave. Jason walked out of the room and informed the security officer with the news.

Ten minutes later, Jason called dispatch from the nurse station on Jack's floor and requested for an officer to stand by to protect Jack. His request was granted and he was informed help would be within the hour. After briefing the security officer of the time frame, they left.

Chapter 48

THREE DAYS LATER, there was no word about the lab results and no word from Gracie. Panic was rioting inside Jade's mind, and sheer exhaustion overwhelmed her body. She could barely eat or sleep since the disappearance of her daughter. Jason had stayed with her continually, being overly protective. She didn't mind. His presence kept her from letting her fears overwhelm her. Jason kept her grounded, and deep down inside, she loved him for it.

Exhaustion weighed heavily on him as each day past. Watching Jade lie awake lost in her thoughts as he lay next to her, he felt helpless, not knowing how to bring Gracie back and at the same time assist the woman he loved through this terrible time. He couldn't even begin to imagine how it felt to lose his child to a kidnapper worst, the kidnapper being a friend of the family, but also a killer. Sighing and feeling defeated, he moved closer wrapping his arm around her for comfort.

⊶═◉ ◉═⊷

Seeing the young child's face in agony as she lay on the large hospital bed, Bob tried to fill out the hospital paperwork, but couldn't focus on it. His Gracie had broken her arm and gotten fractured ribs due to a clumsy tourist at the water park. Gracie had been sitting down in the toddler pool, when a woman tripped over her own child while helping the infant in her arms. The tourist fell back and landed on Gracie. Thankfully, his Gracie was in the process of moving when it occurred. Otherwise, she would have been even more seriously hurt.

He was having trouble filling out the medical paperwork correctly. Surprised by the accident, he had told everyone he was just a friend of the family and was watching Gracie. Now he had to help her, but he had no idea of any of her allergies or all the medicines she was taking.

His heart sank as he remembered he had failed to bring her medicines.

Oh no, no, no, no, no, he thought.

What kind of father am I if I can't even remember my Gracie's medicines?

Silently cursing at himself, he realized he had failed miserably at being a responsible father figure.

"Mommy," she mumbled in her small voice, still asleep.

Her voice caught his attention. He watched her lay helplessly as sweat beads formed on her face. He stood up and looked for her nurse. A few minutes later Gracie's nurse returned and took her temperature. Writing down the results on a chart, she remarked, "You're right, she is coming down with a fever. I'll let the doctor know. By the way, have you finished filling out the paperwork yet?

Looking defeated, he answered, "No."

"Well have you been able to contact her parents at all?" Her voice sounded accusing, as if he was the one to blame for the accident.

Guilt already had settled in, and he accepted the blame. "I've tried, but I can't seem to get a hold of them."

"Sir, I'm sorry but we can't administer anything else to her without her parents' consent. We need you to keep trying, and in the meantime apply a cool wet cloth to her forehead to help the fever." Walking out of the room, the nurse closed the door.

"Damn! Damn! Damn!" he cursed under his breath. Knowing what he had to do next, he pulled his cell phone out and debated. If he called her now, Gracie would get the medical help she needed. If he didn't, Gracie would suffer for his mistakes. The love he felt for the child swelled in his chest restricting his breathing. He had been holding back his feelings and had refused to be upset in front of the strangers. Now his love was threatening to burst his protective wall and shed itself right here and now. He put his cell phone back into his pocket and went into the bathroom to retrieve a washcloth. First, he had to gain control of his feelings then he would call.

⋅⊷⊜ ⊜⊶⋅

The telephone call came in announcing the discovery of a white male adult and small white female child who fit the description on the Amber Alert or Bob and Gracie. Jason had received the call from dispatch. Quickly gathering Jade and leaving in a patrol car, they traveled south with lights and siren on en route to Orlando Regional Medical Center.

"Are they sure it's them?" said Jade. Her heart raced from the excitement as the shock of the discovery hit her full force.

He gave her a sideways glance and smiled confidently.

Joy bubbled in her at the thought of finally finding her daughter. Placing her hands in her lap, she fought to gain control of the trembling her hands had just recently developed.

Afraid of being disappointed she inquired again about the telephone conversation he had with dispatch. "Tell me again what they said, please."

They looked at each other and smiled in earnest. "OK, one more time. A nurse at Orlando Regional Medical Center recognized a man and child who resembled Bob and Gracie from the Amber Alerts that have been going out. The nurse is confident that the male isn't going to leave anytime soon, because of his concern for the child. And there are three officers on their way to the hospital from the Orlando district to assist us."

She muttered hastily, "Why are they at the hospital?"

His fingers tightened around the steering wheel until his knuckles turned white. His expression stilled and grew serious. "The child was brought in for medical problems."

"What medical problems?" Her voice gave away her panic.

"They wouldn't say."

She took a deep breath, and slowly let it out, trying to remain calm. Unconsciously she bit her lip as she fought for control while they continued their way south.

Thirty minutes later, they arrived on the south side of the hospital where the three other troopers had parked. Two troopers had walked inside to find out where in the hospital the suspect was. The other waited outside for them as Lieutenant Mason pulled up and parked beside them. Dressed in civilian clothes, he exited his unmarked patrol car and walked up.

Even in civilian clothes, his presence demanded authority. "I will go inside and check out the suspect," he said, then he turned to the uniformed trooper. "I want you to go to the closest parking lot to this emergency room and look for the vehicle Corporal Davis here will describe. What we want to find is this vehicle. Run the tag to confirm it's the correct one and call me on your phone to let me know you found it." The lieutenant gave the trooper his cell phone number.

Jade wrote down the description of the vehicle Bob drove. With the new information, the trooper left.

One trooper waited at the entrance as the other one walked down to meet them.

Jade turned to the lieutenant. "Sir, I really do appreciate what you're doing, but remember if this is Bob, I'm making the arrest." The flair of anger flashed in her eyes as her determination to capture the suspect gave her renewed energy.

"I understand, Corporal, but we need to do this quickly otherwise we won't be here by ourselves for long. Dispatch had to notify the FBI of the discovery also, and remember, this is a child abduction, so they will be here soon."

"I know. They interviewed me several days ago."

The trooper approached. "The suspect and child are in the emergency section. The child is in the far room to the right." Looking at the lieutenant, he continued, "Sir, what do you want us to do next?"

"All right, I'm going to walk down and look into the room and see if this is our guy. I want all of you to get out of view and wait until I return." He walked up to the emergency room entrance, leaving them staring after him.

Jade's cell phone rang and she reached down and answered it. She turned and walked away from the group. "Hello?"

"I only wanted to make her happy." The voice was hoarse, but she recognized who it was.

"Bob?" She was surprised by this unpredictable man.

"I didn't do this. You hear me!" Excited he continued walking. "Some klutz fell on top of her before I could do anything about it."

"Bob, how's Gracie?" She could hear that he was walking, so she knew he wasn't with her. She looked around, searching for him.

Sighing deeply to maintain his control he said, "Jade she's hurt." An uncontrollable trembling erupted as his control slipped away. He lost when it came to his love for his Gracie. "Her arm is broken and she has some injured ribs." He started crying and couldn't stop. "I'm so sorry. She wasn't supposed to get hurt. I only wanted you to feel the pain that I was feeling and the only way I could get you to feel that was to take her. And now she has a fever and the damn hospital won't give her anything for it." He stopped walking and leaned up against the outside wall trying to regain his composure.

"You son of a bitch. How dare you!" She ground the words out in a harsh tone.

"I stayed to take care of her. I got her fever down, and I was going to call you. They won't work on her without your consent." His tear smothered voice cracked, and he was silent. Finally able to push his emotions aside, he wiped his face and continued walking to his car that was in view.

"I trusted you," said Jade. "I can't believe I did that." Her voice changed and lowered. "You were part of my family, but you decided to take things into your own hands and take my child away from me. Now she's hurt, damn you!" Anger welled up inside and exploded. All she wanted to do was hurt this man for taking her child and getting her injured.

"I loved you, you know, and I would have done anything for you and Gracie." Something clicked inside him as a dark sinister part of him woke up and took over. "If you weren't running into all those men's arms, wanting their attention, we wouldn't be here, would we?" His voice changed to mocking and ruthless.

Realizing something had changed in him, she continued looking for him. "I don't know what you are talking about. What men?"

Walking up to his car, he opened the door and got in. "Don't play games with me. Of all people, I know you the best."

She could hear the engine start and realized where he was. Placing her hand over the receiver, she turned and yelled, "He's at his car!"

Hearing what she'd yelled, he laughed as he drove away.

Placing the phone back to her ear, she heard him laughing. Frustrated by his behavior she barked, "Who the hell do you think you are?"

"Your worst nightmare!" he yelled back.

"Fuck you!"

Laughing, he hung up the phone. Having no choice but to drive by them, he sped quickly past.

Jade pointed to him as he sped by, "There he is!"

Jason turned to the two troopers as they ran to their patrol cars, "Get that son of a bitch!" He waited for Jade as she came running up.

"I'm going inside to be with my daughter," she said. "You go." She kissed him on the lips quickly and left.

Smiling, he jumped into his patrol car and sped off, following the chase.

Chapter 49

THREE HOURS LATER, Gracie was in her own private room. Jade ran her eyes over her child again analyzing the cast arm and the machines around her. The old feelings she use to get when her child was an infant hospitalized for her severe premature birth came back.

Gracie lay asleep and drugged as the machines around her beeped. Relief washed over Jade as she kissed her daughter's forehead. Gently holding Gracie's small hand, trying to give the child comfort, she silently cried. Tears fell down her face as she felt the familiar feeling of almost losing her child again. The first time she almost lost Gracie to death was due to her being so premature, but now abducted and not hearing from Gracie in days, Jade felt the familiar fear trying to settle into her.

A large warm hand came down on her shoulder. She looked to see who it was. Tired from answering the questions for the Federal Bureau of Investigations, her own agency, and the hospital's Jade just wanted to be left alone. Her lieutenant stood behind her.

Looking at him, she waited.

"Jade, I just wanted to come in and check on you." Earlier he had stepped in, taking over what appeared to be an interrogation from the special agents and their own investigators, letting Jade go to be with her child.

Grateful for his presence, she nodded.

Seeing the tear streaked face, he patted her shoulder, not sure how to comfort his subordinate.

"Thank you, Lieutenant, for everything you've done for us." She inclined her head in a small gesture of thanks.

"You're welcome." His smile was courteous. He turned and left them.

Laying her head on her daughter's bed, she closed her eyes from the rush of exhaustion that settled in.

⋯⊷⊶⋯

Jason's anger hardened his features when the shift commander's words replayed over and over in his head. "Ten sixty-six, I repeat ten sixty-six your ten thirty-one with the subject." Then the dispatcher's voice called out a roll call of the troopers involved in the chase to verify they heard the order.

"Shit!"

A sudden swift onslaught of anger rose from him. He reacted by punching the dash hard.

"Shit! Shit! Shit!" Shaking from rage, curses fell from his mouth. Pulling out of Interstate 4 traffic and into the emergency lane, he attempted to calm himself down. Why did their agency always cancel any pursuits was beyond him. There was liability in both cases chasing and not chasing. His personal opinion was to let them chase and be able to use pit maneuvers to take out the suspects, but he knew that would never occur. Images of Jade and Gracie flashed through his mind causing a sense of failure to take over for not catching Bob.

"Oh, God, what am I going to say to them?" Leaning his head on the steering wheel, he sighed heavily.

Distracted, he regarded his throbbing hand, checking it for any permanent injuries. Then a deep, unaccustomed pain in his chest developed, and it extinguished his anger. The pain seeped through every pour of his body, taking over. It was regret. Regret for not being able to arrest the man who caused so much pain for Jade. Now he was free at the moment to figure out what he's going to do next.

Several minutes later, the last traces of anger in him diminished. Focusing back on the traffic, he had to return to Jade and Gracie, but not before he called in a favor.

⋯⊷⊶⋯

The pumping of Bob's heart was exhilarating as he drove quickly down I-4 trying to get away from troopers chasing him. He knew if he didn't lose the troopers very soon, other agencies would get involved. "Think, dammit. Think where to go." Reevaluating the route he was traveling, suddenly he jerked the wheel to the left traveling into the grass median. Traffic on the interstate slammed on their brakes to avoid each other as the onlookers of the chase caused several crashes to occur. Chuckling he braked hard turning his wheel as his vehicle spun around in the direction he wanted to go. Pressing the accelerator pedal hard now, he gained control of his vehicle and entered traffic in the opposite direction. Onlookers quickly changed lanes, giving him room to travel onto the roadway. Looking to his left, he laughed, watching the crashes occur blocking his chasers in. Free from them, he took the first exit off the interstate away from the cameras that watched him.

Now he had to figure out what he was going to do next. His thoughts about Gracie refused to leave and weighed heavily on his mind. A part of him wanted to kill his competition, while another side of him strongly desired to take Gracie away. As for Jade, he wanted to hurt her, yet he strongly desired what her body could give to please him. She was the only woman he loved and wanted only for himself, but she chose not to be with him.

Fine, but she'd pay for the wrong decision.

He drove west away from the cluster of crashes on the interstate to where he could figure out his next move.

⋆⋙◉ ◉⋘⋆

Walking into Gracie's room, Jason saw Jade asleep, leaning over on the bed. Gracie smiled at him as she brought her small finger to her lips, indicating to be quiet. The child's other hand was gently smoothing her mother's hair back from her face. Walking over to the side of the bed, he leaned down and kissed Gracie on her forehead.

"Hi, squirt. I'm glad to see you," he whispered, giving her a smile.

Smiling back at him, she looked like she was in pain.

Still whispering, he asked, "How's your arm feel?"

"Hurts," she murmured.

"And your chest area?"

"Hurts."

"I'm sorry. Anything I can do for you?"

"Candy?" Her eyes lit up as she grimaced from her pain.

"I'll find out from your nurse if you can have some candy, OK?"

She nodded.

He left to find her nurse and inquire more about Gracie's injuries. Jade never stirred, as she continued sleeping in the awkward position.

Chapter 50

THE NEXT DAY, an agent from the Federal Bureau of Investigations and a deputy from the Volusia County Sheriff's Office both pleaded with Jade to cooperate with their plan in capturing Bob. Jason stood quietly beside her. She debated about their idea. "Let me think about it," she said. Frustrated, both of the men left them in the hallway of the hospital as she dialed Lieutenant Mason's number.

A grumbling voice answered, "Hello?"

"Lieutenant, I'm sorry to bother you, but I need your assistance." Her mind reeled with confusion over their agency's policies and the offer of a plan to capture Bob. She did not want to over-step her bounds in this plan. It might violate policies, and with her exhaustion, she realized she needed help. So she was calling on Lieutenant Mason, who she knew was very knowledgeable in this area. Besides, she finally felt a bond with him since his involvement in her daughter's kidnapping.

"What is it?"

She told him everything what the plan entailed, what agencies would be involved, everything. Finally, she asked, "If I cooperate with this plan, would I be in violation of anything with our agency?"

He quietly debated the information, then he said, "I'll run it by the captain and I'll get back with you." Looking at the display on his phone, he saw that it gave her name and cell phone number. "Just keep your cell phone on."

"OK."

She hung up and went back into her daughter's room. She needed to find out from her daughter what she had been doing all this time. Knowing Bob and how he worshipped Gracie, it appeared to her, she had an idea it involved some type of spoiling.

Her anger with him had subsided, now she felt sorry for him. Nevertheless, Bob's relationship with her and Gracie is over forever. He had killed her friends, kidnapped her daughter, and now her daughter is hurt and hospitalized. No there is no way she would let this man ever walk back into their lives, even after how he had been considered to her a member of her family.

It's over, she thought.

Taking a deep breathe, she started questioning her daughter.

⤙⊛ ⊛⤚

Two hours later, Lieutenant Mason called her back.

"I'm sorry this took as long as it did, but I had to inquire with our own investigations section. This is your call, Jade. If you go along with the plan, then our agency is going to get involved. We'll have troopers guarding you until this guy's captured, since you would be placing you and your daughter at risk."

Jason walked into the room and stood before her. Looking up at his face, she saw the deep lines of worry that etched themselves on his handsome features. Before he spoke, she knew what he was going to say about their involvement with the plan. Worried that there would be no rest for her and Gracie with Bob not in custody, she confidently knew what she had to do.

Returning her attention to the conversation with Lieutenant Mason, with indefinable rightness she answered, "I'll do it."

Relieved, he continued, "I'll contact everyone and the news station. I have a feeling Corporal Lance is with you at the hospital. Have him stay with you and Gracie until a uniformed trooper arrives." He'd recognized the look of attraction on Corporal Lance's face when he walked into the homicide room at the station several days ago. He had a feeling the corporal wouldn't leave Jade and Gracie by themselves.

"He just walked in," said Jade. "I'll let him know." She hung up and turned back to Jason.

He pulled her toward him, leaning his head against hers. A look of tired sadness passed over his face as he debated what he would say.

She stood on tiptoe, her lips covered his in a tender kiss.

Her body tingled from the contact as he pulled her body closer against his.

She could feel his warm breath fanning against her ear in their embrace. His behavior had changed since yesterday, he'd become overly protective and didn't hold back displaying his affections for her and Gracie. Burying her face against the chorded muscles of his chest, she settled back enjoying the feel of his arms around her.

He had to tell her. Otherwise, he wouldn't feel right with himself. For a long time he had been attracted to Jade, even before her husband's death, but he tried hard not to show it. Now for the last year he had been a friend, her lover and protector. This time he knew it would be appropriate to tell her how he felt concerning Gracie and her.

Feeling suddenly like a teenager, his blood pressure rose. Nervously licking his lips, he proceeded.

His pulse raced against her ear, and Jade looked up at him, searching his face.

He looked into her eyes. His expression grew serious, and in a low smooth tone he confessed, "I love you, Jade. I've been in love with you for a long time, and it's crazy something like this would cause me to finally tell you."

The surprise showed on her face.

Sucking in her breath, she remained silent and she studied him.

Realizing she hadn't breathed, he reminded her, "Breathe, Jade, and it would make me feel a bit easier if you would say something."

Finally breathing, she answered him. "I love you too."

This time it was him that had the look of surprise on his face.

Three people walked in wearing suits. By their demeanors, Jade recognized them as the agents who spoke to her earlier from the Federal Bureau of Investigations. Taking a step back away from Jason, she gave the men her attention. "Can I help you?"

An Agent handed her a script and informed her that information on it was what she would tell the news media during her interview. Looking over the

8

script, she was ready within a few minutes. Outside her door, the news media waited.

Jason walked up behind her and read the script also.

Gracie woke up and looked around at everyone quietly.

Jason walked over and informed the child in the only way he knew she would understand. "Hey squirt, we're playing a game with these people, do you want to play this game with us?"

Smiling, the child nodded.

"OK, now real soon some other people are going to come in with a camera. When the camera people come in, we are going to talk for a little bit and then lie. For you, the game will be to pretend that you're asleep and make some noises a couple times, as if you're in pain. Can you play the game like that?"

Gracie looked worried and didn't say anything at first. "Game sounds yucky." She made a face of disgust.

In walked the camera operator with a small bag in his hand. Walking over to Gracie, he gently laid the present on her bed.

Gracie looked surprised. She took the bag and looked inside. The smile on her face was so contagious that everyone in the room could feel her happiness. "Mine?" She asked the camera operator.

The camera operator chuckled. "Only if you play this game with us. I promise it'll be really quick."

Looking for her mother, she waited for her approval.

Jade said, "Its OK with me, honey."

Her eyes brightened with pleasure, and Gracie gave a quick squeal and then laughed.

"OK, let's do this," Jade barked, getting everyone's attention.

The camera operator insisted on a practice speech in front of the camera. A few minutes later, Jade played her part by stating what was on the script and pretending she was crying during the interview. Gracie played her part very well, knowing a bag of miscellaneous candies awaited her. Jason remained quiet, holding Jade as she played her part. Ten minutes later, everyone left the family alone finally.

There was restless energy in Jason as he paced through the room. His face clouded with uneasiness at his understanding that the interview would be broadcasted on television. The headline would be Jade's child fighting on her deathbed after being discovered when a kidnapper brought the child in for internal injuries. He was also informed that the story would be headline news in several local newspapers, in case Bob didn't get a chance to view the television.

Eyeing him as he paced the room, Jade found herself extremely conscious of his virile appeal.

Abruptly, he stopped. He looked her way, and his gaze bore into her silently.

Totally bewildered at his behavior, she asked, "What?"

"You know this means we can't leave Gracie. Once you-know-who sees this or reads about it, he'll be coming here." He tried to be evasive for the sake of Gracie who was eating her candy and watching them.

"I know, but we have plain-clothes officers watching over us."

The masked expression of disbelief continued, and it irritated her.

"Look, I want him arrested and out of our lives for good. This morning I checked my voice mail and the results came in from the windshield."

His expression changed as his eyebrows shot up and he waited for her response.

"It was Scott's. You know who the killer is." She answered in a tense clipped voice that forbade any questions.

He walked up to her and put his hand on her shoulder, knowing full well her angry façade was just a disguise. Bob had been a close friend to her and Gracie for a long time.

"I'm sorry for what you've been through." His breath fanned her ear as he pulled her into an embrace.

⤙◉ ◉⤚

Watching the television intently in his room an hour away from the hospital his Gracie was in, disbelief crossed his face. Each word the news reporter spoke about Gracie's condition caught his full attention. "No, no, no, no!" The muscles in his forearms bulged as he clenched his fists in frustration. He struggled with the uncertainty of the knowledge he had when he left his Gracie at the hospital. The reporter stated the fever was started from the internal bleeding. He choked back a sudden unexpected sound of grief. "She's an innocent," he whispered to himself.

Pacing back and forth, he changed the channel to see maybe if the reporter had obtained wrong information. Each channel had the same information, "Damn it!" he roared. A strong instinct rose up inside him, coming back alive. This urge was his over protectiveness of the child. Running his hand through his hair, the debate was over. He had to see her. He had to see his Gracie before she died.

Sitting on his bed, he concentrated on a plan to visit his Gracie soon, really soon.

Chapter 51

LOOKING AT THE clock on the wall, Jason saw that almost twenty-four hours had past. Trying to be helpful, he had returned back to Jade's house earlier, retrieved some clothes for her and Gracie, and then he drove slowly by Bob's residence. He was hoping he would run into the man again so that this time he would place him under arrest. If needed, Jason knew he would shoot the man, but only, of course if he felt his life or someone else's was in danger.

Driving by, he saw his friend Trooper Write sitting in his vehicle two doors down. He had called in his favor and had Bob's residence watched in case he returned.

Now he waited for Bob to return to the hospital.

He sat back and watched the small television on the wall while he waited.

Catering to her daughter was easy. Convincing her to behave sick was another matter. Jade smoothed back the hair from Gracie's face as the child started falling asleep.

He looked up at Jason. He had unlocked her heart and soul being repeatedly there for her. Recalling when she first met Jason, he was going through a bad divorce and fighting over custody of his son. At that time he was definitely good looking, but she didn't spend any time with him then. Because her husband and she worked in the same squad, they had opposite shifts, and it so happened that Jason was on her shift. They became friends. Once her husband's death occurred, not only was Bob there for her, but Jason had told her in private he would be there. Jason had started calling her, making appointments to have their kids play together while they spoke about their cases. Then their friendship had become closer. As time passed, she wanted to be with Jason more and more. She remembered how Susan would pop into her house unannounced. Her friend would pull her away from Jason and Bob's presence and take her out, trying to show her there was a lot more men out there for her to date. She tried to date, since Jason didn't ask her out, but it didn't work out with the guys. Her problem was that she would compare the guys to her husband and then Jason. She smiled as she recalled those memories. She also recalled Jason's reactions when she would adlib about the dates to him in order to see what he would do or say. He was very good at concealing his attraction, at least up until a couple months ago. The only problem she could see in the progression of their relationship was the woman that he had recently been seeing and not telling her about.

Torn by conflicting emotions, and debating whether to ask him about the woman or not, she continued watching him.

Feeling like he's being watched, Jason looked around the room and noticed Jade looking him. The look on her face concerned him. "Are you OK?" he asked.

Nodding, she avoided his gaze and looked back at her sleeping daughter.

Doubt nagged at him over her response. Raw hurt glittered in her eyes as she continued avoiding his gaze.

He stood up, grabbed the chair he was sitting on, and placed it in front of Jade. Turning it around, he straddled the chair, placing his chin on the back of his hands that were resting on the top of the back of the chair. His features displayed an attitude of self-command and studied relaxation. His fingers were cool and smooth as they touched hers.

Her eyes met his and looked at him questioningly.

"Jade, what's bothering you?"

"Nothing." She spoke in a broken whisper.

Not convinced at all, he continued. "I know you too well. There is something bothering you. Let's talk about it." Slightly squeezing her hand for reassurance, he waited.

She answered quickly over her choking, beating heart. "You said earlier that you love me, right?"

"That's correct."

Nervously biting her lowered lip, she said, "Then I've been wondering what type of relationship we are in?"

Confused at her question, he replied, "What kind of question is that?"

She took a deep breath to help her erratic pulse, then she blurted out, "I need to know what kind of relationship we are having... or are we?"

He lifted his eyebrows in surprise. "Why are you asking this?"

"I don't compete with other women, Jason."

"What?"

She realized he was definitely confused, so with all the will power she could muster up she finally let it out, "What I'm talking about is the woman that you're seeing."

Shaking his head, he listened with bewilderment.

She was irritated that he was acting as if he didn't know what she was talking about. "When we started our intimacy a while ago, I called your cell phone and a woman answered."

"Are you sure you didn't call the wrong number?" He stared at her, frowning.

"I'm absolutely sure I didn't call the wrong number. I tried again, thinking at first that I did, but she answered and wouldn't let you talk to me." There. She said it, and invisible relief lifted from her shoulders.

Quietly thinking back, he realized the only time he was around another woman was with his ex-wife when his son was sick. He recalled that he had accidentally left his cell phone at her house, but he had gone back and retrieved it after several days of wondering where it was. He knew now what Jade was upset about.

"Jade, I did misplace my cell phone when Junior was sick. I left it over at my ex's house, and I wouldn't put it past her if she answered and played a stupid game with you. I have not and will not date anyone else while I am with you. Do you understand that?"

He had proven himself by helping her find Gracie and now continuing to be by her side as they wait for Bob to return. Placing her hands back into her lap, she could understand how a woman could be vicious and behave the way his ex-did. Not that she would behave, as cruel and immature, games were not her typical behavior, but the only good man she had lost was her husband. He was a different circumstance he was murdered. Returning her gaze to Jason, she'd let a secretive smile play across her lips.

"Good, that's how I like it."

Standing up, he picked up the chair and set it aside as the one hand that continued holding onto Jade's pulled her to him.

Her body tingled from the contact of his body.

His arms encircled her, one hand in the small of her back as his lips lightly touched hers with tantalizing persuasion. Quivering at his sweet tenderness, his mouth captured hers in a slow drugging kiss. His lips left hers to sear a path down her neck. His body suddenly grew hungry for hers. He fought to regain his control while Jade remained in his arms clinging to him.

She could feel his uneven breathing on her cheek when he held her.

The sound of people approaching the room caused them to separate. Jason took his chair and placed it back, sitting correctly on it as Jade sat back down and waited for the people to enter the room.

Lieutenant Jarvis entered with a smile on his face. His plan had worked. Once the news of Jade's child's health became aired, the other news agencies would grab onto the information and air it on their stations too. Now the lie would sound like the truth. This knowledge caused him to smile.

Jade asked first, "And?"

"It worked. The news has spread on all the local news stations and there is no way our suspect will think it's a trap. God, I love this job!"

Gracie stirred awake from the noise.

"Mommy?"

Hearing her daughter's voice, Jade turned and approached her daughter to comfort her.

Jason looked at his watch and returned his gaze back to his lieutenant. "Now, all we do is wait. Sir, do we have everyone in their positions and ready?"

"Absolutely. We have two in the surveillance cars on each entrance. Then at this floor elevator entrance, we have a trooper in civilian clothes, and you two in this room. How's that for protection?"

"Definitely plenty, but if he got past the deputies at Halifax Hospital and was able to murder Scott, then I'm sure he will be able to get past our people." Jason had already thought about this and it bothered him greatly. Bob was smart, very smart and quick on his feet to convince the hospital staff and the deputies when he gained access to Deputy Scott Kemp's hospital room to be able to murder the man and walk out of the room with no questions asked. He knew how that could have happened. "Now what we have to do is watch the hospital staff too. The only way for Bob to get into this hospital and walk by our people is to pose as hospital staff. Just thought you might have over looked that option, sir."

Frowning, he shook his head. "No way. I already thought that too. Just stay with Jade and the child, and we will do the rest, OK?" Irritated by the way, Jason insinuated that he hadn't thought of all the options, he placed his hands on his hips defiantly. Otherwise, he might have smacked the younger man for his remark.

The tenseness in the air between the two men was thick. Jade stood up and walked over to her lieutenant. "Thank you, sir. We'll stand by and wait. What channel is everyone on the radio?"

Her question distracted him, and he answered.

Grabbing the radio on the nightstand, she turned it to the channel and placed it back down as her lieutenant and hospital security walked out of the room.

Jason turned to her. "Now we wait. Why don't you go lie down for a while, I'll take the first shift."

She was grateful again that he was there. She felt exhausted and figured that Bob wouldn't come to see Gracie that quickly. "Thank you." Walking over to her child, she whispered something in her ear and kissed Gracie before she exited and walked down the hall to the room designated for parents to rest in.

Chapter 52

BOB'S NERVES ATE at his insides as he wondered how Gracie was. He had to see her, no matter what. He would fix everything and have Jade understand.

She would understand.

His love for them would make it all better.

Looking down at his watch, he could see the time from the light of the moon-reading one thirty-three. He had waited at his spot on the backside of the hospital for the last staff member to walk back into the building from their smoke break. He had to plan this correctly so no one would suspect him.

The male nurse crushed out his cigarette and pushed it into the small hole of the pole of the cigarette stand. Done with his break, he stood up, and walked back into the building.

The metal door did not shut right behind the nurse, and Bob grabbed the door and slipped into the building casually. He was wearing a scrub uniform and looked like the typical hospital staff.

As always his plan was working.

Smug with himself, he walked toward the elevators not realizing he had walked right by a trooper who was sitting in a wheel chair at the end of the hall where the view of the only elevators working were in plain view.

Bob walked into the elevator and pressed the button for the floor he wanted. Less than a minute later, the elevator doors opened. The quietness of the floor echoed in his ears, covered by the surgical mask he was wearing. Stepping out of the elevators, he made his way toward Gracie's room, at the same time scanning the area. A person was sleeping on a chair with his head back in a light snore that never stopped as he walked by. Could be a cop, he thought. But he wasn't sure. Gracie's door was directly in front of him as he walked up to the nurses station to see who was on duty and what they were doing.

If the nurses were distracted, he would make his move.

What bothered him was, where was Jade?

A couple nurses were busy writing down their notes in patient folders, but they didn't see him. Turning around, he saw no one, just the sleeping male who was still snoring. A pulsing knot in his neck quickened as he made his move and entered Gracie's room. There he saw Gracie, sound asleep.

Where is Jade? he thought.

Quietly walking over to his precious child, he stood over her, slowly looking her over for injuries. She didn't appear to be as sick as the news had stated. This was good, but also bad.

It had to be a trap!

His adrenaline accelerated into overdrive as he realized what he'd walked into. Jade wasn't here because it was a trap, damn it!

Beads of perspiration formed on his forehead as he looked around for an officer to jump him, but there was no one. Realizing he might get caught, he leaned over and placed a gentle kiss on Gracie's forehead.

Slowly, her eyes opened, and she focused on the person looking down on her. Recognizing who it was, Gracie squealed and smiled.

"Shhhh!" Her happiness was infectious, and he felt it as he leaned down and hugged her.

Then Gracie frowned and she whispered, "Mr. Bob, people here say you bad."

Her speech was difficult for most people, but he understood her very well. He answered, "I know, but what matters is, do you think I'm bad?"

Gracie thought about it for a brief moment and shook her head no.

"Good. That is all that matters to me. Are you OK?" He said in a hushed voice only she could hear.

"Yes."

"Honey, I'm going to have to go. Be good." He smiled at her briefly and turned away toward the door.

Gracie's body trembled as the tears started falling down her cherub face. In a panic, she called out to him, "Mr. Bob!"

He cringed knowing whoever was out in the lobby would definitely hear her voice. Turning back around, he gave her his full attention.

Her little chin trembled as she said, "Love you!"

His heart broke. He watched his precious child lie there injured, and being used as a pawn to capture him. Her unconditional love for him was what helped him through the day, every day.

Steps echoing down the hall caught his attention as he quickly answered her back, "Always remember that I love you." The steps were coming closer. They sounded like the person was starting to run to him. He knew without a doubt, he would never want to hurt Gracie and so he quickly exited the room to be tackled by someone.

The fight was on.

The trooper walked into the restroom and informed Jason that the suspect was in Gracie's room talking to her. Jason walked back toward the room, hoping Bob would leave so Gracie wouldn't see the scenario. As Bob left the room, he had decided the best method of detaining the man was to tackle him. His adrenaline was rushing hard. No way was he going to lose him this time.

Bob grunted from the impact as they both fell to the floor. Bob swung a fist as he turned around to face his attacker. Jason ducked, avoiding the blow. The two men struggled and threw punches as Jade and another trooper came running toward them.

Jason had Bob finally detained and asked for a pair of handcuffs from the trooper who was assisting him in pinning Bob down. As Jason handcuffed him, Bob still fought back by kicking wildly.

"Enough!" The loud voice caught Bob's attention. He stopped and tried to catch his breath.

Jason pulled Bob up to his feet as the trooper called in the arrest on his radio. The voices on the radio squawked back, answering that they were en route to the scene.

Jade was disgusted with Bob and what she had been going through. Seeing him standing in front of her with a bloody lip and his hands handcuffed behind his back, her emotions overrode her logical thinking. Jade stepped up and slapped him hard across the face.

The sound of the slap echoed as other troopers came rushing in. The men stopped abruptly and watched the scene, unsure of what was going on now.

"You bastard!" Jade heard the bitterness spill over into her voice. "I trusted you with my family and our lives, and this is what you do." She slapped him again across his face leaving a red imprint.

"Jade!"

She recognized the warning in the voice as Lieutenant Jarvis.

Laughing, Bob sneered at Jade. His love for the woman turned instantly into pure hate.

"What the hell is so funny, you son of a bitch?" She asked.

"Well, to think I was so in love with you. What a joke." He continued to laugh for a few moments more while Jason read him his miranda rights.

Jade answered back, "Go to hell!"

As quickly as he'd started laughing, Bob suddenly stopped. With a serious look on his face, he continued talking to Jade, ignoring Jason's statements. "So you think I'm the bad guy here huh? Well let's go over the situation again and see who is the bad person here."

Everyone stopped what they were doing as the suspect's continued with his spontaneous statements.

"Let's see, who was it who stayed and helped you after your husband's death? Who was it who supported your every decision even though they were the wrong decisions? Hmmm?" He waited for an answer, but Jade refused to say anything. He continued. "OK, you're going to be that way. Let's see, who was it who helped your daughter to understand her father's death? That was me. Oh, and the answers to my previous questions, of course, were all me." He let out a quick laugh before proceeding. "Who was it who held you all the times you broke down crying all because of your husband's death? That would be me. Who took your daughter to school and picked her up because your job wouldn't let you? Oh, that was me. All the times you were held over due to work situations, who was it that helped your daughter? Of course, that was me. Most importantly, who was it who helped your daughter and you through the roughest times since your husband's death? Me! Me! Me! I've been the one holding your family together for over a year now, taking care of you and your daughter. And do you think you would appreciate it or even recognize the huge amount of responsibility I've taken on since your husband's death? Not just no, but *hell* no!"

Shaking her head, Jade responded in a harsh tone. "No one asked you to do anything, but I did appreciate all that you did. You just expected more than what I was willing to give."

Bob's eyes opened wide at her remark. He didn't believe a word she had said. "Bullshit!"

Jason stepped in. "All right, this isn't going anywhere, you should..."

Bob ignored him and continued. "What? We were a family Jade and you couldn't see that. Gracie loves me like I was her father, and I've been here more than your dead Chuck was. He would be dedicating his time to work more than his own family. I remember you would call him begging him to come home. You know I followed him one night to see what he was up to and guess what I discovered. He was seeing another woman, dear."

Jade reacted angrily to the challenge in his accusation. "You're a liar!"

"Oh no, my dear, I am not. I followed him and found him locked in an embrace, kissing some woman. I followed them to the hotel where they had their fling. By the way, he would go to Daytona for that."

Anger was flooding her every thought as Bob continued with his accusations. Silent tears slowly slid down her face as he answered her fears of what Chuck was actually doing. She had a feeling something wasn't right with their relationship, but they never fought or spoke about separating.

A twinge of regret filled his heart as he saw the tears falling. "My dear Jade, I knew your marriage was a sham, and I couldn't let you or Gracie pay for Chuck's deceitfulness." He took a deep breath, knowing what he was about to say next would change his life forever. Seeing the pain in Jade's eyes and knowing it was him that put it there tore him up, he continued. "Jade, I loved you and Gracie more than my own life, and seeing how you two were just pawns in Chuck's eyes, I wouldn't let him use you that way. I waited until he was working and alone, and I killed him."

At this point, everyone in the room looked at him, hanging on each word.

The tears were blinding Jade as she shook her head. "No."

"Yes, I can tell you how he died if you want, but I know you believe me. I would never lie to you, Jade. You know that. He was a cheating bastard and unworthy of your and Gracie's love."

She continued shaking her head.

"But afterward, when I tried to develop our relationship further, that damn bitch would get in the way. Therefore, I decided she had to go and I killed her too. She was trying to take you away from me and I couldn't let that happen."

Her chest felt like it was going to explode as Bob continued with his confession.

"I hated Susan, and I'm glad that bitch is gone. As for that grab-ass deputy, he had no right disrespecting you and trying to get in the way of our relationship so I had to kill him too. Then your damn partner- the old man- he just got in my way. I realized you had enough evidence against me, so I decided to get away."

Confused, she asked, "So why did you take Gracie?"

He sneered, "To get back at you!" The memory of her in the embrace of the trooper next to him reminded him of the anger he had against her. "You refused to love me back, so I wanted you to feel how I felt. It was easy taking precious Gracie. She willingly left with me through her bedroom window."

Her voice grated harshly, "And now she's here because of you!"

His demeanor changed instantly, softening to a hurt expression. "I did not do this to her. It was an accident at a water park caused by some fat, clumsy bitch. I swear I would never hurt Gracie. You know that!"

"I don't know what to believe."

"Damn it, Jade, Chuck was a bastard and deserved to die. So did your two other friends. If it wasn't for that fat bitch falling on Gracie, I would have raised her on my own."

"You selfish son of a bitch!"

"What? Oh, now I see how this is going to be." By now his left hand slipped through the cuff behind his back releasing him from custody. "Well you deserve having a worthless cheating husband and a whore for a friend." Bob grabbed the lieutenant's holstered gun in one swift motion pushing the older man away and raised the gun at Jade. "Matter of fact, the way you dressed and left willingly with Susan…"

Two shots rang out in quick succession. Taught to double tap when she fired her service weapon, it was automatic for Jade. The smell of gun powder invaded her nostrils as the surrounding men pounced onto her grabbing her weapon as a deputy jumped onto the fallen shot suspect taking the weapon away from Bob's dying grasp.

No more tears fell from her face.

The doubts she had about her marriage with Chuck was over.

The confession was heard by everyone that mattered.

Suspect caught and homicide solved.

The events that followed went in slow motion for Jade. She watched as the hospital staff approached and attempted to save Bob. Her shots found Bob's chest and killed him as he bled out quickly on the hospital floor. The Agents talking to her, she made no sense of what they said, her mind blocked it all out.

Jade fell to her knees as the shock of the scenario, lack of sleep, the stress of her daughter's kidnapping and friends' deaths spun in her head. It was too much for her to handle. Darkness fell as she slumped to the floor unconscious.

Jason went to Jade's side evaluating her injuries and trying to understand what had just happened.

"Shit!" He knew this was not good. This homicide has now turned into an unpredicted circus.

Chapter 53

Two years later...

Jade snuggled into Jason's side as they lay in the hammock in her backyard. They watched their kids play. The cool weather from fall had all of them wearing sweaters as the evening slowly went by.

Placing his hand gently on the swell of Jade's belly, he could feel the baby's movement. Pride spread quickly through him. He knew his child knew his touch, even while inside his new bride. Six more weeks and their child would be born. They were all anxious for the day to come.

Jade sighed.

Worried, Jason asked, "What's wrong?"

Chuckling, Jade turned her attention to her husband. "Nothing. Just thinking it has been just over two years since my life changed."

"And was that a bad thing?" he teased.

Gently swatting his chest, she replied, "No, absolutely not. I finally married a remarkable man who I know is perfect for me, and now Gracie has Junior as a brother who she has adored since she first met him."

"Yeah, and now we're married, and you're carrying our child." He kissed his wife's cheek and settled back into the hammock.

Still unsettled, Jade finally finished her thought "Jason, sometimes I can't help but remember what had happened with Bob at the hospital." She had been seeing a psychologist since the shooting. So far, it had helped her cope with her feelings, but she refused to forget what had happened. Ever since the investigation that cleared her from the shooting, Jason refused to talk about it. He had told her, "The past is the past. Move on with the future and learn from your mistakes."

She has moved on, but refused to forget. A man she had included as a family member murdered too many people she had loved. Never again would she ever let anything like that happen.

Never again.

Gracie had never spoken about Bob since the shooting. Gracie had heard Bob's confession, and when Jade told her daughter that Bob was dead, Gracie had replied, "I know."

Her stomach moved, pulling her attention back to the current time. Smiling, knowing her unborn child demanded her attention more and more now, she gently rubbed her large stomach and soothed her child.

Jason turned to her and said, "I love you."

"I love you too," she answered and she settled back into his embrace.